PROOF of FOREVER

PROOF of FOREVER

LEXA HILLYER

HARPER TEEN
An Imprint of HarperCollinsPublishers

HarperTeen is an imprint of HarperCollins Publishers.

Proof of Forever

Copyright © 2015 by Lexa Hillyer

All rights reserved. Printed in the United States of America.

No part of this book may be used or reproduced in any manner whatsoever
without written permission except in the case of brief quotations embodied
in critical articles and reviews. For information address HarperCollins
Children's Books, a division of HarperCollins Publishers, 195 Broadway,
New York, NY 10007.

www.epicreads.com

Library of Congress Cataloging-in-Publication Data

Hillyer, Lexa.

Proof of forever / Lexa Hillyer.

pages cm

Summary: "Four former friends are transported back in time to a pivotal
summer in all of their lives during a camp reunion"— Provided by
publisher.

ISBN 978-0-06-233038-3

[1. Friendship—Fiction. 2. Camps—Fiction. 3. Time travel—Fiction.
4. Reunions—Fiction.] I. Title.

PZ7.H5648Pro 2015   2014034155

[Fic]—dc23   CIP
                                                                      AC

Typography by Erin Fitzsimmons

16 17 18 19 20   CG/RRDH   10 9 8 7 6 5 4 3 2 1

First paperback edition, 2016

For Ellen Byer Friedlander,
who has always inspired me to read, to write,
and to rage against the dying of the light

PART ONE
HERE and NOW

"Your past is always your past.
Even if you forget it,
it remembers you."
—*Sarah Dessen*

1

FRIDAY

Just do it. Now, now, now, Zoe thinks as she blows loose strands of her blond hair off her sweaty forehead. Don't frogs die like this, from too much heat? One minute they're sleeping, dreaming froggy dreams, and the next they're just . . . fried.

The rickety box fan propped up on the porch railing divides the sunlight into flashes and shadows, its thick blades hacking the sky—before, after, before, after—pulling in the smell of freshly cut grass. Zoe can't help but think of the propeller on a fighter plane. Except no one's going anywhere, and no one knows of the little war inside her.

In the deafening whir, she almost doesn't hear him say it: "This isn't working."

It takes a minute to realize he means the bike.

Calvin has apparently given up on Operation Revitalize Zoe's Wheels. Her bicycle has just fallen in a mangled-looking heap of blue and white metal, half on the porch stairs, half on the concrete path that cuts his front yard down the middle.

"Shit. Sorry." Calvin wipes his greased fingers on his cargo shorts as he straightens to his full height, then swipes his almost shoulder-length brown hair out of his eyes. He is the very definition of floppy. "The chain is too rusted, Albright. Not sure there's much more I can do."

"Well, thanks for trying, I guess." Zoe forces a smile—the kind you give the dental hygienist while biting down on a cold, metallic-tasting X-ray slide. Her cutoff shorts stick to her thighs in the August heat. The maple trees along Jefferson Street wink green and yellow in the faint-but-not-nearly-enough breeze. Down the road, she can see the local church, where she used to go for the free doughnuts. If it's a toss-up between believing in a cozy place in the clouds where you go after death, or doughnuts, Zoe knows which side she's on. When you're dead, you're dead.

Say it, say it, say it, she wills herself. Normally she can't stop talking.

Calvin comes over and kicks the side of her foot. "I can see if my mom will lend you her old one," he offers.

"Don't worry about it. The thing's a piece of thrift-store crap anyway," Zoe says. She feels like she can't breathe. It must be the weather.

"Then what's the matter?" Calvin shades his eyes with his hand, staring down at her from his six-foot-two frame.

"Nothing," she says, too fast. She feels her cheeks getting warm and her throat getting tight. She wants to go back. She

4

wants to go back to three months ago, before prom, before all of this happened.

They were supposed to have gone together just as friends. But then there was the fumbling, sweet, after-party kiss. And everything changed.

Now things *need* to go back, somehow, to the way they used to be. And though she's not sure she'll ever be able to connect the dots and explain why, her unexpected call from Joy today has made this all the more clear. Joy's words still ring in her ears: *I need to see you. Will you come?*

Joy isn't the kind of person you can say no to. Not with that lilt in her voice, that way it has of breaking midsentence from soft to rough, from high to low. Not with that power she has to convince you anything is true, even the idea that life is okay when it really isn't.

Even when she abandoned you two years ago and you haven't heard from her since, until this morning. Even *then*, you can't say no.

Cal raises an eyebrow. "Nothing? Really? I've seen a llama spit more convincingly." He's full of odd phrases like that.

"No, you haven't," Zoe replies, pushing him out of her way so she can sit down beside her bike.

Then his face quirks into a grin. "I know how to cheer you up." He darts around to the side of the house.

"Cal, what are you doing? I have to tell—" Before she can finish, Cal reappears holding the end of the garden hose.

"Never send a human to do a machine's job," he announces, faux-menacing, quoting their favorite movie. He grins again, big. That adorable crooked-toothed grin. Zoe's chest clenches.

"I will kill you if you—"

"Two words, Albright. Dodge this." Cal lets loose.

The water hits her like cold, hard bullets and in a second her top is soaked. She squeals and instinctively goes to tackle him. "No fair!" she cries, trying to wrestle away the hose.

He holds the hose above his head, gazing down at her water-logged shirt. All his references to *The Matrix* seem to vanish from his vocabulary. There's a pause. "You're wearing my favorite bra," he says. He reaches out to flick the neon yellow strap that's peeking out of her V-neck T-shirt, and in that moment she finally gets one hand around the nozzle. But then he grabs her and swings her around so her back is to him and her arms are trapped at her sides. On any other day, this would be normal. This would be fun. This would be fine.

But today Calvin is the only one laughing. "I give up," she says, feeling a sting in her throat.

He continues to swing her around, his face happy. But his expression changes fast when he sees hers. He drops the hose, and it gives one final gush into the grass around her feet. "Seriously, what's up with you? You've been weird all week."

"I just . . . I . . ." *Just. Say. It.* Zoe has done this before. Just not to anyone who mattered. Not to Cal. With Steve Hutz it was easy. Same with Jared Weinbeck. This is different.

"I . . . I don't want to lose you as a friend," she manages to say.

"What are you talking about?" His face turns guarded. "What is this about, Zo?"

Do it. "I don't . . . I don't want to be this. A couple. With you. I don't want that." Zoe takes a huge breath. She feels light-headed but much better. Relieved. She did it.

"What?" Cal blurts out. "Why?"

Zoe doesn't respond. She just stands there, helplessly, wishing she knew. Calvin is her best friend. They've spent hours together, driving around in his Ford, listening to music and talking about nothing. He's been her solace ever since the days when her friendship with Joy came to an abrupt halt. He was there when Joy wasn't.

And yet all it took was one phone call from Joy this morning to send Zoe's head reeling, convincing her that she has to go to reunion night, even though it makes no sense, even though she *promised* Cal they would get pizza tonight—one of their remaining few before college.

"I can't believe this." Calvin starts pacing the yard. "You're *dumping* me? You're dumping me."

"Maybe I'm not made for relationships," Zoe says weakly.

"Zoe, that's bullshit. We're good together," he says, his hazel eyes big and round. "You're seriously going to run away from it now?"

She feels a tiny tide of anger peak and fall. "I'm not *running*, Cal." She moves away and starts fumbling to pick up her bike, but it falls again, the left pedal nailing her in the shin. "Ow. *Damn it.* I don't, you know . . ."

"No, I *don't* know."

She has the bike righted now, the blue, paint-chipped

7

handlebars firm in her hands, which fails to keep them from shaking. "I don't feel it. Anymore. Or ever. I'm not sure. Remember at graduation how you said I was your best freaking friend in the world? That I could always be your metaphorical front man even though I can't sing for shit? What happened to that?"

Calvin stares at her for a second. "What happened to that?" He barks out a laugh. "I'll tell you what happened, Albright. We started *kissing*. I started *liking* you. I *thought* it was mutual. But I guess I'm just your backup guy, right? Your King of fucking Convenience."

"Cal, you know that's not true." She stands there, holding on to her broken bike, wishing she could run, wishing they had never kissed, wishing he wasn't so . . . him.

"So that's it?" he says dully.

She doesn't answer. She swings her right leg over the bike seat and tries to nudge the bike forward, but the misaligned chain causes it to wobble.

Cal hesitates, then reaches forward to catch her. "Zoe, you can't ride that. It's completely busted." He helps her off the bike and she lets it fall behind her, lets him wrap his arms around her. A beat passes where they both just breathe like that, and Zoe tries not to feel trapped.

But she always feels trapped.

"I'm going to miss you," he whispers into the messy knot of hair at the top of her head.

His damp T-shirt presses against her face.

"I should go," she says. Her throat is raw, as if she's been shouting.

Cal lets her pull away. His eyes are wounded, confused. "Let me give you a ride."

"You sure?" Zoe's stomach clenches. She wishes he would yell or something.

"You can't exactly take *that*," he says, managing a quick smile that doesn't touch his eyes.

So she swings her bike into the bed of his old Ford truck, then slides into the passenger seat. As soon as he starts the engine, a mix she made for him pours out from the speakers. Calvin punches the music off quickly, and they drive in silence. Out of long habit, Zoe props her feet on the glove compartment, where there are permanent scuffs in the shape of her flip-flops, and stares out the window at the pastel clapboard houses of Liberty, New Hampshire—the town she's known all her life—flashing by. With a population of about fifteen hundred, they don't even have their own high school; they share Kennett High with a few other towns. *Tiny, tiny, tiny.* This place. This car. Her entire life so far.

"So, back home I presume?" Cal asks, automatically hanging a right onto School Road.

"Actually . . . ," Zoe says, then hesitates.

Calvin sighs heavily. "I hate how you do this, Zo."

"Do what?" she asks.

He turns to face her. She can see the hurt in his wrinkled brow, the pinched corners of his eyes. "That thing," he says.

9

"When you're all broody, but I know there's something you *want*. So just ask me already."

Zoe picks at her frayed jean shorts. Why did she break up with Calvin? Why does she always screw everything up? They should be playing video games in his basement—the coolest room in the otherwise sweltering house. Ordering pizza and watching a *Doctor Who* marathon or working on one of Cal's band's songs, like on any other normal Friday night. Instead, she feels like a little kid who's been put in time-out.

She begins to ramble. It's what she does in uncomfortable situations . . . what she does in *most* situations. "It's Joy. She wants to see me tonight." There's a pause—Calvin knows Joy from freshman and sophomore years, before she moved away and dropped all contact with her former friends. Cal always took Zoe's side, protectively, claiming Joy must've lost her mind to want to ditch her friends like that.

"It's weird, I know," Zoe pushes on, "but that's part of why I think I should go. It's reunion night at camp. She's drawing *all* of us together." She knows he knows what she means—her, Joy, Luce, and Tali. The inseparable four. Once upon a time, anyway. "Except my parents are working. Mom's been stressed. I could text Tali, but you know what the girl thinks of me these days. It's too far to bike and my bike's out anyway and . . . And I need—"

"A ride there," Calvin finishes her sentence.

"Well, yeah. That."

"So what you're saying is you don't want to date me, you just want to use me for my wheels."

"No, Cal, that's not—"

"Relax. I'm kidding."

"Are you sure? Because you're talking like a robot. Or Keanu Reeves."

He smiles now, a little. They mutually hate Keanu but nevertheless consider *The Matrix* the pinnacle of late-nineties filmmaking. "I'll drive you. All right? I've got nothing better to do anyway." Calvin turns his attention back to the road.

Zoe smiles and punches his arm lightly. She tries to let the breeze from the window dry her drenched T-shirt, once again unable to get her phone call with Joy out of her head. The pleading in Joy's voice. Joy never had to *ask* them to listen to her—they always just did. Followed her with a blind faith. She always seemed to be at the center of them, tying things together invisibly. They had this running joke that Camp Okahatchee— aka Camp OK—was the epitome of okay-ness. Even the good stuff was merely okay. "This is all just purgatory, I swear," she'd say. "One day things will be better than okay. They'll be Fantastic." She always said "Fantastic" like it had a capital *F*, like it came with jazz hands.

But ever since Joy moved away the summer after sophomore year, right after camp ended, mysteriously dropping off social media and changing her number, it's like they all fell apart. Tali and Zoe still go to the same school, but they drifted so effortlessly they almost didn't notice it happening at first. As for Luce, it was easier to lose track of her as she became swallowed in her busy private-school life, even though her hometown of Wolfeboro is barely a half-hour drive from Liberty.

It hits Zoe how much she misses Joy—misses all of them, as a unit. She leans back in her seat, hearing the vinyl squeak beneath her legs.

Calvin punches her arm back. "I said I'd give you a lift to camp so you would *stop* brooding. It's seriously tripping me out."

She makes a goofy face caught somewhere between a smile and an eye roll, causing him to snort.

He turns back to the road. "I mean, dude. What would you do without me?" he jokes, though there's an edge to his voice. He taps the steering wheel like a drum.

Zoe shakes her head, watching her hometown turn to a blur. "Ignorance is bliss."

2

Absofuckinglutely not. Tali slips out of her purple silk maxi dress, balls it up, and throws it into the corner of her bedroom. It lands on the pile of half-read magazines on her nightstand, then hits the floor, taking her iPhone with it.

She stares at herself in her floor-length mirror, in only her black push-up and pink and green thong. Sometimes she still can't believe how, well, *good* her body looks now, her long legs finally curved, slightly, in the right places, instead of the awkward, gangly colt legs she had to deal with for years. Her 32Cs look more like C-pluses (*thank you, Pink!*), and her face has just the right amount of roundness in her cheeks but angles everywhere else. Big, dark eyes and long lashes. Pretty, pouty lips. Smooth, brown skin. And hair that, after several rounds of Japanese straightening, shows practically no sign of its natural frizz.

From high up, we all look the same. That's what Tali's dad likes to preach over dinner—that is, when he's *around* for dinner and not off wooing investors. She wants to believe him, but this is plain old Earth—Liberty, New Hampshire, to be specific—and down here it's every girl for herself.

She finally settles on her white skinny jeans—the ones with purposeful rips along the front of the thighs—and a tissue-thin nautical-striped T-shirt from J.Crew that slips off her shoulder. With a tiny bit of cream blush, mascara, and lip gloss, she looks like she's been hanging out on a sailboat all day, minus hairstyle-altering wind.

She puts a beaten gold cuff on her wrist and starts to step into her espadrille wedges, trying to recall if Blake is taller than six feet. Better not take any chances. She tosses them back into the mountain of heels in her closet and settles on her favorite open-toe yellow flats with the ankle buckles instead.

She grabs her iPhone, half-buried under a pile of discarded outfit options. The house is so quiet she can hear the beep of the dishwasher finishing its cycle from all the way on the east end of the first floor. Yrma must have turned it on before she left. Tali's parents are out of the country again, and she feels their absence like a weight. Even though her social life improved vastly over the last couple of years of high school, there's still no one who can make her feel more confident than her mom and dad.

Unconditional love, she told Ashlynn the other day, when Ash was teasing her for still listening to old Britney songs, *is a blessing and a curse.*

Taking a deep breath, she clicks on Blake's face and types a message.

Still going tn?

She waits several minutes, her heart pounding in her throat. She feels like she's going to throw up.

Beep! New message:

It's like my backyard so prob. U?

She smiles, feeling a shiver of excitement. She spends eighteen minutes writing and rewriting her response.

Save a dixie cup 4 me? If cruz isn't being all stalin about the booze lol.

He responds right away. Right away!

haha. Good ole cruz. Sure thing bender.

He called her Bender. This basically seals it. He has called Tali this ever since she used to be into gymnastics. She did all the tumbling programs at Okahatchee for the third through sixth graders. And he remembered.

She takes a breath. Tonight it's going to happen. Blake Green and Tali Webber. Okahatchee's golden boy and ugly-duckling-turned-swan. *Finally.*

Half an hour later, Tali slows her new red BMW—a gift from Dad, symbolizing her strength and independence—and pulls off the highway exit just past Roxy's Diner, where for years she and her parents stopped for chocolate-chip pancakes before they left her at camp. The sun's only just starting to set, sending a cherry-red glare through her windshield; it looks briefly like the mountains are on fire, angry and majestic. Even though it's hidden by trees, she can actually *smell* the lake now with her window down, that mossy, mineral scent that always seems even stronger at night.

Her phone beeps and her pulse reacts. But as she grabs it, she sees it's not a message from Blake. It's a text from a random 603 number.

Wait. A number she remembers. *Zoe.* She doesn't keep Zoe in her phone anymore, not after she rebooted all her contacts after she dropped her last phone in the toilet at the Goose, Liberty's one townie bar. This was sometime during winter of junior year, when Tali started spending more time with Ashlynn Dermott, and Zoe accused Tali of becoming too "cupcake" for her (all frosting, no nutritional value). But Tali's pretty sure their friendship actually expired around the time Zoe started flaking on every single one of Tali's invitations to hang out. It seemed like she was more into holding burping contests with bad musicians in the school parking lot and analyzing her geeky sci-fi novels than spending time with people like Tali, who preferred to, well, grow up.

Funny that she still knows Zoe's number by heart, though. Same with Luciana's and Joy's. Force of habit, even after all this time. She pops open the text with her right hand while steering with her left.

Joy called. She's coming 2 the reunion. C u there?

Tali feels a quick stab of envy. Of course Joy would call Zoe and not Tali. Even when all four girls were inseparable, Tali was always tumbling, or later, running track, while the other three girls were huddled together on Zoe's bunk bed, whispering.

She starts to type a response when her tires hit something and the car thumps. The wheel practically jerks out of her hand, and she gasps, dropping her phone, her heart staggering in her chest. She grabs the wheel, slamming on the brakes, while the car shudders like a wild beast in a panic. The guardrail races toward her as the car skids into the gravel on the side of the road and finally comes to a complete stop.

Holy fuck. What just happened?

The text. Zoe *fucking* Albright. Zoe and Joy, and probably Luce, too. They're all going to be there tonight. She did *not* plan for that. She had only planned for Blake. And now this. If Zoe hadn't texted her completely out of the blue, she wouldn't have been so thrown off, wouldn't have lost control.

Tali opens the car door and stands up. Her legs are shaking just slightly, but otherwise she's fine. No injuries. No big deal. But the car hasn't fared so well. The right front tire is totally busted—it looks like a saggy black carcass.

Okay, think, she commands herself. It's only a flat tire. *How hard can it be to change a flat tire?* She pops the trunk, but there's no spare in there. She remembers taking it out because it didn't leave enough room for her and Ashlynn's shopping bags.

Crap.

Her first instinct is to call her parents. She starts to dial, then remembers they obviously can't help; they're in Belgium. She's tempted to call anyway, but it'll just worry her parents too much—her mom cried before she left for Europe this summer; even though they're always traveling, she never seems to get used to leaving Tali behind. But Tali's usually fine with it—she adores her parents, they've always been there for her when she really needed them, but it's kinda nice to have a big house to herself and the freedom to party and go out whenever she wants.

She sighs. The best option at the moment is to call a tow company and wait for them to come.

Luckily her phone has service. With a quick online search she finds the closest place and calls, keeping her voice steady and professional, like she's heard her mother do a zillion times when she wants something. After she hangs up, she gets back into the car, turning on her lights and radio to drown out the sound of other people racing by her, toward their own destinations, totally oblivious to the girl sitting alone as night comes.

The sun has completely sunk and Tali's starting to get creeped out by the time the tow truck finally shows, its wheels making a hungry crunching sound against the gravel. When the driver pulls over and climbs out, she's surprised to see he's not that much older than she is. Maybe nineteen or twenty. Scruffy facial hair. Clear green eyes. Grease-stained T-shirt and ratty jeans. Blue baseball hat. He smells like car oil.

He squints at her, then gapes a little.

"Don't I know you?" he asks as he loads up her car, then opens the passenger side of his truck for her.

"I seriously doubt it," Tali replies, hardly giving him a second glance. She climbs in while he's obviously getting a good look at her ass. Guys always say shit like that to her—ever since she sprouted the twins, boys will say anything just to get a conversation going.

"I'm not hitting on you," the guy says, looking faintly amused, and basically reading her mind. "You just look really . . . familiar." She stares at him for a brief second. He's actually a little cute, if it weren't for the grease stains and facial hair, and there *is* something vaguely recognizable about his features, but she can't pinpoint it. How *would* they know each other? He's a tow-truck driver! It's possible he's hit on her before, at the Goose or somewhere, not knowing she's a minor. In that case, best to let it drop.

When she still doesn't respond, he shrugs. "My mistake."

Tali ducks her head over her phone, both so that Tow Boy can't see her blush and so she doesn't have to deal with pretending to be nice to a random townie. Fortunately, Tow Boy gets the hint, and they spend the rest of the ride in silence.

The garage is closed, which means the car will have to wait there overnight. Of course. Just her luck. "Don't worry about me," she says to Tow Boy. "I'll get a ride from here."

"Whatever you say." He shrugs and heads back toward his truck. She whips out her phone and calls Kingston Cars, where she has an account. Her parents set it up so she'd never have to drink and drive.

"I'm sorry." The receptionist has a nasally voice and sounds bored. "The Webber account? It has been temporarily suspended. There was a problem with nonpayment."

"Impossible." Tali's hand begins to sweat. She's stranded a fifteen-minute drive from Camp OK and, more important, from

Blake. With her free hand, she fishes out her AmEx and rattles off the number.

There's a long pause. "I'm sorry, miss. The card is declined."

What. The. Hell.

"Run it again," Tali says desperately.

But after another short pause, the receptionist just sighs. "Declined," she repeats.

Tow Boy's truck door slams and his engine starts.

"It must be a mistake," she hisses into the phone before hanging up. Then she waves an arm at Tow Boy. "Hey, wait!"

He rolls down his window. "What's up?"

"Actually . . . if you don't mind, I could use a ride."

The guy raises his eyebrow. "Going somewhere special?"

Tali hesitates. She is not about to roll up to the reunion in a crappy tow truck. What if Blake sees? But she's not giving up on this night, either. No way.

She wipes her palms on her white jeans and squints out at the dark mountains, looming calm and definitive, like an enormous blanket tucked up to the neck of the navy-blue night.

Luciana lives nearby and is almost definitely going—after all, the camp director, Bernadette Cruz, is her *mom*. Even if Luce weren't forced to attend, she wouldn't want to miss an opportunity to show off all of her awards and prizes. Valedictorian of her high school! Nationally ranked debater! Princeton-bound!

But Tali is no closer to Luce these days than she is to Zoe or Joy. Luce has a billion and one extracurriculars at Brewster *and* a perfect boyfriend. And she's made it clear in a thousand ways, big and small, that her old friends have no place in her annoyingly structured life.

Then again, anything is better than destroying Tali's last chance with Blake. So she takes a deep breath and climbs back into the grungy cab of the tow truck.

"I'll tell you how to get there," she says to Tow Boy, then sits back and stares out the window, watching the road curve beneath them like a black snake, winding its way into the mountains, and into her past.

3

Luciana lights the last of the standing oil lamps in the Cruzes' big, sloping backyard. It's cooler now that the mountains have devoured the daylight already—a harbinger of fall. *Harangue, harbinger, haughtiness. Angry lecture, indicator, arrogance.* The SATs are long over, but after hours of tutoring the juniors this spring, the mantras have stuck. She can't believe it's one of the last Fridays of the summer, before her life completely changes.

She carefully picks up a pile of rose petals that have clumped together on the iron garden bench and scatters them to look more natural. She lights the citronella candle in the glass hurricane lantern and centers it on the round, iron table. She swats a mosquito away from her face and straightens out her glossy black bangs, then steps back to survey her work. *Perfect.*

She checks her phone, loaded up with the playlist—or *sexlist*, as her friend Tanya has coined it—all primed and ready to go. It starts first with the sentimental songs, stuff she and Andrew have sung together in karaoke or danced to at homecoming, plus the corny James Blunt song that was playing when they first said *I love you.* Then the smoother, subtle tunes, which were hardest to pick out. Since Luce has never actually had sex before, it's hard to imagine what kind of music's appropriate.

But tonight is the night. In just a week, Andrew will be at Bates and she'll be at Princeton, and the only times they'll see each other will be long weekends and breaks.

Quickly, as though someone might be watching, Luce checks behind the garden gnome to make sure the awkward, lumpy package of condoms is still there, tucked carefully into her bright yellow pencil case. Up until recently, she actually used the case for pencils—she likes them standardized-test perfect—and it still carries that freshly shaven No. 2 scent. She has a brief and disturbing image of a condom being not unlike a large eraser, then closes the case, heading back inside the house, marveling in the silence as she slides open the screen door. Dad's at work. Mom's at camp. Julian and Silas are also at camp, thankfully—she doesn't want to even have to *think* about dealing with her rambunctious twin brothers. Amelia's with her weekend sitter—even though she's twelve, and Luce outgrew sitters by that age, Amelia's a special case. Having a sister prone to seizures means having a mother prone to being too stressed and busy to handle everything all the time. Which means some things fall to Luce. A lot of things, in fact.

But not tonight.

Tonight is *her* night.

In the kitchen, the strawberries are halved and sugared and locked in Tupperware next to her mother's stack of labeled, premade dinners for the rest of the week, and a creepy-looking bag of pork knuckles her dad must have gotten for one of his "traditional" recipes. The Peppermint Patties—Andrew's favorite—are in the freezer.

The stove clock blinks 8:02, and she feels a nervous flutter in her stomach. Andrew will be here any minute. She hasn't seen him all summer—he's been at lacrosse training camp at Bates, trying to get a leg up on the competition, while she stayed in Wolfeboro for one last summer, helping out with Amelia, boning up on the reading list for Freshman Comp, and, well, planning for tonight.

And then the doorbell rings. Her stomach flutters again. *He's here.*

"Lulu," Andrew says, dropping his duffel bag when she opens the front door.

"Happy belated anniversary!" she squeals, practically lunging toward him.

Her inner butterflies instantly fly away as he wraps her in a hug, lifting her off the floor, then setting her back down and kissing her. She gives in to the familiar warmth of his lips as they do their usual—four kisses: one gentle, one deeper, another gentle one, and then a final parting peck. It's practically their secret handshake, except that she's pretty sure he doesn't realize they're doing it. Everything they do is kind of like that—it fits.

"I missed you so much," he says, flicking her ponytail. His

blond hair looks a tiny bit overgrown and the stubble along his jaw is still as faint as ever, which is just how she likes it.

"Me, too," she says, feeling strangely shy. "I have a whole plan for tonight."

Andrew smiles. "You always have a plan." He wraps his arms around her waist. "I thought we were hitting up the reunion so that your mother doesn't have us assassinated." They got together at Camp Okahatchee, midway through that last summer, two years ago, (July 17, to be exact, three o'clock in the afternoon, during free swim, when he hit her with one of the little kids' floaty noodles to get her attention), and it only makes sense for them to go back for reunion night. Also, her mom *would* kill her if she missed it.

"We are. But first I have a surprise for you outside."

He grins as she grabs his hands and leads him toward the back patio.

"Close your eyes," she orders, then directs him through the back door. "*Ta-da! And* I found this in Dad's stash." She extracts a bottle of white wine from a cooler hidden behind a big oak tree. "I don't know if it's any good, but—"

Andrew draws her toward him. "It's perfect. *You're* perfect." He leans down to kiss her again, then takes the wine in his other hand and leads her toward the table. They pour wine into plastic cups, and he moves so that he's sitting beside her on the garden bench. He wraps his arm around her and she leans into his chest, breathing in his familiar smell. The summer so far without him has felt like an eternity. She drinks more quickly than she would normally, trying to calm her nerves—it's just Andrew, this is right, this is perfect—and a warm glow spreads from her stomach up through her head. Soon her cup is empty and she feels loose and happy and giggly.

She puts down her wine cup, then gets up and faces him, moving his cup aside. Then she sits down on his lap, straddling her golden-brown legs around him, and starts to unbutton her plaid shirt. She's not wearing a bra—she rarely needs one.

"Whoa," Andrew says. "Are you sure?"

"What, you don't want your anniversary present?" she teases him. This isn't so difficult. She can do this. She hasn't even *started* her playlist.

"No, no, I *definitely* want it. I'm just . . . happy. Happy *you* want it." He finishes his sentence with a murmur, kissing her neck, while helping her unbutton the rest of her shirt. There's a faint breeze on her collarbones. Andrew groans, low and soft, and she feels a tingle of heat in her stomach.

She runs her hands through his hair, then tilts his face up so she can kiss him again. Long, soft, trying something different. And then, she hears a rustling in the woods beyond the patio. She turns—just as a person stumbles out from between the trees.

"Oh shit!" Andrew stands up quickly as Luce shrieks, too loud, wrapping her now fully open shirt tight around her chest.

"Chill. It's me," says a slightly annoyed female voice. And then some branches part, and there, standing in front of Luce and Andrew in tight white jeans and a blue-striped top, is Tali, looking expensive as always, and even taller and more gorgeous than her Facebook photos suggest.

"Tali?" Luce gapes, half-expecting her old friend to dematerialize again. "What are you *doing* here?"

"Sorry," Tali says, not sounding sorry at all. "Am I interrupting something?"

Luce glares at her, trying to telegraph the fact that she is *obviously* interrupting. But Tali has already plopped down in a chair and picked up the bottle of wine. "Hmmm, I hate chardonnay but it'll do if we're pregaming. It's good to see you, Luce! And you, too, Andrew. Like the hair. Are there any more cups?"

"You came over to pregame?" Luce crosses her arms. She can't remember the last time Tali came over. She can't remember the last time she and Tali even *talked*.

"Actually, I had some issues with my ride to the reunion. You're going, right?" Tali puts her feet up on the other chair and, apparently forgetting about her request for a cup, takes a slug right from the bottle. "My freaking tire popped and then this semi-hot grease monkey had to come to the rescue. My credit cards were acting funny so I couldn't take a car service. I didn't want to show up in a *tow truck*, and I figured since your place is close by we could just go together and I would look slightly more like a normal human being. I rang the bell for, like, an hour, but clearly you guys were too *busy* to hear it." And taking another sip, she adds, "This wine isn't that bad, actually."

Luce feels the usual combination of envy and annoyance— *invidiousness?*—she always experiences around Tali. She really wants to tell Tali to leave. To stop talking to *her* boyfriend. To stop drinking *her* booze. To stop resting her cute yellow peep-toes on Luce's mom's old patio furniture.

Instead, she clears her throat and says, "Well, you should probably call your credit card company and figure out what's wrong. Fraud is a big problem nowadays." Immediately, she hates herself. She sounds like a mom. Like *her* mom.

"What?" Tali squints at her.

"Your credit card company. You said your cards weren't working."

"I'll give my mom a call," Tali says, standing up. "And then we can head over to Camp OK. Yeah?"

Luce swallows a sigh. Her perfect evening—the flickering lights, the rose petals, crumpled from where she and Andrew squished them on the bench—all wasted. What's that saying about best-laid plans?

"Sure," she says, forcing a smile. "That sounds fine."

Tali heads inside, leaving Luce and Andrew alone again.

Andrew wraps her in a hug from behind. In her ear he whispers, "We can pick up where we left off after the reunion."

She tries to smile again but can't get it to stick. She knows Andrew's trying to be sweet, but right now his willingness to abandon the whole plan irritates her. "I'm gonna go get the keys," she tells him, gently extricating herself from his arms.

She heads toward the kitchen but freezes beyond the doorway in the dining room when she hears Tali's voice. Weirdly, Tali sounds much younger . . . and very afraid.

"What are you *talking* about?" Tali is saying. And then, after a pause. "I don't understand. Did Daddy do something wrong?" Another pause, while Tali paces the kitchen, and then, *"Investigation?"* A few seconds later, she blurts, "No, I don't get it. I don't believe you. You're lying! I'm sorry, Mom, it's just . . ." Another pause, as she nods, listening. "Okay, I'll call you again soon. Okay, I love you, too. Okay, bye."

Luce leaps back into the shadows of the dining room, bumping into the end table where all her debate trophies are lined up, almost causing a domino-style disaster. She takes a deep breath, righting the trophies. Then she clears her throat loudly, announcing her presence even before she enters the kitchen.

Tali whips around to face her. She looks as if she might cry. Luce knows how close she is to her parents—whatever's going on now has got to be a big deal.

"Almost ready to go?" Luce asks gently, watching Tali intently, trying to figure out whether she should say something about what she overheard. It's been so long since the days when she would have folded her into a hug.

But in an instant, Tali changes. She shrugs like she's shaking off cold water. "Totally. Let's do this thing."

Seven minutes later, Luce is pulling into the parking lot behind the Camp Okahatchee main offices. She, Tali, and Andrew—who has gamely agreed to sit in the back for the short ride over—clamber out of Luce's dad's old Toyota and cross the familiar dirt-and-gravel lot toward the rec hall. From here they can see a good amount of the Okahatchee compound—between the offices and the rec hall to the right is a sloping hill that leads toward both the lake and the Great Lawn.

Beyond the big grassy field that's home to so many Oka-hatchee sports, concerts, and group gatherings are a string of bunks where the younger girl campers are housed. Farther back, in the dense darkness around the far lip of the lake, are the older girls' cabins. And unseen around a bend, to the left and over a little bridge, is the sandy area where the volleyball nets, the ten-nis courts, a dusty baseball diamond, and the boys' cabins are all clustered together along the water.

Christmas lights and streamers have been strung along the rec-hall roof. Inside, a bluegrass band is playing. A couple of rides and a bouncy castle have been set up on the Great Lawn, with large footlights illuminating them eerily from the perimeter of the field, and a huge crowd of people is milling around. The sug-ary scent of cotton candy fills the warm air, mingling with the algae smell from the lake, which always makes Luce think of the color green, and of the silence of being underwater.

Andrew holds her hand as they walk toward the chaos and noise, which echoes off the surface of Lake Okahatchee in the distance, a smaller offshoot of Lake Tabaldak. Luce is struck by a wave of memories—of sneaking gummy snacks out of the camp kitchen with Zoe when they were nine; of holding Tali when she cried for hours after her dad and mom had that terrible fight in the summer before sixth grade and she thought they were going to get a divorce. How weird it is that this used to be her home every summer for nine whole years.

Just like that, things change—the faint, filmy bubble of summer pops, September's cool breath whooshes in, and life moves on.

Next to the rec hall, someone with short hair is standing alone in the darkness, leaning against the fading red siding, smoking a cigarette, which Luce is positive is not allowed. The tip cuts an arc through the night, like an orange lightning bug or one of those phosphorescent amoebas. *Phenomenon, philanthropy, phosphorescent. An occurrence, charity, light emitted without burning.*

As they start to move by her, Luce gasps.

Tali recognizes her at the same time. "Holy shit. *Joy?*"

Their old friend smiles with her mouth still around her cigarette. She is even paler up close than she at first appeared, though she was always fair. She looks so much *older* without her long, light brown, wavy hair, which Luce remembers she used to wear in braids, sometimes woven around her head like a crown. Joy looks like a completely different person now: from her extremely short pixie cut, the tiny silver stud in her right nostril, and the dark red lipstick she's wearing—which has left a stain on her cigarette—to her clunky green army boots, faded black jeans, and holey gray sweater. She takes her time dragging on her cigarette, then lets the smoke slip out between her scarlet lips like she's hesitant to let it go.

Only her smile is the same.

"You came," she says.

4

Everyone always says it's the little things in life that really matter: a gentle kiss, a just-opened tulip, a half-eaten peach, hearing someone you love laugh openly and freely . . . blah, blah, blah.

Joy has never really gotten that. Sure, life is one jumbled collage of moments that each play their modest role in the greater outcome, just like the body is made up of cells. . . . Nerves, arteries, and veins snake through us like tree branches. Capillaries. Muscle and skin. Marrow. Blood. Bone. Water.

But we don't *experience* things that way. It's the *big* things that matter; that's what Joy believes. Mountains and oceans. Encounters and accidents that forever change us. Ultimatums. Epic fights. Wars, even. Doomed love affairs. Death, especially: its mysterious blackness licking at the edge of existence like a tide creeping in at night, seeping into the sand and slowly taking over.

So when Joy showed up at Camp OK, she wasn't struck by the way the spice from the roasting nuts vendor tickled her throat, or the way the needles of the tall firs on the outskirts of the lawn pricked the night with a sharp odor of pine just like a car air freshener, or how the paint on the main headquarters was starting to crumble, giving the buildings that look of classic New England rusticity.

Instead, what mattered to her, and what she still can't shake, is the *epicness* of it all: how when she stands back from the crowd, the lights and balloons and the rides twirling around and around all blur together over the Great Lawn in one big mess of sparkle and flail.

For a long time before tonight, Joy worried her old friends would be mad at her, if they came at all—that Tali would ignore her, that Luce would scold her about her absence from their lives over the last two years, that Zoe would have forgotten their secret handshake and inside jokes. Joy has changed a lot since that last summer at camp, but she hasn't forgotten a single thing.

At some point, though, Joy's mind started to clear and all those doubts and worries vanished. Tali could ignore, Luce could scold, Zoe could forget—she simply wanted them to be together again.

This, she thinks, is the whole point of reunion night—putting people together in the same place. It's like reopening one of those dorky, clunky, old puzzle boxes and dumping all the pieces into a pile, like her grandmother does during Sunday visits. Some won't fit together, but that's okay. There's a vision in there, a Big Picture somewhere amid the mess of jigsaw shapes and edges.

That's what she's pondering—the Big Picture—when she sees

them. Tali first: tall, put together, her crisp white clothes accenting her not-quite-ebony skin. Joy is struck by how much she looks like a *woman* now. Behind her is Luce: tiny, perky, in what appears to be an all–L.L.Bean outfit, including a plaid button-down, khaki short shorts, and sandals with a slight wedge. She's holding the hand of a slightly scruffy, well-bred-looking blond guy in a soccer jersey. Andrew. So they *did* stay together all this time. It gives her a small jolt. When Joy shut down her Facebook account, on some level she believed everyone else's lives would shut down with it.

But reunion nights are known for their miracles—the time someone opened a pesky vent and an entire nest of baby birds flew out. The time there was an upside-down rainbow that no one was able to capture on camera. The time, according to legend, that two Camp OK-ers, years ago, walked all the way across the surface of the lake, as though it were frozen, and found themselves safe and dry on the other side. Maybe tonight there'll be a miracle, too.

Maybe this *is* the miracle.

Joy breaks into a smile, even as Tali gasps and squeals and starts toward her.

"You came," Joy says, an incredible sense of power surging through her: She has done it. She has gathered the elemental forces from the corners of the world together tonight. Or at least, from the corners of New Hampshire and Maine. Close enough.

Now they just need Zoe.

She pushes off the wall with her boot and hugs Tali first, who smells of Ralph Lauren Romance, then Luce, who smells like strawberries and jojoba—and slightly of lemon surface cleaner.

"Why'd you chop off all your hair?" Luce blurts, at the same time Tali asks, "So how's life in Portland?"

Joy laughs. "Portland's cool—the ocean's right there, which I love. And yeah, the hair," Joy says, touching her almost-shaved head with a flicker of insecurity. "Believe it or not, it's kind of a popular look in the crowd I hang with these days. You know, moody, artsy types."

Joy bends down to pick up her shoulder bag, which is heavy.

"Well, you *were* always an art freak," Tali says.

Luce looks at her skeptically. "Yeah, but more of a make-your-own-lanyard-out-of-hemp artsy, not hack-off-your-own-hair artsy." She isn't trying to be mean, but Joy can see she's baffled. Of all of them, Luce is the one who handles change the least well. "I mean, it looks cute," Luce hastens to add. "I was just surprised."

"It's no big deal," Joy says. There's an awkward silence. Joy can sense the discomfort between them—not tension, exactly, but not coziness either. Her old instinct kicks in, to try to make it better. Only, for the first time she doesn't know how.

"So." Luce plasters a smile on her face. "We're all here."

Joy nods, starting to feel even more self-conscious.

Luce shrugs. "Who wants cotton candy?"

"I could use a beer if we can find any," Tali announces, her eyes looking cloudy. "I sort of have someone I'm supposed to meet up with, actually."

Luce is already waving at a figure she recognizes in the distance. Joy is hit with a sudden ache in her chest—it's clear the girls don't really *want* to be here. At least not for the same reasons she does. Already, the powerful feeling is slipping away. She doesn't want everyone to scatter, not yet, not so soon. This used to come to her so easily.

"Wait," she says. "We have to wait for—"

"HOLY. CRAP. Is that *you*?" Zoe is jogging downhill in her flip-flops, her messy blond bun coming undone. She's wearing cutoff jean shorts, a loose white men's T-shirt, and an overlarge zip-up hoodie—no makeup.

She fires off a dozen questions at once. "When did you get here? What did you do to your hair? Where have you been all this time? What have I missed? Is that Jason Moran over there with Holly Snegman? Do you think they're hooking up? How gross! Is anyone else *starving*?"

Joy laughs, which feels good. It eases some of the tightness in her chest. "Andrew, can you give us a second? Guys, there's something I kind of need your help with."

Tali looks up from her phone. "What kind of help?" she says, an edge of impatience in her voice. Joy can only assume the "someone" she's supposed to meet up with later is Blake. Old habits die hard.

"It'll be easy," Joy says. "You just have to follow me . . . for old times' sake," she adds.

There's a split second of silence.

"I don't mean to be rude," Tali blurts, "but I haven't heard from you in, like, two years."

Her words land like a pile of rocks at the bottom of the lake.

"Tali," Zoe spits out, as if her name is a curse.

Luce jumps in to mediate. "Sure, Joy," she says, with a smile that looks a little too forced. "For old times' sake." She speaks like she's at a college interview, not talking to her old friends. But it's enough. For now.

As they move down the hill and into the crowd, someone bumps into Joy and she temporarily loses her footing. Disappointment creeps in around her, chilling, like the damp of the grass seeping into her leather boots. Where has all the ancient childhood magic gone, the kind that seemed to keep her, Zoe, Tali, and Luce within its protective netting? It used to seem as if campers would simply part, Red Sea–like, so that the four girls could pass through them. Now she feels like an injured lieutenant, leading troops through the chaos of a battlefield, uncertain about whether they're on the winning side or the losing. Uncertain what a victory would even look like.

The night is humming with activity, the din so loud you can't hear the normally deafening chirp of crickets. When Joy was little, she associated the sound of crickets with stargazing. Her mom would take her out onto the back porch in their old Liberty house, shut off all the lights, and tell her to wait until her eyes adjusted to the darkness. While she waited, watching the stars blink their way into existence, she heard the crickets' *chk-chk*, and believed it was actually the noise stars made when they clicked on at night, one after the other.

But now, with the many floodlights and blinking red and blue bulbs lining the rides, and the smoke from various food vendors filling the air, the night sky just looks like a blackboard, starless, smudged gray with a lifetime's worth of chalk. A little girl runs past Joy, trailing a bunch of streamers, which brush lightly across Joy's face as she pushes her way forward, their damp ends dissolving away like tears.

"So you want to tell us where we're heading?" Tali says, after they've left the crowd behind and crossed down to the sandy part of the shoreline.

"Almost there," Joy says, wishing she didn't sound so pathetically urgent, wishing she weren't the only one for whom this night actually *means* something. "Just trust me."

There's a deep ache in her chest, as if she has just smoked too much, too fast. These girls, with whom she once shared so many of her most significant moments—getting her braces off, learning to ride a bike, that time she almost drowned by Forest River Falls, countless slumber parties, the first time she got her heart broken by a boy, the list could go on and on and on—these girls are barely more than strangers to her now.

Her fault. All her fault.

They finally get to the Wellness Cabin, Okahatchee's optimistic name for its infirmary. Joy pulls them behind the boxy unit, leading them to the small wooden structure tucked into the edge of the woods next to the Agro Club's garden, which is really more of a sad, square patch of rotting squash vines.

"Remember?" Joy says now, turning around to face her

friends. This close to the lake, the air is cooler, the darkness thicker.

Zoe gets down on her knees on the forest side of the shed and overturns the pile of rust-colored rocks next to the leaning birch. From underneath the rocks, she unearths a silver key. "How could we forget?" she says, her face looking ghostly in the darkness.

"The Stevens," says Luce, laughing softly, placing a hand on the shed wall as though to verify it's still solid. Tali used to sneak in giant bags of the candy Luce's mom kept in the main offices for the younger campers when they inevitably got homesick. Then they'd gather at the shed and tell secrets they didn't want the rest of their bunkmates to hear, and they'd divide up all the candy evenly. Luce would insist that they share "even-stevens," which became their secret code.

"This is so surreal," says Zoe, straightening up. "God, I haven't thought about the Stevens since we were, like, Bunk Coyote."

Tali raises an eyebrow. "I hope you're not going to suggest we gather around on the floor like we used to. I'm wearing white."

"I think the shed is actually *used* now, for storage," Luce says thoughtfully. "According to my mom, Agro is actually becoming a *thing* recently. They just got some major funding."

"Maybe Camp OK is finally becoming Camp Fantastic," Zoe says wryly.

Joy smiles. It's the thing she always used to say. It never even used to seem optimistic—that things would get better, that those summers at camp were only okay compared to what would come next, compared to *fantastic*. It always just seemed like a given, a fact of the universe. Things are constantly spinning toward better and better outcomes, is what she thought. Now, as she thinks about the idea of fantastic, she can't help but shake her head, unable to believe she's the same person who once thought that. Unable to believe she was that naive.

She opens her bag, determined not to lose her nerve. "I brought some things . . . you know, things we made, stuff I collected—memories—and I thought we could bury it under that loose floorboard in there where we sometimes stashed notes to each other." She feels her face heating up and is thankful for the darkness.

"Like a time capsule?" Zoe offers, sounding skeptical.

"Exactly, a time capsule." Joy takes a deep breath. Even standing so close to the shed, she's hit by the musty smell of old garden gloves and moldy wood—the signature scent of the Stevens. "Let's face it. We've grown apart. We have," she adds bluntly, when Luce starts to protest. It hurts, but at least it's the truth. "Our camp years are forever behind us. I get that. But I know, deep down, that you guys have to be sad about that, too. That it meant something to you, just like it did to me. And this way, a little piece of our camp experience—of *us*—will live on in the future."

It isn't exactly an apology. Joy wonders in their silence if the girls resent her, if they will ever *really* forgive her for leaving, for dropping away. If she'll ever be able to admit why she did it.

For a minute, no one speaks. Then Zoe says, "What'd you bring?"

Joy reaches into her bag, into her stockpile of notes, wrappers, bottle caps, ticket stubs, miniature toys, shells, friendship brace-lets, and pictures. She removes a thin envelope and opens it. Tali pulls out her iPhone to see by its light.

Inside the envelope is a narrow strip of photo-booth photos, four in a row. They were taken that last summer of camp. In the photos, all four girls are posing for the camera with huge, goofy grins. In one, Tali is making a sexy-pouty kiss face at the camera while holding up a pair of Batman boxers, and Luce is tilting her chin up in faux indignation. In another, Zoe is sticking her tongue out while waving a gold medal at the camera, and Tali is stealing the tiara Joy is wearing in the two photos above. Luce has her merit badge proudly displayed on her shirt.

In all of the photos, Joy has her long, flowing, light brown hair down around her arms, her cheeks are flushed pink, and her eyes look big and tearful and happy. Even now, looking back at her former self, Joy feels a flutter of that old happiness in her chest, just a quiver of it really, but fastened down with guilt, like a pinned butterfly.

Tali, Luce, and Zoe huddle together around Joy to get a closer look. If someone were to observe them from afar, they might actually believe the girls were still best friends.

"Why are we doing this?" Zoe asks at the same time Tali says, "Ugh, I look like a freaking idiot."

Luce touches Joy's arm gently. "I *love* this idea," she says, her voice soft but firm. Whether or not she actually means it, Joy can't tell, but she's grateful anyway. "It's the perfect way to say good-bye to camp."

Joy nods. "A way to say good-bye to all of it."

Luce takes the key from Zoe and steps forward to test it on the lock.

The key sticks. Luce gives it a hard shove, and the whole wall of the shed shudders, but the door doesn't give.

Joy's throat squeezes up. She didn't come all this way to have her plan ruined. She takes her turn trying the lock. Still no luck.

"Maybe we should just pick a different spot," Tali offers, looking antsy.

"Hold on." Zoe marches around to the side of the shed, getting the determined look on her face that Joy remembers so well.

A second later, they hear a grunting sound, followed immediately by an alarm.

"Zoe! What the hell did you *do*?" Luce cries.

Joy darts around the side of the shed, with Luce and Tali right behind her, to see Zoe sticking a pin back into her pocket, looking a bit guilty—and also a little amused.

"I thought maybe I could jimmy the lock." Zoe shrugs. "Cal showed me how . . ."

Joy wants to smile but her whole plan is spinning away, and it makes her almost dizzy with frustration.

Zoe throws her hands up. "Anyway, I didn't think it would be alarmed."

Tali snorts. "Since when is the Stevens so valuable? What are they keeping in there?"

"Dynamite?" Zoe offers.

"Cocaine?" Tali suggests.

"Guys," Luce urges. "We need to get *out* of here! I'm so not getting busted for this. Come on!"

Joy has no choice but to follow them. The screaming of the alarm pierces her ears and brain like a bratty tattletale on the playground. *Nah-nah-nah-nah-nah.*

It used to be that the four of them were invincible. Between Tali's charm, Luce's practicality, Zoe's cleverness, and Joy's innocence, they could get out of *anything.*

But that was then and this is now.

They cut through a portion of the woods so as not to be caught, hurrying the opposite way around the Wellness Cabin, then skirting the sandy beach and racing back to the Great Lawn, where once again the bubbling sound of laughter and friendly shouting and the jingle of Ferris wheel music drowns out everything, including the sound of the Agro storage shed's fancy new alarm. Including, too, the sound of Joy's racing heartbeat.

Running out of breath, she slows down. It's then that a sharp but familiar voice calls out her name. "Why, *Miss Freeman,* it's so *lovely* to see you here tonight!"

Joy turns. Barreling toward her is the Cruz, aka Bernadette Cruz, in head-to-toe camp director regalia: khaki shorts and a matching tan, collared, short-sleeved shirt with the Okahatchee logo emblazoned over the heart, featuring an image of a green mountain, a blue lake, a yellow sun, and a totally un-PC Native American tomahawk. *Where all the right elements unite* is written in script over it. She is also carrying around her clipboard. Why she needs that thing for reunion night, Joy has no idea, but she suspects it could be permanently attached to the Cruz's hand.

The Cruz smiles at her. "I'm so glad you came. I know Luci-ana has thought a lot about you since you both graduated from Okahatchee." The Cruz always refers to campers who make it all the way to the age cap as "graduates." Her eyes sweep over the other girls. "And Misses Webber and Albright, too! Looks like the whole gang's back together again. Now, where were you all scurrying off to in such a hurry?"

Luce, Tali, and Zoe hang back guiltily, avoiding eye contact.

"Mom," Luce begins, obviously trying to help. "We were just, um . . ."

Zoe jumps in: "Heading to the photo booth!" She pulls the old photo strip from Joy's hand—she's been clutching it since they fled the Stevens. "You know, for old times' sake," Zoe adds.

"That's a fantastic idea." The Cruz beams. "We could use more images for the memory wall. I'll walk you over there; I was just heading that way."

Before the girls can protest, the Cruz herds them toward the photo booth, with its steady stream of campers and alums alike filing in and out, their pictures spitting out of a small slot on the outer wall like a long tongue.

"Now go ahead," she says, giving Joy a slap on the back that actually stings. "Enjoy yourselves."

Zoe shoves Joy inside the booth and pockets the old photo strip. Luce pilots Tali inside after them with a final awkward smile at her mother, who is hovering there, waiting to see their photos come out.

The curtain swishes shut behind them. Inside the booth it's hot and sticky and as narrow as an upright coffin. It smells like bubble gum and burning rubber. Luce and Tali manage to claim space on the small plastic seat, leaving Zoe and Joy to hover uncomfortably on either side of them, cramped and piled on top of each other.

Joy's back hurts, her heart hurts, and it's all she can do to muster a smile. She notices graffiti all over the inner walls:

Sammy & Gina, '12.

Dave is da bad ass. Crossed out to read: *Dave is an ass zit.*

Eat me.

Long live the Cruz.

For a good time call Emily Fargo. (Poor Emily.)

Indigo Perez is a ho.

But her eyes are searching for something else. There it is:

Z, J, T & L, friends forever. She feels a pang in her gut.

Luce grabs the remote control tethered to the camera by a long cord. "Ready? Set, go!" she says.

Joy's heart rate peaks. *Ready, set, go.* Just like in the camp relay races they used to run.

"Luce, I wasn't ready!" Tali squeals, frantically readjusting her top and in the process jostling Joy with her arms.

SNAP. The first flash is blinding, and Joy blinks, trying to clear her vision, which has gone totally white. She can hear Zoe laughing, saying, "Redo! Redo!" It's hot and hard to breathe, but for a miniature second, Joy feels like it's old times again—the four of them goofing off while a line of other campers builds up outside the booth.

Just then, they hear a whining sound and are thrown into utter darkness.

"What the hell?" Tali says, standing up and jostling the three other girls again. "Zoe, what did you do?"

"It wasn't me," Zoe says. "Ow, that's my *foot!*"

Suddenly, it's chaos inside the tiny space—a thick blackness tentacled with sixteen sweaty, sticky arms and legs.

"I think we broke it," Joy says, as someone—Tali?—elbows her in the stomach.

"We are on a streak of destruction!" Luce exclaims. Then: "Ew, what *is* that?"

"My boob," Zoe says. "You just grabbed it."

Tali chimes in, "I can't breathe. Let's get *out* of this thing."

Finally, the four of them manage to push through the curtain one by one. Joy squeezes out last, stumbling out of the confining space, gasping for air.

For a second, she thinks she must still be staring into the flash of the camera. She's hit by near-blinding brightness. She blinks a few times and rubs her eyes, feeling dizzy.

The laughter around her has abruptly died out. All four of her former friends are blinking, silent, stunned.

The sunlight is blazing. It's daytime.

She swivels around and gasps. The photo booth is nowhere to be seen. It has completely *vanished*, like some trick of the light.

"What. The—" Zoe turns a full circle.

"What's going on?" Luce says in a trembling voice.

Joy starts to register that the campers around them are not waiting in line for carnival rides and cotton candy—they're *running*. Someone—a black-haired girl, faintly recognizable—whizzes past her carrying a Hula-Hoop. As Joy watches, the black-haired girl hands off the Hula-Hoop to another camper. She, in turn, starts running, tearing across the Great Lawn, where hundreds of other campers are racing and jumping around, tagging one another and wearing bright-colored T-shirts.

Just like they used to do on relay day, back at camp.

Joy feels like she might puke.

A loud whistle pierces the air. Joy's chest seizes.

Jeremy Farber, counselor and asshole extraordinaire, is marching over to them from around the side of the offices. "Get a move on, girls!" he shouts. "Stop slouching. You're giving the Orange team a bad name!"

"What—what's happening?" Luce's eyes are wide. She looks like she might cry, which is impossible, Joy knows, because Luce *doesn't* cry. Her life is too efficient for tears. "What *is* this?"

Zoe shakes her head, dazed. "Relay races," she whispers.

It occurs to her that they're all wearing orange T-shirts. Every summer, on the Monday of the final week of camp, they would divide everyone up into five color groups for the relays.

Jeremy blows his whistle again. "I said *move*. This is a race, not gossip hour!"

Just then, a camper named Petra Manger, whom Joy hasn't even thought about in two full years, is in her face. She grabs Joy's shoulders. "Joy! I *said*, Take. The. Baton! We're losing."

Instinct kicks in. Joy grabs the baton numbly. Her heart beats so hard it threatens to knock her over. Petra gives her a shove toward the center of the field. With no time to process, Joy begins to run; the only thing on her mind is the boy in an orange T-shirt, waving his arms at her, screaming, "Come on, come on, they're beating us!"

Her arms and legs are moving, but her mind is stuck in mud, churning forward at a thousandth of the pace. As she runs, her footsteps pound out a chant in her head: *What. Is. Happening. What. Is. Happening. What. Is. Happening.*

She can see now that the boy in the orange shirt is Gene Yung. He's waiting for her to pass the stupid baton.

Her neck is hot and she feels something clinging to her shoulder blades. It takes her a minute to realize what's causing that sensation: her hair . . . at its full, former length, grazing down her back.

Just like she wore it every day when she was fifteen.

PART TWO
REMEMBER WHEN

"The past is never where you think you left it."
—Katherine Anne Porter

5

MONDAY

Farber's whistle must have been perfectly designed to replicate the sound of Satan ushering a person into hell. The instinct to react when Okahatchee's jerkiest counselor blows his lid is immediate.

Zoe's thoughts jostle around in her head with every step, as if they're being dislodged by her pounding feet. What the hell is going on? It's like she had a complete blackout. The last thing she remembers, she was piled into a hot, sticky photo booth at the reunion with Joy, Luce, and Tali.

Did she get drunk last night during the reunion carnival and pass out? But her head doesn't ache, and she doesn't have that pinched feeling in the pit of her stomach that she got when she and Cal drank all of his dad's Jack Daniel's after a Lumineers concert last March.

As she hits the soccer field, she begins to recognize a whole host of other campers, shouting and waving their arms and taking part in the race, some in purple, some in yellow, some in green, some in orange. Samantha Puliver is leaping over the final in a series of hurdles and tagging James Larsing, who takes off in another direction, rolling a tire. Zoe's head is spinning. This is *definitely* the end-of-summer relay course.

It doesn't make any sense. None of it makes any sense.

As Zoe slows down, someone with long hair darts past her, and it takes her a second to realize it's Joy, surpassing her on the field.

Joy with long hair.

At this, Zoe stops completely, floored and confused.

"Move out of the way!" someone shouts behind her. Before she can react, the person rams into her from behind. She goes flying to the ground with Ricky Mandelson on top of her.

A sharp pain shoots through her right knee when it makes contact with the ground, and the wind gets knocked out of her. She rolls Ricky off her, disentangles herself, and sits up. Ricky has hit the ground, and his ankle is now twisted at a funny angle. "Dammit. Shit." He's gripping his ankle with one hand, his face contorted with pain.

"Are you all right?" Zoe asks—a stupid question, since it's obvious he isn't.

Now more whistles are blowing and everyone is shouting. Campers and counselors start crowding them, babbling, giving Ricky competing instructions—*try to stand up* and *don't move.*

Zoe feels like her head will explode. Two years ago, Ricky twisted his ankle during relays. That time, it was because he'd tripped on a hurdle. She remembers because Luce was the one to stop running and help him off the field, and in return she earned the merit badge on the last night of camp. . . .

Wait a minute . . .

As Ricky stands up, leaning heavily on two other campers, Luce, Tali, and Joy heave Zoe off the ground. Her head is spinning.

Am I losing my mind?

"Something's wrong," she croaks out. She stands up on legs that feel unsteady now. "I'm having the worst déjà vu. But it won't go away. What *happened* last night?"

"It's not just you," Luce says. She looks over her shoulder to make sure no one's listening, then lowers her voice. "It's happening to me, too."

"Same," Tali says. "What the *hell* happened in that photo booth?"

"I don't know," says Joy, "but I'm pretty sure I know what's happening now."

The three girls stare at her.

"Isn't it obvious?" Joy says when no one speaks. "We're fifteen again."

"WHAT?" Tali squeals, and Luce leaps up, trying to clamp her hands over Tali's mouth.

"Just calm down, okay?" Luce instructs her. "Let's all think about this rationally. . . ."

"*Rationally?*" Tali screeches as she twists away from Luce. "There's nothing *rational* about this." She whirls on Joy, eyes blazing. "Is this some kind of prank? Was this your big reason for getting us back together, so you could pull this stunt? Because it's not fucking funny!"

Joy shakes her head, looking stricken. "I'm just as confused as you are."

"No one thinks it's funny!" Zoe practically hisses at Tali. *Why is it always about Tali and what's inconvenient for her?* "Has anyone stopped to think Joy might be *right*? I mean, look around us!" She can't believe she's saying it. She clears her throat again, trying to keep it together.

Suddenly, Tali screams. "My boobs. They. Are. *Gone*," Tali says, a sound of real terror in her voice, grabbing her chest like she keeps hoping her Cs will materialize from her shirt. "Oh shit. Oh *shit*."

"And what about my hair?" Joy says, pulling on her long, light-brown ponytail as though it's a foreign creature that has attached itself to her head.

Zoe stares at Joy. Her old friend Joy, who looks so much more familiar than the Joy of the present. Or the past. Or future. Whatever it is. Was. *This* Joy has all the same old vibrancy she had that last summer at Okahatchee. In fact, they all do.

"So somehow we went . . . back," Luce blurts. "But how?"

"Okay." Zoe tries to think it through, doing her best to stay calm, even though she feels like her brain hopped onto a roller coaster and it wasn't properly buckled in first. "This is like this one *Dr. Who* episode, where the professor travels back in time and—"

"Zoe, this isn't a sci-fi TV show," Luce says rather harshly. Zoe can see that her whole body is shaking. "This is *real* and it's our *lives*. And we need to figure out how to fix it."

"We need to get back to reunion night," Tali says, growing semihysterical. "I had *plans*!"

Another wash of annoyance spreads through her. "Tali, I hate to break it to you, but this isn't all about *you*."

"Guys, let's not fight," Luce interjects. "Please! We're in this together, so we need to just figure out what to do next. Okay? And let's move off the field, where we can talk in privacy."

She leads the way toward the line of trees behind the rec hall.

As they walk, Joy looks around. "Actually," she says, her face going contemplative. "Maybe this isn't as crazy as we think. . . ."

"What do you mean?" Zoe asks, hoping her input is actually helpful this time. Now that they're hidden in the cool shade of a couple of oaks, she's starting to feel less nauseated.

Tali gives her a slight glare.

Joy goes on. "What I mean is, haven't there been strange things that have happened on past reunion nights?"

"What, like alums getting drunk and throwing up in front of their own kids?" Zoe says, fully aware that she's babbling, that *she's* the one being unhelpful now. She sits down on the grass, and the other three join her, gathering cross-legged, just like they used to.

"She's right," Luce chimes in. "There was the time Minna

Spencer's dog came back."

The memory, though dim, creeps back into Zoe's mind. "That's true—the cocker spaniel?"

"Yeah," Luce says, nodding thoughtfully. "It ran away when her parents dropped her off in June, and she was devastated that summer. Then it came back two whole months later, on reunion night."

Zoe sighs. "That's definitely a bit odd, but not quite up there with time travel."

Tali looks from Zoe to Joy and Luce, then back at Zoe again, as though she has just confirmed that time travel is real.

Which she basically did.

"True," Tali adds, "but there was also the time Petra fell off the spinning swings and everyone thought she could have broken her neck and died, but she turned out to be miraculously fine."

Luce nods. "She didn't even have a bruise."

"So," Zoe says, tugging a piece of grass out of the dirt and twisting it between her fingers. "What we're agreeing on here is that this is just some awesome reunion night *fluke*?"

"My mom told me once that Okahatchee translates to something like Water of Possibility."

Now it's Tali's turn to roll her eyes. "Next you're gonna tell me some brochure B.S. about the natives who believed photographs steal your soul."

"Huh. That gives me an idea," Joy says. She's doing her best to stay positive, and Zoe feels an instant wave of gratitude. She speaks slowly, as if she's working it out as she talks: "It all comes back to the photo booth. It *must*. Remember how it short-circuited while we were inside it?"

"I don't get it," Luce says, looking panicked.

"We need to get back into the photo booth," Joy says. "Maybe we can somehow undo all this."

"But the photo booth isn't even *here*." Luce crosses her arms as if she's freezing, even though it must be mid-eighties. "Mom only brings it in for reunion night. And if today is the relay, then it's a Monday. And we still have five more days before the Friday of reunion night, when we can even *try*."

Tali gapes at her. "So . . . you're suggesting we hang around in the past for five days and then . . . take a bunch of glam shots in the photo booth and hope it works like a time machine in the other direction? And how do we know we're *really* in the past in the first place, not just some—"

"Alternate reality?" Luce fills in, wide-eyed.

Tali rolls her eyes. "I was going to say drug-induced hallucination."

"Well, we do look *exactly* like we did two years ago," Zoe says, fumbling in her pocket to see if the old photo strip—the one Joy had wanted to bury—is still there. "I'll show you."

She pulls out the photo strip . . . and gasps.

"What?" asks Joy.

"It's . . . it's . . ."

"What?" Luce asks.

Tali grabs the photo strip from Zoe's hands and says it for her. "It's . . . blank."

"The photo from two summers ago?" Joy asks.

"The photo from *this* summer," Luce says slowly.

"Right." Tali nods. "It's totally erased. Gone. Like it never happened."

Zoe stares at the blank photo strip over Tali's shoulder. It's true. It's like some giant eraser has come and smudged out the images of their smiling faces . . . and with them, the last two years of their lives.

"It's blank because it *hasn't happened yet*," Zoe says.

"What are you suggesting?" Tali frowns.

Zoe shrugs. "I don't know . . . maybe we have to, like, take it again."

"Take *that* photo again?" Luce asks.

An idea starts to unfold in Zoe's mind, shining brighter and brighter, like the sun as clouds part to reveal it. "Yeah. Maybe we have to *re-create* the photo. Maybe we have to re-create our pasts in order to get back to the present." It makes an insane sort of sense as she thinks about it. "The photo booth did this. Instead of taking a *new* photo of us, it caused some sort of glitch in the time-space continuum. It *untook* the old photo of us, thereby reversing time, and—"

"This is absurd," Tali says, crossing her arms.

"How can we know it would even work?" Luce adds.

"Well." Joy looks at all of them. "Do we have a better idea? Anyone?"

"True," Zoe says. "It's as good a plan as we've got. Although . . . if we have to duplicate it exactly"—Zoe realizes what this actually means and feels sick—"I need that fencing medal from the photo."

"Oh crap," Joy adds. "I'll need that stupid talent-show crown! And Tali will need those boxers. . . ."

Luce adjusts her weight. "I was wearing the merit badge, which I earned for helping Ricky—*shit*. Shitshitshit." She squints back out at the playing field where the counselors are breaking down all the relay equipment. "Someone else *already* helped Ricky. How am I going to get that badge?" Her voice breaks again, and Joy reaches out and squeezes her hand.

"You'll find a way. You have to," Tali says bluntly.

"But we need to be careful," Zoe says. Of the four of them, Zoe knows in her gut that she's the one who really *gets* it. She didn't spend most of sixth grade obsessively watching and rewatching all of *Dr. Who* for nothing. If this really is the past—and she still isn't completely convinced of it—then it has become clear that *already* things are not going the way they did that last summer. And changing the past—no matter *which* sci-fi movie you're watching—is never a good idea. "Whatever we do, we've got to be sure not to rewrite history. If this *is* the past and we somehow got thrown back into it, then we need to do everything *just* like we did it before, until we can find a way to fix this. Do you guys understand me? This is important."

Tali nods. "She's right. We need to get to that photo booth and retake those photos. We've got to try. I mean, what if we end up getting *stuck* back in time? Would we have to relive the last two years all over again?"

Zoe shudders. "Possibly. I'm not promising it'll work, but it's not like we have much of a choice. We have to move forward, and hope this plan works. And like I said, we need to try to follow the past exactly like it happened the first time. Otherwise . . ."

"Otherwise what?" Luce demands.

Zoe wishes she wasn't so afraid. She wishes it didn't feel like the trees were closing in on them, like the world was spinning just a little too fast. Part of her keeps thinking: *This can't be real, this can't be real, this can't be real.* But the words that come out of her mouth make it sound real as hell. "If not, then we could stay trapped in the past forever."

6

There's something very "Circle of Life" about the dinner call at Camp Okahatchee: a blaring horn at exactly 6:30 p.m., which sounds like a mix between an enormous trumpet and one of those old-school conch shells, and then the ensuing flood of campers—the seven- to twelve-year-olds herded in organized lines from their bunks by their head counselors; the thirteen- to fifteen-year-olds converging from their afternoon sports and activities; everyone flowing together like tributaries into a larger river, headed toward the chaotic delta of the dining hall's barn-style double-door entrance.

Luce always had dinnertime down to a science: expertly navigating the steady stream of other campers, surging ahead so she could secure a spot at picnic table 17, the one farthest from the bathrooms and the busy food line, the table with the best light in the early evening.

But today, she feels like a leaf pulled along by the

current—undirected and uncertain, unable to stop. Unmoored. *Unmoored, unprecedented, unwitting. Without an anchor, never having happened before, unconscious.*

After the relay race was curtailed due to Ricky's injury—a fractured ankle, just like two summers ago (just like *this* summer)—the girls were eventually sent back to their cabin, Bunk Blue Heron. (Nobody knows, not even Luce or her mother, why the girls' bunks are named after animals and the boys' bunks are simply numbered.) Now she shuffles toward the dining hall—wearing the purple and yellow flip-flops she found tucked neatly under the corner of her bottom bunk, waiting for her like a pair of obedient puppies—as though compelled by a malicious force. She feels itchy and antsy, sticky and confined, as though she's been forced to put on an old, still-wet one-piece.

The other girls may be referring to what happened as another one of Okahatchee's reunion night "miracles," but Luce personally does *not* want to be back, does not want to have to consider the repercussions this could have on the time-space continuum, as Zoe put it. She does not want to pretend to be someone she's not: her former self.

As soon as she steps through the giant entryway, inhaling the smell of limp pizza and squishy, mayonnaise-drenched pasta salad, Andrew calls her name.

"Luce! Hey, Luce!"

The relief is immense; his voice anchors her, finally, and she's so drawn in, she doesn't even bother to scan the crowd for Zoe, Tali, and Joy. Another thing she isn't prepared to do: pretend to be close again, like they were that summer. *This* summer.

Luce weaves her way through the packed dining hall, careful not to bump into anyone's tray. As she nears table 13—square in the middle of the mayhem—Andrew's grin grows so wide it seems to take over his whole face. He looks almost exactly the same, except for his facial hair, which is basically nonexistent. Luce feels something pull inside her chest. She realizes that in Andrew's mind, they have probably been together for only approximately five weeks. Five weeks! The idea seems crazy to her now, after more than two full years. How is she supposed to act around him?

Will he know something's wrong?

This Andrew is still getting to know Luce. He has never seen how ridiculous she gets when watching corny old Disney movies. He hasn't yet held her hand while she cries, waiting for Amelia to undergo surgery. He hasn't even seen Luce's boobs. Second base is still a few weeks away, in his dorm room at Brewster. . . .

"Hi, babe—er, Andrew," she says, trying to seem casual. She's already completely unsure how to behave. Do they call each other babe yet, or did that start later, at some distant point post–second base?

Luckily, he doesn't seem to notice. He slides down on the picnic bench to make more room for her, then immediately throws his arm around her shoulders and kisses her cheek. She leans into him, marveling at how good it feels to be next to him. His smell is a little different—more sunscreen and less of the sharp spice of the deodorant she knows he'll switch to eventually.

"You aren't hungry?" he asks.

She realizes that it didn't even occur to her to get a tray for dinner.

"I guess not. Mind if I just have a bite or two of yours?" She reaches over his tray and grabs his plastic fork, skewering a slice of pepperoni straight off his pizza. It leaves a gooey trail of cheese behind, which Andrew doesn't seem to mind. He never seems to mind.

"They didn't have any pineapple," he says apologetically. "I know it's your favorite."

Luce stares at him for a second, midchew. She *still* orders her pizza with extra pineapple. Usually she likes how Andrew tries to take care of her. No one else ever does—people always assume Luciana Cruz doesn't need help.

But this feels wrong—shouldn't there be those heady, crazy sparks between two people when a relationship is just beginning? Shouldn't she be harder to read? What always felt wonderfully comforting and easy now feels *too* easy, like a downshift, or when they make those crappy PSATs that are way too unchallenging to be the real deal.

"So I heard the Orange team would have come in first place, if it hadn't been for the Ricky thing," Andrew says, going for a giant bite of his pizza.

"Yeah, well, we wouldn't have won anyway, after I botched the whole baton pass. I was pretty, um . . . distracted, I guess."

Andrew finishes his pizza in one final bite, his Adam's apple bobbing like he's a snake downing a mouse. It always amazes

Luce how quickly boys can put away food.

"Apparently the pain was so bad, Ricky actually started crying," he says. "It's broken, I think. Jade and Mark had to practically carry him to the infirmary." Luce knows that Jade will go on to transfer to a performing arts high school for her senior year—she's always had a flair for drama. In fact, she's always had a flair for being at the center of *other* people's drama.

Andrew finishes another bite of pizza. "She got the merit badge right on the spot."

Luce's heart stops. *Jade got the merit badge.*

He registers the look of complete shock on Luce's face. "Hey, what's the matter?" he asks, touching her back lightly. "Should I go get you some salad or something? You probably shouldn't skip dinner after relay day."

"No, no, I'm fine, it's not that, it's just—" Luce pauses, trying to figure out how much to tell him.

"Just what?"

"Just that I was kind of hoping *I'd* get the merit badge this year, is all. I really, *really* wanted it." *I need it in order to undo a cursed photo booth incident and bring me back to the present!* "What am I gonna do now?" She starts to feel queasy. Briefly she toys with the idea of telling her mom. After all, if there's one person who understands the mysterious workings of Camp OK better than anyone else, it's her. But then . . . would her mom get mad? Would her mom even *believe* her?

It's too loud in the dining hall; too hot. Zoe said they had to be super careful—they had to act exactly like they did the first time around, but here she is, failing already.

What can it mean? Will we ever get back to our real lives, or will we be caught in a time loop forever, permanently paused at fifteen? Will we have to start over from here? The sounds of campers shouting and laughing and the clang of trays being slammed down onto tables and milk cartons being punctured by straws all converge into a single wave of sound, threatening to drown her.

"I'm sure you'll get a different badge, Luce," he says gently. "You get one every summer. 'I do what I can to honor the values Okahatchee has taught me' and all that. Right? So don't put so much pressure on yourself."

Luce gapes at him. "You remember that?" He just directly quoted her acceptance speech—the one she has repeated three summers in a row, once when she was an Eagle, once as a Hawk, once as a Wolf. And if all was going to happen like it was supposed to, she'd be giving that same exact speech again this year as a Blue Heron. It never struck her before how repetitive summer camp had been for her. Always the same badge, always the same speech, always the same tepid applause, always the mild sense of accomplishment that got quickly washed away like a shell by the tide.

Andrew smiles at her sheepishly. "I remember it all, babe. Everything about *you*, anyway. Besides, it's one of the things I like most about you."

"What, how freakishly predictable I am?" she asks, half-wondering if this is in fact what he means.

"No, Goofy," he says, touching her nose. "How you always

do the right thing." He touches her chin now, moving her face slightly closer to him, and starts to kiss her. The kiss is sweet—tender and nervous. An early Andrew-Luce kiss. He tastes of salty pepperoni, mozzarella cheese, and root beer. She tries to enjoy it. This is Andrew—*her* Andrew. The one she fell in love with two years ago and is still in love with to this day . . . whatever *this* day actually is.

But for some reason, his words bug her. *You always do the right thing.*

She has got to stay focused on her goal. Stay in control. Somehow or another, she must manage to win the badge back from Jade—do something so honorable that it forces her mother to change her mind and reassign the honor to Luce. There's got to be a way to undo this mistake. It can't be that hard. She can still fix this.

Luciana Cruz can fix anything.

7

Unsurprisingly, Tali takes the longest time to shower, despite the fact that the rickety wooden stall is lined in a faint slippery sheen of green mildew, its corners draped with ancient-looking spiderwebs. By the time she trudges back to her bunk with her plastic shower caddy in hand, wrapped only in a threadbare standard-issue camp towel that feels far too meager for her body, the other girls have gone to dinner without her.

Other than Sarah Hawking, rummaging fruitlessly for a lost sock behind her bed, the rest of the cabin is empty. Even so, Tali feels self-conscious as she towels off and slips into her bra, an A-cup, one strap at a time, trying hard not to look at her young, not-fully-developed-yet boobs and her awkward, bony shape. She misses her subtle curves, her ability to raise one shoulder slightly at a guy or give him a certain look, and know, deep down, that she can have him if she wants him. It's like she's been completely stripped of her superpower, and now she's back to gangly-skinny-loser Tali. The Tali who doesn't get noticed by boys and doesn't get invited to the best parties and who, when she steals her mom's credit card to buy a new outfit, is then teased for trying too hard and wearing the wrong thing. It took years of effort to *learn* how to be effortless.

And now it's all lost, like some higher being accidentally hit a big fat PREVIOUS PAGE button on the invisible screen of life.

Camp Okahatchee has a serious lack of mirrors, but she can easily tell by touch that her hair is frizzy. Once it dries, it will be *too* frizzy. She rummages through her top cubby, the one filled with all the products she can't cram into her shower caddy, looking for her magic hair balm. Her heart starts racing. She can't even *remember* the last time she was seen in public with her hair like this. She removes every bottle and tube from the cubby, lining them along her top-bunk blanket. *It's not here. It's not here. It's not here.* Was it really fewer than two years ago that she discovered the best product to civilize her pre-straightening locks? This cannot be happening. The panic that's been hovering like a dark cloud threatens to break into a full-on storm.

And then, with a whoosh of relief, she locates the pink and black tube. As she pulls it out, a delicate gold chain comes unloosed and clinks to the floor. She stoops to pick it up. It's the necklace her dad gave her for her tenth birthday, a tiny Taurus symbol. He always called her his stubborn Taurus. She hasn't seen it in years; she lost it here at camp that last summer, doing something or other—maybe she took it off to swim or it came off in the sand or broke during a run or who knows what. Maybe it just got lost at the very back of her cubby and she forgot to look for it.

As she clasps it around her neck, the phone conversation she had with her mother right before heading to reunion floods back to her, filling her chest with anxiety all over again. Her dad. Fraud. Investigation. Their assets frozen, at least for the moment. None of it made any sense at all. Tali's dad is one of the best people she knows—he always talks about how important it is to treat everyone equally, and he shows kindness in small ways that others would never think of, whether it's bringing home surprise gifts or remembering details of a story you told him years before, or just going out of his way to make you comfortable. No matter how bad things got at school, during her gawky, ugly, miserable phase, she always felt safe at home. Her dad believed in her, said she could do anything she put her mind to—anything she put that bullheaded spirit into, more like it. She even used to joke sometimes that his unconditional love and support was going to make her soft. But she meant it—not everyone sees her the way her parents do. In the real world, she's had to work for it.

For the first time, she wonders if her dad ever had to work for it, for the way people just gravitated toward his big, warm smile and generous spirit. She can't believe he'd ever lie about anything. Sure, he traveled a lot for business and would sometimes tell her that things were rocky or that his company was taking big risks . . . most of it would fly over her head. But anyway, she trusted him implicitly. It simply never occurred to her that he could ever do anything wrong.

Thinking about it now sends her spinning. She *can't* think about it. Because the only word she can come up with to describe how she feels is cold, harsh, and definite: *betrayed*—a word that lands hard as a rock at the pit of her stomach.

When she arrives at the big barn-style dining hall entryway, she's struck by the familiarity of the scene: the clatter, the crowdedness, the unmistakable scent of aging wood, and the rubbery tang of lumpy food kept warm in metal chafing dishes. Tali navigates the circus of pre-sixth-grade boys jockeying for the attention of their female counterparts (the Bunk Fox girls), the chatter of pre-third-graders (the Chipmunks) writing messages in washable marker on one another's arms, all the way through to the circling Hawks, prowling Wolves, and, finally, the Blue Herons.

Joy and Zoe are bent toward each other in a distinctly intense-looking huddle over table 17, Joy's long, brown hair and Zoe's matching blond—both of which Tali always envied—tucked behind their respective ears.

Tali plops down next to Zoe; Joy smiles and nods at her tray. "I see you've found the Camp OK dinner just as they've left it for us," she says, not feeling particularly hungry.

"The only question is whether the food's from two days ago or two years ago, right? Not sure I'd be able to tell," Zoe adds, poking at her noodles, then giving up and going for her slice of pizza instead.

"I vote two years ago," Joy says with a slight smirk.

"Whatever," Tali says, forking a bit of salad. "It's a far cry from fantastic, but it's edible."

"I wonder if this pasta would stick to the walls if we threw it," Zoe says.

"I bet I could find out," Joy says, and reaches over to pick up a noodle from Zoe's plate.

Zoe's face gets serious, and she puts up her hand to stop Joy, then leans in closer. "Wait. We should be more careful. Remember? We don't want to do anything out of the ordinary. What if we accidentally caused a food fight or something?"

Tali looks at her skeptically. "Aren't we basically doomed to screw up?" She stabs a meatball. "There's no way we can perfectly replicate everything we did two years ago. I can't even *remember* most of that summer."

Zoe nods her head seriously, like she has already anticipated Tali's skepticism. "We just have to do the best we can. Camp ends in only four days. We have to focus on getting all of the objects we need for our date with the photo booth. For Joy, that means getting the talent-show tiara. For me, it means winning the fencing tournament again. And for you . . ." She trails off and looks at Tali. "Well, you have it the easiest."

"I do?" Tali asks, popping the meatball into her mouth.

"Sure. All you have to do is explore Blake's nether regions, like you did two summers ago—aka *this* summer," Zoe says, smirking.

Tali coughs, regretting the meatball. She grabs her Diet Coke, taking a long sip.

"What she means is you need to get his boxers from him

again," Joy clarifies, as if Tali doesn't get it.

"I know what she means," Tali replies quickly. "You're right. It's no problem." She forces a big smile. Inside, her heart is beating fast. For a moment, she debates telling her former friends the truth.

But maybe, she thinks, Zoe is wrong. Maybe it's never too late to change the past.

Tali can smell the smoke from the bonfire before she can see the flames. Isn't that what they always say of fire? Funny how from afar it looks so pretty. Harmless, even.

Tali may not really be the rustic type, but bonfires always remind her of the large beach fires her aunt and uncle in Rhode Island would build on their private strip of sand, back when she was too tiny to even be allowed within five feet of the flames. The Safety Point, they called it. Back when things were simpler, when security could be counted in child-size steps.

Back when she believed people were exactly as they seemed. People like her own father.

"You guys," Luce says beside her, pulling Tali out of a dangerous spiral of thoughts. "For the first time since whatever the hell happened to us this afternoon, I just . . . I don't know. I got an incredible feeling. I think it's all this." She gestures toward the bonfire, its flickering light dancing on her golden-brown skin.

Joy smiles, toying with her side braid. "I know what you mean. Being back here. It almost seems like it wasn't an accident. It's kind of . . . exciting."

Tali has to admit, through the thick layers of stress hovering in her mind like smog—the lies, the unanswered questions, the tasks ahead of them, the utter surrealness of it all—somewhere amid that she can feel what Luce and Joy are talking about: that spark. That Okahatchee magic.

Zoe shrugs as the four of them cross the rest of the grassy field toward the barren, cleared-out area where the fire roars, surrounded by a thick crowd. "I still think I should be practicing for the tournament, rather than, ya know, basking in the weird time warp—"

"Sh!" Luce turns to Zoe with a finger to her lips.

"Sorry, sorry," Zoe mutters, and Tali can't help but crack a tiny smile. Despite all her convictions about this time travel business, there's one area in which Zoe Albright could never follow her own advice—subtlety. Zoe simply cannot keep her mouth shut. It's one of her most annoying, and lovable, traits. Back in middle school, Zoe and Tali could wander the streets of Liberty for hours, getting lost and eating ice cream and rambling about nothing and everything. Once, in eighth grade, they bought a fifty-cent bottle of red glitter and decided to sprinkle it all over the benches along Main Street, so that anyone who sat down would have glitter on their butts. It was dumb, but the two of them cracked up about it all afternoon, despite the fact that Zoe kept giving away their secret and apologizing to various people with sparkly rear ends.

It's crowded enough around the bonfire that Tali can't really get a grasp at first of who's there and who isn't. All the thirteen-year-olds are vying for the best s'mores angle, their roasting sticks clashing like they're at one of Zoe's fencing tournaments. She takes a step backward to avoid getting skewered by one of them.

"Hey," a male voice says, touching her arm. "Careful." It's Jacob, broad and built like a jock, one of Blake's closest friends. Tali's heart thrums in her chest. Blake *must* have come if Jacob's here.

And all at once, she spots him, directly across the fire, laughing broad and easy while pounding another guy on the back, his dirty blond hair tousled and damp as though he's come directly from a shower, his white T-shirt accenting his deeply tanned skin.

Tali realizes she's sweating.

"Thanks," she says distractedly to Jacob. He has barely registered her—this is the curse of the twin As—and is already about to make his way over to Blake and the rest of his friends. "Hey, where'd you get that?" she asks, her voice sounding awkward even to her as she nods toward what *appears* to be a Dixie cup full of something very likely spiked.

Jacob raises an eyebrow. "Blue cooler behind the sprinklers. Blake brought a stash. Benefits of being a day camper. Help yourself, if you want. Just don't tell anyone."

Before she has a chance to thank him, he's gone. But it doesn't matter. This is her *in*.

"Come on, guys," she says, turning back to her crew. "We are going to need some liquid courage."

Tali tries not to catch Joy's eye, but it happens, and what passes between them wordlessly makes Tali's pulse still for a second. It's like Joy *knows*, just from a look. She knows Tali's nervous. It's possible she knows even more than that; knows about Blake. But in that same moment, it's also completely understood that Joy won't say a word.

Tali always used to take this quality of Joy's for granted—that she understood people in a way no one else did. That she would keep your secrets for you even when you didn't realize you had them. But now Tali wonders how Joy does it, how she can hold so much of other people's dirty laundry. She wonders what happens to *Joy's* emotional hamper.

She wonders why Joy left them. But part of her doesn't want to know the answer.

The four of them find the barely concealed blue cooler, and Tali gives a silent prayer of gratitude to whatever gods control underage drinking at camp. They always seemed to take a particularly lenient view of Okahatchee. Inside the cooler, melting ice sloshes from side to side as she plunges her hand into the achingly cold water and retrieves a three-quarters-empty liter of Russian vodka. She sees a bottle of cranberry juice as well, but upon further inspection discovers it to be empty. Straight vodka it is, then. She pulls four flimsy Dixie cups apart from the rest and begins to fill them each to a centimeter below the top, but Luce makes a face. "I'm not drinking that without a mixer."

Tali shrugs and keeps the fourth cup in her hand—she can bring it to Blake. "Suit yourself!"

Then she swivels the cap onto the bottle and stashes it back in the cooler, glancing over her shoulder to make sure she hasn't been spotted by any of the counselors.

Zoe takes a sip, winces, coughs, and laughs.

Tali rolls her eyes. "Can we *try* to play it cool? You may recall I'm on a mission to seduce someone." She didn't mean to sound so bitchy, but Zoe shakes her head, like she's not surprised.

"Whatever," Zoe says, pouring out the rest of her drink. "I need to practice fencing anyway. I don't need to be parading around with you on a quest to get some ass." She starts to march off.

"Zo—" Tali calls out, but it's too late. Zoe has disappeared into the crowd.

"I'll check in on her later," Joy says, shifting her weight. "Come on, let's go find your boy." She loops an arm through Tali's, and Tali feels a tad better.

As they approach Blake's side of the bonfire, they almost run straight into Jeremy Farber, biggest contender for the Douchiest Counselor of the Year Award. Luce gasps, backing up, and Joy giggles, hiding her Dixie cup behind her back.

Fortunately, he doesn't see them, since he's lost in conversation with the head of Bunk Otter, Suzanne Simonson. Tali boldly takes a sip from one of the cups she's holding. The vodka stings her lips and burns a trail from her throat to her stomach, then settles, warming her from the inside.

They dodge through the cluster of fourteen-year-old boys currently pegging one another with balled-up bits of tinfoil, and all of a sudden, Tali's heart is in her throat and she feels like she can't swallow. Blake is only three feet away. She's way past the Safety Point . . . stunned by how hot he is up close. It has been two full years since she has seen him in person.

He and a couple of his friends, including Jacob, are sing-shouting something indiscernible in a half huddle. They erupt in laughter. That's when Blake's blue eyes catch hers. Time seems to slow as recognition registers, and then the unthinkable happens. He winks at her. She offers a tiny smile in response, moving toward him and causing Joy's arm to unwind from hers. Then she lowers her shoulder just enough so that her bra strap slips down.

"Hey!" he says, throwing an arm around her as they approach, causing her to lose a little more vodka from both her cups. "It's the hot gymnast!" He says it sort of to her and sort of to his friends, as though making an announcement. Heat rushes through Tali's ears and down her body.

Joy and Luce exchange quick looks of skepticism, which Tali tries to ignore. A moment ago, she was relieved to have her old friends beside her. Now, she kind of wishes she'd come alone, instead of having them stand so close to her, like petite body-guards.

Still, she laughs, giving a friendly nod to Jacob, Soffi, Sam, and the other people she doesn't remember as well. "I'm not a gymnast *anymore*," she qualifies, "but I can still do splits."

"Hear, hear!" Jacob says, holding up a cup to toast with. "To the splits."

Tali lifts one of her cups, too, and that's when she sees it: that signature, fried-blond bob, weaving its way toward them. The girl is wearing an all-pink outfit—*all pink*. How could Tali have forgotten?

Rebecca Ross. Bunk Wolf. Tennis prodigy, just like Blake. Adorable, aggressive, annoying . . . and Tali's biggest roadblock for Blake's affection.

As far as Tali knows, Blake has never been *that* interested in Rebecca. They were never actually together, at least not officially. But she was always hanging around. Tali is flooded with memories: Rebecca swishing over to him in her tiny tennis skirt, Rebecca taking Blake's arm and begging him to dance with her at the Midsummer Formal, Rebecca in her tiny bikini, trying to capsize Blake's boat during sailing lessons.

Tali takes a deep breath. Things will be different this time around. *She* will be different.

Rebecca stops on her opposite side, facing Blake and practically trampling Luce. Tali can't help but notice that she's poking out her ample chest. She puts her hand on Blake's bicep. "There you are! I couldn't *fiiind* you before," she says to Blake in a whiny voice, wearing the most irritatingly cute pout Tali has ever seen. "Have you been holding *out* on me?"

"'Course not, Bex," he says amiably. "I saved a cup just for you," he says, handing her a half-full Dixie cup.

Before she can lose her nerve, Tali turns, inhaling the musky, heavy scent of Rebecca's floral perfume. "Hey, *Bex*," she says. It's the first time she has ever directly addressed Rebecca in her life.

Rebecca tilts her head. "Hey, what's up?" Now her voice

sounds normal—apparently she saves the simple syrup for the boys.

The lies come fluidly, easily: "I just saw Cherry Brentworth. I think she was looking for you? Over there by the main office?"

Rebecca rolls her eyes and turns back to Blake. "Looks like I have to go babysit a friend. Wanna come?"

Before Tali can even protest, Blake's hand is in Rebecca's and she's yanking him away from his friends, away from Tali and Joy and Luce . . . away from the glowing circle of fire.

Just like that, Tali is a nobody again—no, the ghost of a nobody—hovering in the darkness, just on the brink of everything she wants. The heat is overwhelming now, the smoke choking.

"What a ho," Luce announces.

Joy looks at Tali, her eyes both searching and a little sad.

Tali cannot stand that look. "I . . . I gotta go," she says, then promptly turns and weaves through the clamoring, shouting crowd, toward the quiet sanctuary of the line of trees in the distance, not bothering to stop when vodka sloshes all over her hands.

At the edge of the woods, she stops and throws back what remains of her vodka. She cringes. It tastes like nail polish remover and hair balm, but after a few seconds she feels calmer, steadier, more like her old (new?) self. The alcohol isn't enough to make her drunk or even dizzy. All it does is make her feel smooth, as though she's gliding over the surface of the earth like an air-hockey puck.

She was never supposed to feel this way again: what it's like to be plain. What it's like to be invisible.

She doesn't remember walking back to the bunk. The lit-up cabin leaves a halo on the matted grass surrounding the screened-in walls, and the air is filled with a low hum she can't quite pinpoint. She blinks rapidly, trying to remember which Tali she is—modern Tali or past?—and steps through the doorway, where the unidentifiable hum gets louder. It's Hadley Gross, blaring into her French horn, her black hair snaking behind her in a long, fat braid.

Why Hadley feels the need to practice just before curfew, in their bunk, Tali will never understand. She's good, as far as Tali can tell, but there's something almost obscene about the way her thick lips press up against the lip of the horn, the way the big brass instrument wraps itself into her lap, the way her face gets so red as she blows into it.

Tali glances around but notices with some relief that Zoe is not in the cabin. She must be making good on her vow to practice.

Suddenly there's a gloating face right in front of her: Paige McAlister, who has been passing around camp mail. "No letters," Paige tells her. Paige reeks of a cheap, vanilla-scented body spray. "But you've got a Feddy." Paige holds out a small box.

"Thanks," Tali says, her spirits lifting. Everyone loves a Feddy. Maybe her mom has sent her something good, like Italian truffles or nice Swiss face wash.

She takes her box and heads out the back door of the cabin,

sitting down on the back porch to open it. As she's tearing open the cardboard, she hears Joy's voice, quiet, in the distance. She looks up. Joy is crossing back toward the cabin alone, her cell phone pressed to her ear. She must have left Luce at the bonfire, probably with Andrew.

Tali considers offering an apology for ditching them, but Joy pauses, turning around in the darkness near the trees, cupping the phone close to her face. Tali stops ripping at the cardboard so that she can faintly make out Joy's end of the conversation.

"No, I . . . I'm not leaving early. We only have a few days left. I *want* to stay." Joy's voice is hushed but urgent.

Tali sits there, puzzled. She's startled when only a moment later, Joy is beside her, the phone stuffed into her back pocket.

"Hey," Tali says. "What's up? What was that about?"

Joy turns to her, and the usual warmth in her eyes—that ability to make you feel like you're the only person in her world at that very moment—is gone, replaced by something else. Something that startles Tali and even scares her a little. Something animal. She wants to call it *anger*. Without thinking, Tali backs away slightly.

But just as quickly, Joy's expression changes in a single blink. "Nothing," she says.

Tali pauses as a creeping sensation worms through her: *She's lying.*

What's going on? She wants to call Joy out on it, but something stops her. What did Tali miss that last summer at camp? What changed? Joy obviously has some sort of secret, and Tali

82

senses it's connected to why she disappeared at the end of this summer, leaving not just their school but all of her friendships behind.

She clears her throat. "Well . . . if you want to talk about it, I'm around," she says, though the words feel like lead—more lies. She and Joy haven't talked, *really* talked, in two years. Why would they do so now?

"Thanks," Joy says, her voice rough. She tosses her side braid over her shoulder and heads inside.

Tali sits there on the porch for another minute or two, trying to process. Around her, the night air chatters and gossips, full of leaves rustling and insects mating and campers' voices carrying over the wind. Finally, she returns to opening her Feddy.

Inside the box is a Steiff teddy bear and a note from her dad. *For your collection, sweetie. We miss you. Hope you're soaking in those final camp days.* Her stomach tightens.

The note goes on, asking about the end-of-summer relays— he remembered her story about tripping on a Hula-Hoop last year—and how her friends are doing and saying he can't wait to see her when he gets home from their trip, just in time to pick her up from her last day of camp. But Tali's eyes have glazed over, her conversation with her mom once again returning to haunt her.

Your father's company is under investigation.

No.

Your father *is under investigation.* Her mother's voice had wavered, like she'd been crying.

Tali pulls out her cell phone and heads for the Dumpsters

behind the counselors' lounge, remembering that there's a spot over there where she can usually get better reception—and privacy. She wants to call her mom back and make it all go away. She wants to call her dad and demand an explanation. But how can she? Whatever her father did, it won't really happen until two years from now. So what is she supposed to say?

Instead, she tries to dial Ashlynn but realizes she doesn't have her number in her phone. Right. Of course. Because they aren't even friends yet . . . and won't be until junior year, after Joy moves away, after Luce becomes busy, after Zoe becomes a band groupie and starts looking at Tali like she's some kind of fraud every time she so much as dares to sit with the popular kids.

As she paces the periphery of the counselor cabins, Tali's chest aches more and more. What's so wrong with her that she has no one during what's turning out to be the scariest moment in her entire life?

Everything her dad worked so hard for, traveled so far for, stayed out so late on weeknights for, will vanish. So what was it all for, really? Shouldn't he have known better? Doesn't he know most people don't get a second chance?

She can't keep her father's gift. She won't repeat the past—not when she knows it's going to lead to such a horrible future. Not when she knows now that it's founded on a bunch of lies.

She lifts the heavy lid on one of the Dumpsters behind the lounge cabin and drops the box, letter, and teddy bear into it. Then she lets the Dumpster clang shut with a metallic bang.

She feels the faintest hint of tears on her cheeks as she jogs back around the dark side of the counselor cabins, only to run directly into someone.

"Whoa, whoa. You okay?" says a boy's voice. Her eyes have begun to get used to the darkness, and she sees a boy's bare chest and a whistle glinting around his neck. Standing this close to him, she can smell the strong, familiar scent of super-high-SPF sunscreen, coming off his whole body in waves. A lifeguard, obviously.

"Fine," she mumbles. She starts to dodge him, but he stops her, placing a warm hand on her arm.

"What are you doing out here so late?" he asks.

Tali is about to respond that it's none of his business, but when he turns slightly she can make out the planes and angles of his face. He's taller than her and the moon is behind him so at first she's convinced she has it wrong. . . .

She must be gaping, because he crinkles his brow and says, "What?"

"You're . . . you're Tow Boy!" Tali blurts out, connecting the dots. No wonder he'd recognized her, if vaguely.

"Excuse me?" the boy says, looking even more confused.

"You work for the local tow company. You know, cars, accidents, popped tires? Right?"

The boy shakes his head, but now she's *sure* it's the same guy who picked her up the night of the reunion. He's got to be only a couple of years older than her. Eighteen or nineteen, max. "I have no idea what you're talking about," he says, and she realizes of course he doesn't because they're in the past. "This is my first summer at Okahatchee. Look, you should be in your bunk. I could give you a demerit for being out after curfew."

Tali's surprise turns rapidly into annoyance. "First of all, only counselors give out demerits. Not *lifeguards*. *Secondly*, I had to take care of something important, which is too much to explain—"

"What, you had to throw away a teddy bear?" He grins, one of his eyebrows slightly perking up, like he's trying not to laugh at her.

Tali feels a flush of heat across her face and is grateful for the darkness—hopefully he can't tell. "Were you following me or something?"

"I was on my way back to my cabin when I saw you racing by with a teddy bear in your hand. I feel sorry for whoever sent it." In the dark, it's hard to make out his expression. "What did he do to piss you off?"

"What is this, the Inquisition?" Tali puts her hands on her hips, trying to seem in control of the situation. Still, she can't help but be pleased. Tow Boy—it *is* Tow Boy, she's sure of it, even if he's not yet aware of his own future calling—assumes the teddy bear came from a boyfriend. She won't correct him. "Anyway. It's just . . . I found out he was lying to me. For a long time."

Technically, that's true, even if Tow Boy doesn't know she's referring to her father.

Tow Boy watches her through narrowed eyes. "I get it," he says with a nod. "You're the pretty-girl type."

"What do you mean?" She can't stop from thinking: *He thinks I'm pretty.* And that's the *pre-pretty* Tali.

"I've seen you around this summer, flaunting yourself in front of the guys. If we're not perfect, we're not worth your time." He shakes his head.

"You don't even know me," Tali says quickly, self-conscious. She can only dimly recall him from two years ago—Okahatchee is a revolving door for lifeguards, even hot ones. But *he* has noticed *her* all summer? It makes her feel unsettled, off guard. He's obviously cocky and full of himself. The last thing she needs to deal with right now.

"True," he says, crossing his arms.

"But you know what *I* know?" she says, taking a step closer to him. She's so close she can smell something else besides his suntan lotion—a musky, slightly sweaty *boy* smell. She picks up his whistle, her fingers brushing against his bare chest ever so lightly. "It's girls like *me* who keep boys like *you* employed."

With that, she lets the whistle fall back against his annoyingly hard chest, spins around, and walks off.

It was mean, sure. But then again, he needed to get the hint and stop stalking her. And anyway, she won't ever have to see him again, once she gets the hell out of the past for good.

8

Pompeii looks like this—a giant pile of black ashes.

With a charred stick, Joy pokes at the soft mound that was once the bonfire, picturing a miniature city perfectly preserved underneath it. Some embers are still smoldering, glowing red like lava.

Few people know that Vesuvius is an active volcano even now—when it erupted so violently a couple thousand years ago and destroyed the city of Pompeii, that wasn't a one-hit-wonder thing. It could still have a big comeback, and something like three million people live close enough to it that they'd be killed almost instantly. Those three million people must simply be willing to take a gamble on their lives.

She drops the stick, wiping her hands on the back of her shorts. She is supposed to be focused on getting the talent-show tiara, which she earned two years ago through a pity vote. She knows it. She didn't even *participate* in the talent show—she was the behind-the-scenes coordinator. And if there's one thing she's certain of now, it's that she does not want pity votes this time around.

After the unexpected phone call, she had wandered the campgrounds for a while, trying not to run into anybody. By the time she made her way back over to the bonfire, it had died down and everyone seemed to have returned to their cabins for curfew. In fact, she should probably do the same.

On her way toward Blue Heron, though, she hears the sound of girls giggling somewhere in the trees. She stops and watches as three girls from a younger bunk—probably Hawk or Wolf—clad in bathing suits, dart off toward the path that veers straight into the woods, around the right side of the lake. To Red Cliffs.

The cliffs she was always too afraid to leap from, down to the water forty feet below, even though there's a tree with a tire swing up there, and kids much younger than her are brave enough to try it every summer. The cliff swing is an Okahatchee tradition.

The three girls appear to be around twelve, and Joy wonders if she knows them—*knew* them. Whatever. It's likely she led them in arts and crafts, years back. She was always doing stuff like that with the younger campers—teaching them how to weave shells and feathers into their friendship bracelets and lanyards. She's always found kids easy to be around. Even when they're brats, they still have a certain sweetness, an innocence. They don't think about the future, they just think about now. And, for the most part, like Joy used to, they believe in *fantastic*.

Curious, she turns left at the path instead of heading straight toward the cabins, and picks up her speed, occasionally glancing over her shoulder to be sure she hasn't been spotted. It has always been easy to sneak around Okahatchee at night. She's pretty sure the night counselors are too busy drinking or hooking up to notice the campers breaking rules.

Soft pine needles poke at her feet around the sides of her flip-flops and the cool night air invigorates her as she follows the trail of voices and laughter, high and light and carefree, toward the edge of the water.

She runs faster now, breaking into a true lope, feeling the blood pounding in the veins of her legs and throat and ears. Suddenly she's afraid to lose them, afraid they'll jump too soon, afraid one of them will get hurt. Don't they know how dangerous the cliffs are, especially at night?

When she breaks through the clearing in the woods and sees the tree and the little *O* of its tire swing dangling below, swaying just slightly, for a moment she's surprised by how quaint the whole scene looks. Not dangerous at all. The three girls are huddled together and one is whispering urgently while another giggles, and the third wraps her arms around herself, obviously cold and a little scared. She hears them count down, one of them squealing quietly, and then she takes a harsh breath as all three grab hands and race over the edge, disappearing completely.

Joy's heart seems to stop pumping. *Gone*. They're gone—three birthday candles blown out.

But then she hears the almost simultaneous set of splashes, and another minute later, the tinny sound of distant gasps and voices, fading away.

Slowly, Joy inches into the open clearing and approaches the ledge. As she reaches the lip of the cliff, she carefully leans over, peering at the water. In the cool, mossy darkness, the drop seems even farther. She can barely see the shapes of the three girls, who are clambering over the rocks a little ways down, shivering.

She grabs the rope of the tire swing, sliding her legs through its mouth, and kicks off the ground, swinging out over the ledge, testing her nerve. Wondering if now's the time. If she should take the leap, too. She may not get another chance, after all.

What is there to lose? she asks herself, though some other voice in her head responds: *Everything.*

She shakes her head slightly, trying to shut out that voice.

But it has curled its way throughout her chest like smoke, making it hard to breathe.

She allows the swing to slow to a stop.

Then, with a heaviness, she slips out of it, and moves away from the ledge. The tire swing sways listlessly, exuding disappointment. The wind turns chilly, and Joy hugs herself as she turns and walks back toward her cabin.

She has changed, she reminds herself. She *has.*

And she's got an opportunity to relive the rest of this summer. It should be different this time—better, happier, freer than ever before.

But she needs more time.

She stares up at the sky through the trees. *How did you get so far up there, moon?*

No answer comes.

The tiny sliver makes her think of one of Uma Finkelstein's clipped toenails.

Don't you know how easy it would be to fall?

9

TUESDAY

The final sprays of dirt fall over Zoe, blocking out the rectangle of light above. She tries to scream, but no one hears her. Cool, damp walls of earth surround her, keeping her arms pinned to the sides of her body. Trapped. She can't move, can't escape, can't breathe. She tries to expand her lungs, inhaling dirt. She'll die out here, buried alive, alone, unheard, unseen.

The voice that always comes to her in this dream comes to her again now: *Give up. There's no point in struggling. There's no way out.*

Zoe wakes up with a hard gasp, almost falling out of her bunk. Her bunk. *Right.* She's at camp. Safe. Alive.

I have to tell Cal I had the dream again, she thinks. And then she remembers, all in a rush, that she broke up with Cal, that he was hurt, that he gave her a ride to Okahatchee anyway, that he even said he'd go grab a burger and come back for her later that night if she wanted a ride home from the reunion.

Zoe sucks in a deep breath, taking in the familiar scent of the Camp OK cabins—mildewed towels and a strange comingling of Body Shop body spray and mosquito repellent. So. This isn't part of the nightmare. She really did dump Cal. And she really is here . . . and fifteen again.

For a second, she can't help but be a teeny, tiny bit pleased. She always *suspected* time travel was a real thing, not just the stuff of sci-fi. In a way, it was all delightfully, surprisingly elegant—no fuss, no fancy machinery, more like a simple hiccup in the normally forward trajectory of a life.

She's going to be hailed as a genius when she proves this really happened. BU's physics department is going to go ridiculously nuts. She'll probably get the rest of her tuition covered by scholarship without even having to apply for one. She won't have to pick up any more shifts at Tasti D-Lite during breaks. She'll be a campus legend, a hero . . .

When she *gets* to college, that is.

Zoe looks at her green plastic watch. *Crap.* Almost time for the breakfast bell. She had been meaning to wake up early so she could squeeze in another workout, but this whole time-travel thing has her off her game. This is *not* the sort of quandary she normally wakes up to—usually it's more like Eggo waffles versus Crispix.

She throws on the first items of clothing she can locate and jogs over to the dining hall, knowing she'll be one of the first campers to arrive. Her calf muscles are screaming. Between the impromptu relay yesterday and the hour after leaving the bonfire that she spent re-teaching herself the basics of fencing in private, using only an inadequately short stick, Zoe's exertions may have been a bit overkill. She also did forty push-ups, and her arms feel like limp noodles.

She has practically inhaled her whole breakfast by the time she sees Tali, Joy, and Luce walk through the broad, bright barn doors to the dining hall.

"Good morning," Joy says cheerfully when they all bang their trays down on the table.

Tali frowns at her. "Did anyone else have a horrible time trying to sleep last night?"

Joy shrugs. "Despite Sarah's snoring, you mean?" she says, just as Luce throws in an "Ugh, yes."

"I feel like it's so messed up, what's happening to us right now. Like, why us?" Tali asks.

"Who knows?" Zoe sits up straighter, trying not to let Tali's victim attitude bother her—or the memory of how rude she was last night at the bonfire. "But we can't sit around angsting about it. It's already day two of being in the past. We need to stay positive and focused on what to do to get *out* of here."

This was clearly the wrong thing to say, because Tali glares at her. "I'm not *angsting*. And who appointed *you* the ghost of summertimes past?"

"Tali," Luce puts in, "I think Zoe just meant that we're all in this together, right?"

"Yeah, sure," Tali says. But she's still glaring at Zoe. "I just think I'm allowed to be disturbed by the recent sequence of events."

"Or lack of sequence, technically," Zoe says but regrets it again. How come literally everything out of her mouth ends up being the exact wrong thing?

Tali rolls her eyes. "Whatever."

"Well, I for one could use some help," Luce says then, putting her fork down, grayish scrambled eggs leaving a sad trail across her Styrofoam plate. "I'm supposed to get the merit badge but Jade Marino already *got* it. So what do I do? Is there some way to fake it?"

It crosses Zoe's mind that they could just try to find a way to *steal* the badge, but she doesn't tell Luce that—it goes against all her goody-two-shoes morals, and besides, they should be *trying* to stick to the script as much as possible. Even though the more she thinks about it the less confident she feels about her whole plan. What if it doesn't even work?

"You can't fake history," she informs them, although she's not one hundred percent sure if that's true. Still, she's definitely sure that it isn't worth the risk of finding out. "But maybe you can do something nice for Jade, and she'll *let* you have it?"

Joy clears her throat and finally speaks up. "Or you could talk to your mom and see if she can make an exception this year. Tell her how important the badge is to you. Something like that," she offers.

Luce is nodding. "I can try," she says, but she sounds

unconvinced. "What about you guys? Joy, don't you need to sign up for the talent show?"

Joy doesn't look up from her soggy cereal. "Yeah. I can go to the planning meeting today." She nods, as though to reassure not just her friends but herself. "That's the easy part, anyway. The hard part will be getting everyone to vote for me again. I'm really not sure how I pulled that off before. Plus I have one day less than you guys, remember? The talent show is on the night *before* reunion. The tournament is the day of reunion. Same with the badge ceremony."

Luce cocks her head. "I'm sure you'll win again, Joy. Everyone thinks you're sweet. Don't worry about *that*."

"Besides," Tali adds, "if we have to . . . help the votes along, we're not above it." She grins at Joy. She means this to be supportive, Zoe knows, just like Luce's comment about Joy being "sweet," but it doesn't come off that way.

Fortunately, Joy seems not to mind.

Luce cuts the crust off her toast with precision, like her life depends on it. "What I'm more worried about is whether this plan is even going to work or not," she says. She looks over her shoulders as if to make sure no one is listening—but with the typical morning chaos of the dining hall, it would be near impossible for any of the other campers to overhear them. "What if we really have to relive the last two years? Or what if we get back to the present but everything has changed?"

"I don't have an answer for that. All I know is that a plan is better than no plan. And that I am seriously behind on my end of the bargain," Zoe announces. "Last night I literally tried to do a balestra into a lunge and ended up in a corps a corps with a freaking ash tree."

Tali snorts. "I *literally* have no idea what you just said."

"I'm basically a mess," Zoe clarifies.

"Don't worry, we have your back," Joy says. "We'll figure this out. We all will. If the relays were yesterday, that means we still have four days left until reunion night, including today."

"All right." Zoe stands and picks up her tray. "I gotta go. The countdown is on."

Joy looks up at her. "You're leaving?"

Zoe pauses, tempted to blurt out: *You're the one who left. Two years ago. You left all of us, with no explanation. Why did you do it? Why did you drop us?* But for once, she bites her tongue. She has to focus on the problem at hand. "I need to get back in mental shape if I'm gonna win this thing."

Joy seems deflated. "Okay."

"And I need to go talk to my mom about the badge," Luce adds.

"But we should all reconvene later," Tali says, finishing her yogurt. "Tonight's Casino Cruise Night, remember? Blake was there two years ago. So obviously we *all* have to go."

"Why do we *all* have to go?" Zoe asks, still standing there with her tray of dirty dishes in her hands.

"Well, I'm not planning on going *alone*," Tali answers. "How unsexy would that look?"

This is precisely one of those statements that people who

understand popularity make all the time, while people who are *not* Most Likely to Be Asked to Prom find completely selfish.

"So you expect us to be your backup dancers?" Zoe says sarcastically.

"Come on, Zoe," Tali says, turning her head just enough to make eye contact and smirking slightly. "You know you want to. This is your chance to see what the notorious Cruise is really all about."

Zoe is perfectly aware of the Casino Cruise Night rep—it's basically an unofficial booze cruise, because the counselors are famous for smuggling alcohol on board the big boat, which departs just after sunset and glides across the lake and back, taking a couple of hours. In fact, it *is* the perfect occasion for Tali to hook up with Blake. He'll be trapped.

Of course, being trapped is exactly why Zoe didn't go on the Casino Cruise two summers ago. Or more specifically, *Russ Allen* is the reason she didn't go. After that awful, fumbling hookup on Water Wars day, he'd been all slobbery and clingy for the rest of the summer. She knew he'd corner her out there on the cruise.

But this time around she hasn't even glimpsed Russ yet. And she has enough breakups under her belt by now to know how to handle Russ if it comes to that.

The image of Cal trying to help fix her old junker of a bike flashes into her mind. The look on his face when she told him it was over. His offer to give her a ride anyway. Maybe she should say she's sorry. As soon as they get back, she will. She owes him that. Her chest aches from missing him, but she tries to focus on what's happening now.

Zoe sighs. "Fine, I'm in. But only because I understand the immense importance of you getting some tonight so we can all get the hell out of here in one piece. Anyway, why are you strung out about this? You have the easiest job of all of us—been there, hit that. Right?"

Tali had never been super explicit about what had happened between her and Blake, but the possession of his boxers had said enough.

Tali shrugs, turning back to her tray. "Of course. But an entourage never hurts."

"Great!" Joy says, with real enthusiasm.

"It'll be fun," Luce adds, though whether she means it or is just trying to convince herself, Zoe can't tell.

Zoe is still aching and exhausted by the time she files into line with the other girls on the fencing team and slips on her helmet. She forgot how sticky and clammy it is under these fencing masks—hard helmets with firm metal mesh covering the entire face area. She already feels off her game, and practice hasn't even begun. Coach Patelski walks up and down the double lineup of girls—each of them facing a random opponent—checking off names and verifying that everyone has appropriate equipment.

Zoe is facing Samantha Puliver. It's hard to tell which girl is which with the masks disguising their faces, but Sam is all muscle—one of the strongest girls at camp, in fact—and Zoe recognizes her pregame foot bounce, almost like she's about to start boxing or something. *Great*. Zoe doesn't even get to warm up on someone easy.

They begin sparring. Just as she expected, Sam is a beast, but Zoe parries decently and Sam gets in only one direct hit. Every two minutes, Patelski blows his whistle and makes everybody switch partners—the north line stays still while the south line does an about-face and takes a stride to the right, facing a new opponent. Zoe takes the moments between bouts to adjust her helmet, remembering how she used to love the sense of anonymity and power that came with wearing one. Now she just feels humid and damp.

Sam steps down and next Zoe's facing Indigo Perez, aka camp slut. Zoe would feel bad about the label, but Indigo seems to be into it. She breathes a sigh of relief. Indigo sucks at fencing—Zoe has literally no idea why she continues to sign up for it, summer after summer. Zoe easily bests her four times before the whistle blows again.

"Hold on, women," Patelski shouts before they begin their next engagement. He points to Zoe and her new opponent. "I want everyone to check out Zoe's back foot. Zoe and Ellis, you two alone, please."

The other girls turn so they can watch, while Zoe begins her bout with Ellis, a girl she only dimly remembers. Ellis isn't in Bunk Blue Heron with them, which means she's either younger or a day camper. Zoe can make out her sharp blue eyes through the mesh mask—if Zoe has to guess, she'd say the girl looks pleased to have the attention.

"See how she tracks that back foot, people?" Patelski says, and Zoe experiences a rush of pleasure. At least she hasn't forgotten *everything*. "It's right under her, every time. That's how she's able to make those lunges with so much control. See what I'm talking about?"

Zoe feels a blaze of heat in her face. Confident, she lunges again, more aggressively than before. Ellis is surprisingly agile and easily deflects with an opposition parry, never losing contact with Zoe's épée. Zoe racks her mind to recall her strategy—how did she beat Ellis last time?—but comes up blank. Even the stronger fencers, like Sam, have their weaknesses. Sam is too eager in her attacks—she loses her footing in the forward momentum. Sarah Hawking is bold but erratic and can't keep her lines. Cherry Brentworth and most of the other Bunk Wolf girls are simply easy to intimidate—once you get them focusing on defense, they become scared, powerless to make a hit, and give way too much space.

But this girl is different. She doesn't back up when Zoe attacks, and her rhythm is unusual, making her appear like a humming-bird, flitting in and out of Zoe's range seemingly at random. She can't anticipate Ellis's next move, and she's starting to lose her balance. Thankfully, Patelski blows the whistle again, just as Ellis leaps past Zoe's sightline, attempting a flèche. Zoe quickly steps backward, out of bounds. Ellis would have scored her hit had it not been for the whistle.

Zoe realizes she's been holding her breath. *Shit*. She may not recall Ellis from two summers ago as anyone special, but if she's that good at distracting Zoe this time around, it's very possible she'll be Zoe's biggest competition for the gold.

Zoe brushes herself off and readies for the next bout of sparring, but in her mind she keeps turning over that last flèche, how Ellis breached the space between them as though she were invincible, flying out of Zoe's peripheral vision in a flash of white and rendering her completely off balance. If there's anything Zoe hates, it's the inability to see what's coming next. Especially when she's about to get hit.

"Are you serious?" Tali asks that evening after dinner, standing behind Zoe and staring at her in the single, highly coveted bunk mirror. "At least fix your hair," she insists, and reaches up to yank on Zoe's ponytail.

"Ow!" Zoe spins around and slaps Tali's hand out of her face. The demands of the day are catching up to her and her patience is about as thin as Tali's trendy little tissue T-shirt. "I *will* let my hair down, and I *will* come on the cruise tonight, but that is the *last* thing I'm agreeing to tonight, 'kay?" she says, keeping her voice tense but low, so Tali will get that she's serious.

"Fine," Tali says with a shrug as she walks back over to her cubbies, as though she hasn't been harassing *all* of them about their outfit choices for the last half hour. "Here, you can use my brush."

Zoe reacts quickly, reaching for the brush Tali tosses to her. "How generous."

She turns back to the mirror and catches Joy's eye in its

reflection as Joy slides gloss across her lips. It's just a momentary glance, but it makes her feel better. And then the soothing feeling turns into something else—a sharp pang in her chest. When Joy disappeared, the threads that held them together unraveled. The friendship between the four of them fell apart at the seams like an old sweater. So how is it that after all this time, Joy can still have that same effect on her—an instant calm, like staring into the lake itself?

While Zoe fixes herself up in the mirror, she can see Uma Finkelstein repainting her toenails and Hadley straightening her hair. Zoe has a sudden memory—that is, a flash from the future. She remembers that Uma will get into Brown with some sort of prestigious scholarship for brainiacs. It's posted all over the internet. Or it will be, in two years, when it happens. Zoe real-izes she never even *noticed* that Uma was so smart. She's the kind of girl who always has her head down, whether she's focused on her toenails or achieving academic greatness. Not for the first time, Zoe's awash in that *Twilight Zone* feeling, causing her skin to tingle. Everyone around her—everyone on earth, in fact—is constantly pursuing his or her own separate journey through life, going mostly unnoticed. She's just one of infinite possibilities and realities. She plays a minor, passing role in Uma's life—if that.

Finally, they're all ready. Tali is wearing a lime-green tissue T-shirt through which her black bra is visible and a pair of Luce's black shorts, which look *super* short on Tali (which was, appar-ently, the whole point of borrowing them, even though Tali has her own black shorts as well). Luce is in a simple yellow sundress and wedges, and Joy has on a flowing, patterned top Tali insisted she wear, along with her skinny jeans and sandals. Bringing up the rear is Zoe, in—surprise, surprise—cutoff shorts and a men's white T-shirt. She holds her breath, ducking through the cloud of peach- and passion fruit–scented body sprays as she heads out the cabin door, letting it slam behind her.

They trek across the grass with their flashlights toward the pick-up spot on the docks at the far lake. Okahatchee is too small for the cruise, which always takes place on the far bigger and more famous Lake Tabaldak. As they approach, the noise of other gathering campers and the flames of various lanterns fill the night with a buzzing energy. Zoe can make out the basic shape of the boat, strung with Christmas lights, and one large, blinking sign that reads, in cheesy-looking cursive, WELCOME TO VEGAS.

Just as she's starting to think this was a bad idea, Joy turns around and smiles. There's something about Joy's smile—it's unlike anyone else's. Maybe it's the way it causes her eyes to turn down at the sides, radiating sympathy. Maybe it's the way she can hold a gaze, making it more than clear that she's not just listening, she's *absorbing.* "Isn't it kind of perfect?" Joy says, gesturing at all the activity surrounding the bobbing boat and the steps leading up to it from the dock.

"Perfect how?" Zoe asks quietly. Some part of her is terrified by that smile, afraid to let Joy back in.

Afraid to lose everything all over again.

"You know, this whole experience. The idea of a gambling night. Don't you feel like we're kind of gambling on our fates? Like we're cheating the house somehow? I don't know." She shrugs.

Zoe takes a deep breath, inhaling the mineral smell of the lake and the citronella of the torches. "I guess, when you put it that way," she replies. "We *are* getting a do-over."

"*Exactly,*" Joy says with a laugh, following the other girls onto the dock. "And we're getting away with it. Pretty awesome, when you think about it."

"Yeah," Zoe says. But then, under her breath, she adds, "At least, we *think* we're getting away with it."

As soon as the boat leaves the dock, Zoe's heart rate picks up. There's no running back to the safety of the cabin now. Andrew appears almost immediately and whisks Luce away to play one of the casino games, grabbing their allotment of fifty chips each and leaving Zoe with Joy and Tali. But it doesn't take long for Tali to spot Blake, who is, as usual, hanging out with Jacob-something (Zoe always thought that was funny: Jake and Blake, douche-bag besties), and some other guy whose name Zoe forgets.

Tali grabs Joy's hand and pulls her toward the boys, and in turn Joy grabs Zoe's. Zoe is so startled she almost stops walking for a second. She hasn't held Joy's hand in two years—probably not since they rode the spinning-swings ride and reached out to try and slap each other's hands, spinning farther apart and then closer again, dipping in and out of sky. She hasn't had that feeling since, the ghost of which returns to her now: belonging. Being one with her friends, connected, inseparable.

Moving like that, in a chain, they snake across the crowded deck, through the clinking and blinging of slot machines and betting tables.

"Ladies, ladies," Blake says, his grin big and rich looking (why do rich kids always have *such* big white teeth?). "What happens in Vegas, stays in Vegas. Am I right?"

"Including the herpes," Zoe reflexively quips, then cringes, then tries to turn the cringe into a smile. She *still* doesn't understand why Tali can't see what a total douche Blake is. These are not her people. She's doomed to keep saying ridiculous crap the longer she's around them.

Jacob laughs, baring equally bright whites, and the other guy leans toward the girls conspiratorially. "We have the goods, by the way, if you all want some. Just don't tell too many people or we'll run out."

Blake eyes Tali. "Don't worry. Bender and her friends are safe, right, girls?" Is it Zoe's imagination, or does Tali blanch slightly when he says *friends*? "As long as Mini Cruz doesn't tattle, that is."

"She'll never have to know," Tali says, like Luce is some lame stray dog who follows the rest of them around instead of one of their best friends. Instantly, the feeling of belonging passes. These people are disgusting—they remind Zoe of that horrible friend of Tali's from school, Ashlynn, and the douchey lacrosse players they usually hang out with. Their mere presence seems to instantly turn Tali into one of their clones.

To Zoe's surprise, Joy touches the arm of no-name guy, almost flirtatiously. It's a small thing, but it bugs Zoe, like Joy is taking Tali's side over hers. "So show us where to find it?" Joy says shyly.

The guy shrugs and waves an arm. Joy follows, and so does Tali. Not interested in getting stuck with Jake and Blake, Zoe once again trails behind, but not before overhearing Blake say to Jake: "I've got dibs on the one who can do the splits."

"Wonder what else she can do," Jake says back, with a laugh.

"Hopefully a flying leap away from creeps like you," Zoe mutters, though neither of them hear her. Zoe almost feels bad that Tali has to hook up with Blake again. But Tali must know what she's getting herself into.

As the three girls trail Blake's no-name lackey (it turns out he does have a name: Soffi) toward the cabinet belowdecks where he and his boys have stored the booze, Zoe scans the crowd. Rebecca Ross, a Bunk Wolfer, floats past her up the stairs in a midriff-baring top that's more bra than shirt. Cherry Brentworth and Emily Fargo are not far behind.

"I see you brought your two friends," she observes as Rebecca passes. Rebecca casts her a look like *Who are you, anyway?* Luckily, she doesn't seem to pick up the fact that Zoe was talking about her exposed cleavage, not her actual friends. Zoe can't believe even the fourteen-year-olds dress like that, but immediately she chides herself, realizing even in her head she sounds old and lame. *Kids these days,* she imagines Cal whispering to her. She grins and then is hit by a wave of sadness. If only Cal were here to entertain her, to help her make fun of all these people, these people with whom she used to feel totally normal, comfortable, like she belonged. Instead, she's the weird girl muttering bitchy comments for her own amusement. Old Tali would have laughed at Zoe's sarcastic jokes. New Tali . . . well, New Tali has left her in the dust, just like she has for the past two years.

She's so distracted she doesn't spot Russ Allen approaching her until it's almost too late. *Ugh.* There he is with his stupid waterproof sandals and that stiff crew cut and the backpack he brings everywhere with him, containing, Zoe recalls, his inhaler and a spare set of waterproof sandals. Because the only things hotter than waterproof sandals are two pairs of waterproof sandals. She cannot for the life of her recall why she ever kissed him at Water Wars (and let him reach under her bikini top afterward with his gross, fumblingly big hands). Talk about major mistakes.

Quickly she ducks behind a counselor headed in the opposite direction and weaves her way toward the snack bar, without a chance to tell Joy and Tali she's no longer on their trail. She wonders whether they'll notice she has disappeared. Maybe they'll be glad. Maybe she's just being lame.

What she needs is a serious salt and sugar high. Zoe is pleased to see through the cluster of heads in front of her that the snack bar is impressively stocked, and not with normal Okahatchee fare, either. Instead, it looks like they've raided the best vending machines north of Boston—the table is littered with chips, candy, and chocolate that hasn't even started melting yet. *Sweet.*

But just when the person in front of her absconds with two Snickers bars and a package of Oreos and Zoe is about to take her spot at the bar, a figure darts in front of her.

"Hey," Zoe says. "No cuts."

The boat bobs slightly under her feet as the girl whips around and Zoe comes face-to-face with two piercing blue eyes and an expression that seems to say *Try me.* But her expression quickly changes to one of surprise when she recognizes Zoe at the same time Zoe recognizes her—it's Ellis, the girl from fencing, the one who distracted her earlier today, darting about like a hungry hummingbird after liquid sugar. The one who almost—*almost*—bested Zoe when they were sparring. Zoe can see that without her helmet on, she has messy-looking, wavy, dark hair down to her shoulders, bright red lips, and chiseled but petite features with a somewhat pointy nose—not unlike a hummingbird, in fact.

"Looks like you still need to work on your speed," Ellis says. She winks at Zoe.

Before Zoe can react, the girl has disappeared back into the crowd. Zoe tries to follow her path with her eyes but can't.

Zoe turns back to the snack bar, which now looks far less appealing than it did just a few minutes ago. Is it her, or have the big lake's waves gotten rougher? Over the railing, she sees the shoreline getting farther away. All she can think about now is that brat Ellis, who is clearly determined to be her primary competition, the main hurdle between Zoe and a gold medal; the one factor that could hold her back from ever returning to the present—that is, if her plan even works.

As the wind whips Zoe's face, the only certainty is that she is, once again, trapped: out here on this boat, and, quite possibly, in her own past.

10

"It's right back here," Tali says, the sickly-sweet schnapps warming her throat. She pulls Blake's hand, shoving the back door of the storage unit open to the secret staircase at the front of the boat. *Still here,* she thinks, just as she remembered it. No need for anyone to know how she found the secret door two summers ago—that she'd been hiding in that closet, crying, after Rebecca Ross accidentally-on-purpose spilled grape soda on her dress in front of Blake. This time around, Tali came prepared.

She hiccups quietly, hoping Blake can't hear. She doesn't want him to think she's only doing this *because* she's had so many sips of the sugary liquor, which has made her tongue thick and her head feel soft on the inside.

The front stairs rock beneath her as the boat lurches. She lets go of Blake's hand and grabs the banister, laughing. Tabaldak is a huge lake—one of the biggest in the state—and far more impressive than dinky old Okahatchee, one of the many smaller ones that surround the big one like parasites. The waves here can be surprisingly strong.

She feels a wash of nervousness. Can she actually pull this off? And will it even help? How do they know that re-creating the photo will bring them back to the present?

And then again, does she even *want* to return? What's she going to say to her dad? What's she going to do when they lose everything?

"Should I trust you, Bender? Or is this some sort of suicide mission?" Blake asks.

"Almost there," she insists. "Do you wanna see it or not?"

"Well, I'm pretty sure I've got the best view in the house right now," Blake says, and she silently thanks Luce for lending her the short shorts. She may not have her boobs yet but at least her butt is decent. With every step toward the private deck, she's more confident.

"Patience, patience, boy!" she teases, marching up the final couple of steps and giving the door handle at the top a firm turn and shove.

Sure enough, the trapdoor pops open and she emerges onto the private front deck, technically off-limits except to staff. Thankfully, no one's out here to stop them.

"Come on up," she calls down to Blake, who skips a step and swings himself out onto the deck after her, brushing off his jeans.

It's much colder up at the very front of the boat—even in late August, the mountains have a way of cooling down the air at night. Out here on the lake, the wind is strong and wild. The water stretches out into the darkness beyond the ring of light formed by the boat, sloshing and whispering.

When Tali swivels around to stare at Blake, some small part of her feels unhinged, like she's wearing heels and the strap just broke. To steady herself, she puts her hand on his arm, where his Izod meets his biceps, lean and strong from years of tennis. Blake. This is Blake. The boy she has, on some level or another, held out for over two long years. And now he's real again; she can touch him. He's grinning at her, the breeze making his sandy-colored hair dance on his head. Not like his usual manicured perfection. And that just makes him even hotter.

"I have to admit, this is pretty dope," he's saying now, looking around at their mini private deck. "I can't believe the guys don't know about this. And now it's our last summer to take advantage of it."

"I know, right?" Tali says, the warmth spreading from her throat to her face. "I knew you would like it."

"You did, huh?" He raises an eyebrow at her and passes her what's left of the schnapps. She holds her breath as she takes a swig.

"Yeah. Great minds think alike," she says, fiddling with her gold Taurus necklace, trying to channel New Tali. Trying to channel confidence. Spontaneously, a thought flashes through her mind—*I wonder if he's wearing the Batman boxers tonight.* She doesn't have the guts to ask.

He grabs the belt loop on her short black shorts and draws her closer to him. "It's funny," he says.

"What is?" Her heart is racing.

"Every summer here, you discover something new." His eyes trace her body, then return to her face.

"Just when you thought camp was getting boring . . . ," she fills in.

"Exactly. *You* appear. In the nick of time. Bender. Who would've thought." He smiles, wrapping his hand around her waist, and pulls her even closer so that now their hips are almost touching.

Who would have thought. The words sting, just a little. She doesn't think it's *that* shocking. Hasn't he noticed how she's been looking at him all summer? *Hasn't* she been looking at him all summer?

But she doesn't have time to process further, because now he takes one hand and cups the side of her jaw. His mouth is so close to hers she can smell the syrupy peach booze on his breath.

"The little gymnast, all grown up," he says, and kisses her jawline.

A wave of heat rushes through her body and her lips tingle. She wants to pull his face to the right and kiss him hard on the mouth, but she resists, letting him take his time.

"I like that," she whispers.

"What, this?" he asks, kissing her jaw again, while running his other hand down her back.

"That, too. I was gonna say the fact that you call me Bender. It's cute," she says, smiling as she feels his hand trying to sneak up the inside of her T-shirt. He moves fast, she realizes. Faster than she expected, actually. Briefly, she wonders exactly how far he *does* expect this to go.

He wraps her arms around his neck, then picks her up by the waist and sits her on the railing, so that their faces are at the exact same height. The boat bounces and a tinge of worry flickers through her. Her head feels mushy and her vision is a little blurry. She smiles at Blake, but he doesn't notice. He's too busy kissing her neck.

She goes from feeling cold to feeling hot—*too* hot. It's too much, too fast. He's too urgent. She likes it better when she's the one completely in control of the pace.

"Hey, Blake, slow down," she says, trying to push his shoulders gently back, to give herself some space.

But he just groans and drags her hips closer to him so that her butt is balanced at a weird angle on the railing. "Come on, don't be like that now," he mutters, then goes in for a kiss.

"Don't be like *what*?" she asks, jerking back.

And as she does so, he backs up, surprised, and she loses her grip on his shoulders. Before she has any idea what's happening, the world gets pulled out from under her. There's a sharp bang against her calf—the railing—and then she's truly falling, falling through the cold spray of the waves against the boat, wind whipping into her face.

Water slams into her and she goes under. It's much rougher and colder than the water in Camp OK's cozy swimming alcove. For a second, she thinks she must be dreaming. Then she gets the first, jarring gulp of lake water and instinct kicks in.

She thrashes to the surface. From this angle, the boat appears enormous. She can't see Blake. She can't see anyone. "Help!" she shouts, waving an arm, not sure if she's more scared or angry.

Amid the waves—each about a foot or higher, rougher because the boat is still moving, she realizes, pushing the current out at her—she could swear she hears Blake call out, "Tanya!" And for one second, it occurs to her that he might not know her real name.

Could that be why he calls her Bender all the time?

"Blake!" she cries again.

This. Is. Not. Happening.

Then another figure emerges beside Blake. There's some shouting followed by a loud splash, and soon, an arm is wrapping itself under her armpit and around her neck, holding her head above water.

"Calm down. I gotcha, calm down," a voice shouts in her ear.

It doesn't quite sound like Blake, but at this point she doesn't care. She's freezing, and completely and utterly overwhelmed with exhaustion—or mortification. Definitely one of the two.

The guy—she can't make out his face in the dark and sloshing water—has brought along one of those floaty rings, and he shoves it down around her head.

"Can you hold on to this?" the voice demands. And then again, almost angry: "Can you hold on?"

Tali nods, and then the guy dips under the water and reappears a couple of feet in front of her, pulling a lead rope. Gradually, she is brought closer and closer to the boat, though it takes much longer to cross the space than she expected. No wonder she was struggling. The waves are big tonight.

The guy lifts her onto an emergency ladder, then waits until she has a solid grip on the rungs—which takes a while because it's slippery and she feels drenched and awkward, her arms and legs shaking from the cold.

After she emerges over the railing, bringing a puddle of lake water with her, a cheer goes up throughout the crowd. Tali feels dizzy—why are they applauding her? And then she realizes they're clapping for the guy who saved her—the guy who is right now climbing over the side of the boat behind her.

The lifeguard. Aka Tow Boy.

Tali's heart plummets deep into her gut, sloshing around down there with the schnapps she now regrets. Nausea creeps through her, threatening to make her hurl.

"All right, all right, everyone," Tow Boy shouts out, wringing water out of his completely soaked shirt. "Show's over. Go back to your games. Everything's under control."

Still, it's all he can do to carve a path through the thick crowd, with one arm around Tali's back, holding her up. Tali keeps her head ducked. She doesn't want to see anyone, *especially* not Blake.

Suddenly Joy, Zoe, and Luce are all surrounding her, talking over one another in a jumble.

Joy: "Are you all right? What can I get you?"

Luce: "How did you fall? Were you scared?"

Zoe: "That was crazy, even for you!"

The lifeguard, aka Tow Boy, waves her friends away, then

leads her to the staff room and deposits her on a narrow, scratchy couch.

"You okay?"

"I'm . . ." *Sorry? An idiot?* Shakily, she settles on "I'm fine," completely unable to make eye contact.

He sits down on the arm of the couch, his clothes dripping quietly onto the floor. It takes her a second to remember that he's soaking wet because of her. Because he just had to go leaping into the freezing lake after her.

"Can I ask you something?" he asks.

Instinctively, Tali tenses. She hates when people ask if they can ask things. Don't they realize they're already asking something? But all she says is, "Sure, what?"

He shrugs, looking away. "I'm just wondering why you were crying."

"Excuse me?" She shivers. The boat bobs beneath her.

"Last night, by the Dumpsters. After you threw away that bear. I didn't want to call you out on it, but I could tell you'd been crying. I was just wondering if there was something, like, bigger going on." Even though he's still gazing at the far door, she can *feel* his presence, as potently as if he were staring right at her.

Tali's chest feels like it's been loaded with two tons of lead. "Why do you care? I told you, I'm fine."

Finally, he turns to face her. His green eyes are flecked with light. "That's not what it looks like from my vantage point," he says quietly. "Let me go get you some water. Stay there."

He walks out of the room, and leaves her wondering: What exactly *is* his vantage point? Has he been following her around again? It occurs to her that she should be grateful. Maybe if he wasn't keeping an eye out for her, things would have gone differently tonight. . . .

"Mr. W is pissed," he says, returning with a plastic cup of water and handing it to her. "He knows you guys were drinking."

Tali almost chokes on the water. *Really?* She nearly drowned—sort of—and he has the balls to lecture her?

"I think you'll get off with a warning," he goes on. "I know that those guys—the day camper and his friends—smuggled the booze on board. That girl Luciana reported them. So Wilkinson says he'll go lighter on you than on them."

"Whatever." Tali picks at the couch with a nail. This couldn't be more humiliating and she just wants it all to be over. The guy is lecturing her like he's ninety-five instead of nineteen. And what did he mean by *something bigger going on*?

"But he's going to ban *all* of you from using the lake for the rest of the summer."

"What?" she gasps, finally looking up. *No no no.*

"If you ask me, he's letting you off easy," says the boy, taking the empty water glass from her hand. "Oh hey, you're, um—" he says, pointing at her chest.

Tali looks down and sees that her tissue-thin T-shirt is now more like nonexistent-thin against her lacy black bra, which leaves very little to the imagination. Even with her A-cups, she's still looking extremely, well, exposed. She yelps and covers herself with her arms.

Infuriatingly, the guy just laughs, like it's all some big joke. Then he goes to a basin across the room and extracts two spare Camp OK T-shirts. "Not quite as stylish, but you should change anyway—you'll freeze."

He turns his back so she can change into the dry shirt and she notices, with surprise, that the completely soaked one he's currently wearing says the Lost Tigers across the back. It's a Swedish pop band. Tali's not great with remembering musicians—usually she just knows the songs she likes, not who wrote them. But she remembers the Lost Tigers because they were relatively new to the indie scene a few years ago and Zoe liked to claim she was one of the first to "discover" them. She dragged Tali to one of their concerts sophomore year, back when they still hung out together. Seeing the shirt on Tow Boy now somehow makes her even more annoyed with him. How dare he like a band that *her* best friend—or former best friend—worships?

He pulls off the Lost Tigers shirt so he can change, too. He's broader than Blake, she realizes. Even with his back to her she can feel his arrogance oozing off him in waves.

"Are we almost back to shore?" she asks, feeling sick and miserable.

He turns back around. "I would think you'd be a little more grateful."

"Excuse me?"

"Well, I mean, I *did* just save your life." He cocks his head, like he's trying to figure her out.

She sighs and looks away. He has a point, but can't he see how horrible she's feeling? Since when does rubbing it in ever help? "It *is* your job, ya know," she mutters. Because it's true. That's what lifeguards do—they jump in and rescue girls like her, girls who are foolish enough to get in over their heads.

"Oh, I know. And you wouldn't miss an opportunity to remind me," he states, icy now, before turning and leaving her alone in the staff room.

Whoa. Sensitive much?

She kind of feels like apologizing, but at the same time, it's probably *he* who should be apologizing to *her* for being so presumptuous.

She lies back on the couch and throws an arm across her eyes to block the overhead light. Okay, so maybe she did come off as slightly ungrateful. But what was she supposed to do, kiss his ass? No way.

Everything is going from bad to worse. She and Blake have both been banned from the lake.

And this means he and his friends won't be swimming there tomorrow afternoon, like they did two summers ago. They won't be swimming there at *all.*

For a moment, Tali wishes she'd been honest with her friends, that she'd told them what really happened that last summer at camp. But admitting the truth—that she'd never hooked up with Blake at all, that she'd simply stolen his boxers from a pile of his clothes lying in a heap by the lake—would have somehow sealed the deal on her past as a loser. It has always been so much easier to let them believe what they already assumed.

Now she has no backup plan.

Which leaves only plan A: seduce Blake.

Blake—who apparently thinks Tali's real name is Tanya.

And after tonight, she has just three days left to do it.

11

"Spotty," Andrew says, his face serious. The lights strung around the boat bob and sway gently as they pull back into the dock. For a moment, Luce could swear that this is all a dream, that the memory of Andrew—her Andrew from before, fifteen-year-old Andrew—has returned to her in some hazy, glowy vision.

"What? No way," Luce says now, holding a plastic giraffe at an angle and staring at it pensively. "Spotty's way too obvious. How about Puppy," she suggests, recalling it's exactly what she said two summers ago. She still has Puppy in her bedroom—packed away already as a Princeton-worthy item.

Just thinking of Princeton gives her a spike of adrenaline. She didn't say it over breakfast, but one of her biggest fears is that they are going to somehow change the past enough to screw up the future—and possibly risk her acceptance to Princeton. Luce worked hard for everything to go exactly according to plan, and she doesn't want to risk ruining all that now.

"You're gonna name a giraffe 'Puppy'?" Andrew teases, flicking Luce's ponytail. He wraps his arm around her and she tucks her head into the crook of his shoulder.

The night has darkened and the air carries a new chill to it. She's getting tired. It has been a long day, from the meeting this morning with her mom right after breakfast, during which she begged her to reconsider handing Jade Marino the merit badge (fail), to the long afternoon swimming session, to the unappetizing dinner of "fish dogs," to Tali's dramatic premature exit from the cruise—the girl is the very definition of *overboard*. Still, she is anxious to make sure Tali is *really* okay—Luce distinctly does *not* recall her falling overboard two summers ago. She was whisked away so quickly, Luce didn't have a chance to confer about what it all meant. The counselors had assured everyone else on deck that she was fine, just a bit "rattled and wet."

Zoe and Joy go off to fetch Tali as Luce and Andrew disembark from the boat. When they return, Tali looks okay, if embarrassed. She's wearing a big Okahatchee T-shirt that's practically twice her size and still has on the black shorts she borrowed from Luce. Luce assumes she won't get an apology for the sodden shorts, then chides herself for thinking that way. Tali could have died out there. Who cares about her shorts?

Joy has her arm around Tali, and Zoe walks a few feet behind them. Her long blond hair is tousled from the wind, and Luce can't help but notice how pretty she looks—pretty in a totally disheveled, natural way. And Joy, too, with her honey-brown hair in a braid. It's touching, seeing them the way she used to. There's just something so innocent about all three of them, so . . . intemerate.

Intemerate, intrepid, inveterate. Pure, brave, habitual.

"Back to Blue Heron, team," Joy says.

"One day down," Zoe adds under her breath.

"Maybe I can just bury my head in the sand for the next decade," Tali mutters.

"I'm so ready for bed," Luce puts in, starting to catch up with them, but Andrew pulls her back.

"Already?" he asks.

She turns to him. "It's almost curfew."

"I know, I know, but hold on, I have something for you," he says, his grin slightly mysterious in the darkness.

"But you already got me Puppy," she says, fiddling with the plastic animal in her hand.

"Something else," he says. "Please?"

She swallows back a sigh. "You girls go ahead," Luce says to Joy, Tali, and Zoe, who trudge off through the sand, looking almost as weary as she feels. "What is it?" she asks, turning back to Andrew.

"Come over here," he says, pulling her toward the tree line.

"Andrew, I'm *really* tired," she says, trying to keep her voice light. It's unlike Andrew to be spontaneous, and she's not sure if she likes it or not.

"Hold on," he says, then kneels down in the dirt, as though tying his shoe. Only he's not tying his shoe.

Oh crap. He's proposing!

Wait—Luce reminds herself that makes no sense. They're

fifteen. But he is definitely on one knee, and holding his closed fist out to Luce. "Go ahead," he says.

And now, she remembers. It happened differently that first summer—he'd cornered her in the dining hall. But still, she has a pretty solid instinct that she already knows what's coming next. She tentatively peels back his fingers, to reveal a bright purple plastic ring with a creepy-looking smiley face on it. All her tension is released in a quick laugh.

She was right.

The question now is: How is she supposed to react? Should she act happy or embarrassed or just surprised?

"Aw, thanks!" she says, hoping for some combo of all of the above.

"I promise to be good to you forever," he says, his smile wavering slightly, as he pushes the plastic ring, which is a tad too tight, onto her finger.

Luce feels a mixture of warmth and annoyance. Why does he have to be *so* thoughtful, and yet so . . . oblivious? How is it that he can't tell how *different* she is?

And she feels something else, too . . . almost like an eerie sense of déjà vu, kind of like what Zoe described yesterday on the field. When he says he'll be good to her forever, she *knows* he means it. She's *seen it happen.*

She knows she should consider herself lucky—how many other girls her age can say they've found the One? That their boyfriend will always treat them right, that he'll love them forever?

Still, something about it just feels . . . wrong. Or if not wrong then, well, she hates to admit it, but . . . *boring.*

Luce feels a piece of tension inside her snap, like a twig breaking underfoot, or a trapdoor falling open. She pulls Andrew up
off the ground. "Don't you feel like doing something insane
tonight?" she asks, the words coming out of her before she can
really think too much about it. "Something totally unlike us?"

Andrew puts both of her hands together and uses them to
pull her close to him. Then he kisses her. "I like us how we are.
Besides," he says, "I thought you were tired."

"I am. I mean, I was. It's just . . . We have so little time left,
before—"

"Before camp ends forever?" he fills in.

"Right, yes, precisely." She feels a rush of relief. He *does*
understand. She briefly thinks again of what Zoe said—that
changing history might somehow change the future. But how
could *anything* involving her relationship with Andrew change?
Besides, she feels so itchy, so stuck in her own skin, she *has* to
react. She has to make this feeling go away. Just for a little bit. She
needs to be able to breathe again, to think clearly.

"So what do you wanna do then?" he asks, cocking his head
and looking at her with a mixture of surprise and amusement,
like she's a plastic carnival animal who has learned to talk.

"I hadn't gotten that far," Luce admits.

"How about we approach it like Clue. You suggest a place,
I'll suggest an object, then together we'll figure out the crime."

Luce smiles, so big she can feel her cheeks stretching. *This* is
why she loves Andrew so much. "Location: tennis courts," she

says in a shout-whisper, then begins to run.

They race along the tree line. When the coast is clear, they dart across the sandy beach, and Luce can feel childlike giggles escaping her throat. They make it to the walking bridge, then past the volleyball area, with its nets drooping like the flags of some fallen moon-country, and then onto firmer ground, around the Stevens, where Luce knows there will one day be a thriving Agro community, but for now there is just a three-foot-by-three-foot patch of uncultivated land . . . and there they are: the tennis courts.

As she slows down, Luce notices the moon hanging overhead like the half smile of some creepy voyeur. *Voluminous, voracious, voyeur. Spacious, ravenous, secret observer.*

The pale green of the courts looks ashy gray, its white lines strangely phosphorescent. The smell of fresh tennis balls and body odor lingers, and it's so quiet out here that Luce almost wishes she had a ball to bat around—its *pong pong pong* breaking up the silence.

She turns to Andrew, catching her breath. "Okay, so what's the weapon of choice? I don't think we'll find any wrenches or candlesticks around here."

Andrew runs a hand along one of the nets. "What do we have to work with? There's Spotty—er, Puppy—"

"I will not turn him criminal," Luce says.

Andrew shrugs. "What else do we have to work with? Our shoes, clothes, and some spare betting tickets . . ." Then he turns to her, and even in the darkness she can see the look in his eyes. "Our *clothes.*"

She puts a hand on her hip. "So what's the crime, then?

Strangulation by sock?"

"I was thinking something a little less violent. Strip Tennis?"

She laughs. "You're changing the game! Besides, we don't have balls and rackets."

"Okay, so just *strip*." Andrew has his arms out and turns around in a circle. "In the great wide nighttime that is ours for the plucking, or whatever."

"You should be a poet. How about Strip Twenty Questions," she suggests. A thrill of excitement and nervousness runs up Luciana's spine. This is it—this is being spontaneous. This is living in the moment, doing something new, something they never did that last summer at camp. The fear comes racing back up to her head—is she about to screw up her future? But so far, the universe has not come to any sort of dramatic screeching halt. Maybe this really is some magic bubble, a dream, even. Maybe none of it will matter when she wakes up tomorrow.

"Fine, sure." Andrew grins. "My turn. What is Strip Twenty Questions, and what are the rules?"

"That's two questions," Luce says. Andrew cocks his eyebrow at her. "Fine," she relents. She takes off her knit sweater and her sneakers.

Even in the darkness she can see Andrew roll his eyes. "Oh, come *on*," he teases.

"Whatever, it's *my* turn now. Question . . . what's the craziest thing you've ever done?"

"That's not a yes-or-no question." He picks up her sweater and swings it around like a lasso.

"So?" Luce demands.

"I guess we're really winging it now. Well, the answer is: this." He pulls his shirt over his head.

She laughs. "That's all you've got?"

"I will if you will," he says, putting his hands near his fly, slowly starting to remove his shorts.

Luce hesitates—but only for a second. *This is it—your last chance.* The words keep running through her mind, drumming through her blood, making her feel breathless and reckless. Before she can stop herself, she wriggles out of her shorts. Now she's just in her tiny underwear and T-shirt. "I have another question," she says, feeling bolder by the second.

"What?" he asks softly, taking a step toward her.

"My question is . . . can you catch me?" And then she's off and running, darting around the nets to the other side of the court.

It takes him all of a minute to catch up to her, just as she's about to try and dodge past him again. He wraps her in his arms, laughing, and then goes quiet as he sets her down.

"So what do I get for catching you?" he asks, his voice low.

Before Luce can say she has lost track of the rules, or even the game, there's a rattling at the far end of the fence, the crunch of footsteps, and her heart catches in her chest.

Even before they turn, she knows: they've been caught.

So much for the merit badge is the last thing she thinks before the piercing beam of a flashlight lands directly on their faces.

12

WEDNESDAY

Joy's thighs burn as she puts one hand before the other on the rough cliff face and pulls herself up another notch, following the color-painted course. She feels for the next groove with her sneaker, tests her weight, then pushes again. Again. With each surge upward, she feels more powerful, more alive. Ever since watching the younger girls leap into the lake the night before last, alone in the darkness, everything seems like it's happening in fast-forward. Did time *always* move this quickly, or is it different in the past somehow? She has always thought that time can stretch and expand on a long sad day of ceiling-staring, and contract in an instant as soon as you're having fun, but she never thought that was actually a function of time itself so much as of the mind. Now she's not so sure.

"Tali, your rope is tangled in mine," Zoe whines from

somewhere just below and to the left of Joy.

Tali looks down from her stance several feet higher. "Lucky for you, I'm almost at the top and then you won't have to hang out in my shadow anymore."

Luce rolls her eyes. "I'm just dreading finishing the course. My mom told me I need to come in for a 'disciplinary meeting' before dinner tonight," she says, making air quotes with one hand and nearly losing her grip on the side of the rock. She already explained to the other girls over lunch today how she and Andrew got caught half-naked last night on the tennis courts, goofing off. The whole situation is completely *non*-Luce—Joy's never thought of her as a big supporter of nudity, or spontaneity in general—but her stress over getting in trouble brings Joy right back to the old days. Luce is always stressed about something. Of course, Zoe made it worse by freaking out over the fact that Luce was "changing history."

And even though she should probably be worried, too, Joy can't help but smile. Maybe everything's going differently, and maybe that will have disastrous consequences on the future . . . or maybe it won't. Either way, it just feels so familiar—and so right—to be in this mess together.

The rock-climbing course is set up along one of the lower cliff faces, around thirty feet high. And waking up this morning, Joy knew she had to conquer it today, if only to make up for her fear two nights ago. Even if it meant dragging her friends practically against their will. And despite their protestations and complaints, she feels . . . light. Like when she was a kid and would ride on the handlebars of Zoe's bike without holding on, paint her face in mud, eat a ladybug on a dare, or stick a fork in the microwave to try and make it explode. Before she got scared, worried about getting hurt or embarrassed. Back when she always believed things would turn out okay, or even better than okay: fantastic.

Right now, life *does* seem like a promise, the sky touchable. And she knows—she's *certain*—she's going to make it to the top of the course. So certain, in fact, that she can't help humming as she climbs, a few words slipping out.

"Good song," a male voice startles her.

She's thankful for the harness holding her in place.

The boy, whom she vaguely recognizes, is hot in a rugged but slightly awkward way, with messy red hair and red-blond eyebrows that seem to dance of their own accord. He pulls himself the rest of the way up to her level.

"Doug Ryder," she says with surprise.

Luckily they are both so red-faced from the effort that he probably has no idea she's blushing.

He shakes his head. "Nobody ever calls me Doug. I practically forgot it was my name."

"Sorry."

"No, no, it's a good thing. It's refreshing," he assures her.

They both continue to climb. She can tell by the fluid way Doug moves that he's an experienced rock climber—she's pretty sure she saw him complete the course once already today. Campers have been going up in groups of ten or twelve. Some have rappelled back down to start all over, like Doug. Some are resting at the top, enjoying the view. She assumes he is going to continue to surge ahead, but he lingers beside her, keeping pace.

"Nice pipes, by the way," he says.

She snorts, but grins. "Thanks, but not really."

She looks around to see if her friends are noticing their interaction. Tali seems to have disappeared over the top of the rock and Luce, still below Joy, shrugs apologetically before rappelling back down to the ground with Zoe, who gives Joy a totally obvious wink.

She turns back to Doug. "I used to sing in choir but, like, ages ago. They basically kicked me out for not blending."

He raises an eyebrow at her. "They kicked me out of church, too, but for different reasons."

She laughs. He is definitely flirting.

"So what *do* you prefer?" she blurts.

"Huh?"

"I meant, name-wise," she says, inwardly scolding herself. *Don't blow it. Be cool.* She wasn't ever very focused on guys at Okahatchee, she realizes now. There was always too much going on with her friends. And maybe she never really thought they noticed her. She tended to be more of a magnet for the younger kids. She dimly recalls how two summers ago she didn't participate in the rock climbing, but she volunteered to help, making sure the younger campers got properly tied into their harnesses and distributing water bottles. Usually, that was her comfort zone—after all, sometimes blending into the background is the best way to really see everything for what it is. In every group, someone's got to be the observer, the one who takes it all in, who remembers the details, who listens.

"Most people just call me Ryder," he answers, cutting into her thoughts. "So I'm not famous in the Bunk Blue Heron sphere of gossip? That's a shame."

Ryder. She *does* remember him. He was always doing athletic stuff, while Joy was busy doing exactly what he just implied— gossiping with her best friends. But now she's up here, on a cliff face, temporarily without them. Being flirted with by Ryder. And flirting back, too.

"This part's a little tricky," he says, pointing her to a closer hold.

"I'm good," she says, ignoring the offer. The last thing she wants right now is to slip back into the old Joy, the girl who is scared, who needs help, who needs to be drawn out of her shell. As she pumps her thighs, trying her best to keep up with Ryder, she imagines that shell falling off on its own, tumbling into the dust below.

Ryder starts talking again, to her relief—something about his older brother and the rock climbing they did together in Mexico during winter break.

She's momentarily distracted by a rough patch of rock she can't quite get a grip on, and the next thing she knows, Ryder's saying, "So are you?"

"Am I . . ."

"Entering. The talent show."

Joy's stomach tightens. It's already day three of the past.

Tomorrow night is the talent show. The following night is Friday, reunion carnival.

"Technically, I'm on the planning committee," she responds, hedging.

They're almost at the top now. Only a couple of more feet to go. She can hardly believe it, and she's hit by a small wave of panic. She doesn't want the climb to be over. Everything's going so fast.

But then Ryder smiles at her. "Well, I'm in kind of a bind. See, Jade bailed on me. First she begs me to sign up with her, then she changes her mind." He pants a little, adjusting his belay device. "I guess winning that merit badge went to her head. Apparently she's been angling for that thing for like the last five summers."

Joy remembers Ryder's performance at the talent show that last summer now. He'd played some cheesy song on his guitar—a tune that had been made ridiculously popular due to a TV show. Jade sang along with it, big and bold like a Broadway star. Joy was the stage manager and had been surprised Ryder was even friends with someone like Jade, someone who gets into everyone's business. But maybe he was just too nice to say no.

This time around, history is rewriting itself. Jade won the merit badge instead of Luce, leaving Ryder without a talent-show performance. It's a minor change, but it tickles the back of Joy's mind. She recalls what Zoe keeps warning, about how they shouldn't mess with the past. Is it already too late? Will there be some sort of terrifying cosmic punishment for all this?

Does she care?

"I was thinking about skipping the whole thing, but my dad did drive all the way down here from Vermont to drop off my guitar last weekend," Ryder goes on, stopping again, almost as though he, too, is hesitant to reach the summit, "and I have a new song I've been working on. But it would require, well, you."

"Me?"

"I need a singer," he says. "It's decided. I'm signing you up." She's about to balk but he says, "Uh-uh. No 'buts.' I've already heard how good you are."

Joy laughs. Is this the camp equivalent of being asked out? "Well, I guess if I have no choice, then it's settled," she says, climbing the remaining few inches and then throwing herself gratefully onto the ledge. Her arms and legs are shaking.

She rolls over onto her back on the dusty ground and hears Ryder clamber over and do the same, both with their harnesses still on, the metal carabiners clinking with their movement. The campers waiting at the top are milling about, picnicking on the supplies that some of the counselors have set up. A bunch more are in the process of finishing the climb.

For now, Joy doesn't want to move. She doesn't want to do anything other than stare at the bright sky, where big white clouds are billowing past, gentle and easy, like fat tufts of cotton, while she takes in giant gulps of the fresh, clear air. They lie like that for several minutes, saying nothing.

"Come on." He sits up, then squats over her, offering her a hand.

She takes it, and lets him help her up to standing. A quick gasp escapes her as she looks out at the landscape, taking an instinctive step back from the ledge. They may not be *that* high, but the view is breathtaking: the dark green sway of treetops, the ramshackle rows of cabins, the lake shimmering and blinking in the sun. "Who knew Camp OK was this beautiful?"

"I know, right?" he says, wiping his hands off on his dirt-covered shorts. "A lot of surprises today," he adds, and she senses he's talking about *her*.

She grins like an idiot while they unbuckle their harnesses, drop off their equipment in the truck stationed nearby, and grab fresh water bottles, chugging them. She glances around and her grin fades. All three of her friends have left. *Your fault,* she thinks fleetingly. She let them down two years ago. Why should they forgive her? This whole trip into the past, maybe it's all make-believe. Maybe they're just playing along, humoring her. She can't re-create the past—not *really*.

There's a truck waiting to take the last of the climbers back to the main part of camp, about a couple of miles away—a wagon, really, with a big open bed full of hay in the back for kids to sit on. A boy and girl, around nine years old, are struggling to get into the back of the wagon as Joy and Ryder approach. It's the Ferguson twins. She's surprised—and happy—as the names slowly return to her. She and Ryder each take the hands of the two kids and boost them into the back of the truck.

They hop on behind the twins and head down toward the main camp area, letting the breeze dry their sweaty clothes and revive them. As they pass through the densely wooded area between Lake Tabaldak and Lake Okahatchee, Joy breathes in the deep pine smell and lets the rumble of the truck beneath them relax the tension in her muscles.

On the way over, she felt such a strong sense of certainty. But now, as the sun flickers through the leaves and pine needles overhead in quick blinding flashes of white, she's filled with the exact opposite—total uncertainty, total openness to whatever may come. She closes her eyes and finds herself leaning slightly into Ryder, who is sitting next to her, their legs touching. She watches the light dance behind her eyelids.

"Go ahead, just make yourself at home," he jokes. "Mi casa, su casa. My shoulder, your pillow."

"Sorry," she says instinctively, opening her eyes.

"No, I meant it." He puts his hand on her arm and pulls her back toward him, so that now her head really is resting on his shoulder. They stay like that the whole way back, and even though Ryder is barely more than a stranger to her, Joy has the completely irrational sense that as long as their bodies are touching, she's invincible.

By the time they reach the campgrounds, the sun has begun to sink. Joy and the other climbers head toward the dining hall, anxious not to miss another night of fish dogs and twisty fries. She's eager, too—to rejoin her friends. Whether or not they care. Whether or not any of this is real.

"Joy, wait."

She turns around. Ryder runs a hand through his hair.

"I was thinking we should probably practice. The talent show is tomorrow." There's a light mist starting to come in over the mountains now, making the sunset behind him a blur of pinks and oranges reflected back by the lake. It reminds Joy of her mother's blush compacts, the mirrors always stained a dusty salmon color, through which her reflection would come back distorted ever so slightly.

"I'm starving," she says. "Can we practice *after* we eat?"

"Actually, I have a better idea," he says. "This way."

He takes her around to the far side of the dining hall, and through a narrower door at the back of the kitchen, crossing through patches of tall overgrown grass and weeds with tiny purple buds. As she follows him, she can't help smiling to herself. Already this second-chance summer is unfolding in new, mysterious ways. She knows Zoe probably wouldn't approve. This is breaking her time-travel rules and regulations. But Zoe isn't here at the moment. And Ryder *is*.

He leads her through a small hallway into the back of the kitchen itself, where several weary-looking servers in hairnets are bustling about with giant, heavy chafing trays. She's hit by a burst of steamy, fishy, broccoli smell, mingled with burning metal.

Ryder turns back to face her, making a *Sh!* signal with his finger. They pass by the servers unnoticed and into a new hallway, and then into a small, grungy lounge area where there's a beaten-up old plaid sofa, wood-paneled cabinets, and a refrigerator.

"They have a staff stash," he explains. "I found out about it once, when I had to run back here for an EpiPen for Eamon Fitz."

Joy nods knowingly—Eamon Fitz is a younger camper famous for his asthma and allergy attacks.

Ryder swings open the refrigerator and removes a bottle of Sprite. Then he moves to the cabinets. "Bingo," he says, procuring chips, granola bars, and cookies. He tosses a bunch of the stuff to Joy. They crouch down like criminals as they slip out of the empty lounge room and back the way they came.

They keep running even when they hit the lawn behind the dining hall, tracing the tree line toward the boys' cabins. Joy slows automatically as they approach Ryder's cabin. Even though Joy, Luce, Tali, and Zoe have snuck over here numerous times throughout the years, there's still something sort of sacred about the separation of the boys' cabins from the girls'—a certain mystique, defined by strange foot and body odors as well as the overall sense of complete chaos that rules within the boys' walls.

The stories of gore are seemingly endless. There was the time Jason Moran and Dave Krauss duct-taped Gene Yung's sheets down while he was sleeping and he woke up completely trapped in his own bunk, screaming. There was the time Sammy Green got in a fight with Elliot Burr and ended up sending Elliot's head straight through a bunk-bed ladder, splintering it—Elliot received eighteen stitches and Sammy had to leave camp early that summer. There was the time someone apparently jerked off into Soffi Sorento's sock—no one ever took credit for that one; some speculated it was Soffi himself.

Even now, as Joy waits just inside the door of the empty cabin for Ryder to retrieve his guitar, she can practically feel the testosterone emanating off the tangled sheets, the strewn towels, the twisted piles of muddy clothes and athletic gear. The air inside is heavy and still and vaguely yellow-hued, like the eye of a storm.

"Guys are pigs," she says, shaking her head, vaguely wishing the other girls were here with her as witnesses.

"And you wouldn't have it any other way," Ryder replies with an easy smile. "I know where we can go that's private," he adds, leading her back out of the cabin and toward the lake. They head past the volleyball area and she wonders fleetingly if he's taking her to the Stevens.

When they get to the footbridge, he stops and gestures to the boulder that juts into the water just past the bridge. "The little waterfall over there kind of drowns out the noise, so it's a good spot to practice."

They clamber up the side of the boulder so they're mostly concealed and set out all the snacks. Then Ryder reaches into the guitar case and hands Joy a wrinkled, folded sheet of paper. "Here," he says, "I have to tune up." He bends his head over the guitar, adjusting and tightening the strings. She notices how gently and easily his hands move across the frets.

Joy unfolds the paper. In the waning light, she struggles to make out the lyrics to his song, labeled at the top: *Disappear.*

"So it's two verses, chorus, one verse, and a final chorus, okay? I'll play it to you first so you can get a feel for what it's supposed to sound like," he says. "Obviously my voice sucks so just bear with me on that."

His red hair appears darker as the last of the sun slides behind the mountains with a final gasp of pale blue light. He doesn't make eye contact with her as he plays, plucking at the strings percussively and staring out over the water. Joy almost feels bad for being here, as if she's invading his private space.

But when he starts singing, all thoughts of regret flee her mind. He's obviously not much of a singer—his voice is rough and strained—yet somehow that only adds to the honesty of the sound.

I call and you aren't there,
Empty room at the top of the stairs,
All your things untouched
The ribbons that you loved so much—

I pick up the books, the shirts,
Things you'll never use again.
Sometimes even sleeping hurts,
Driving myself crazy again.

And it's clear, oh so clear
You'll never be here
Because every day, a little more
You disappear, you disappear, you disappear.

Now I climb another wall,
Look out from another height,

Trying to remember it all
Scared that I just might.

But it's clear, oh so clear
You'll never be here
Because every day, a little more
You disappear, you disappear, you disappear.

Joy is shocked to feel tears pricking the backs of her eyes, and for a while she can't say anything, almost afraid to break the moment, like it's a bubble that a single wrong word could pop. The song is so much more than she expected—so much more beautiful, smart, and raw.

Eventually, he's the one to end the silence. "I know that last transition still needs some work . . ."

"Are you kidding?" She shakes her head. "It's perfect. It's so good. I almost don't feel right, singing your words. . . ."

"Oh, you have to," Ryder says, finally locking eyes with her. "That's the whole point. If it's any good, you'll make it great."

And so they begin practicing, at first tentatively, then with more precision and confidence. They even figure out a harmony for the chorus. The whole time Joy senses how important the song is to Ryder. She's aching to ask him what it's about—*who* it's about—but doesn't dare. After a while, she has the lyrics memorized, and begins to relax into the music, enjoying watching the way Ryder's hands move across the guitar, sometimes softly, sometimes with quick, rapid confidence.

They take a break to pass the Sprite bottle back and forth and finish off the last of the cookies.

"You ever mixed rum and Sprite?" he says, at the exact same time she blurts out: "So what's it about, the song?"

He screws the cap back onto the bottle. For a long time, he doesn't answer. "It's about my sister. She died three years ago."

"Wow, Ryder." Joy looks down, her throat constricting. "I had no idea. I'm so sorry, you don't have to tell me—"

"It's okay. I mean, it's *not* okay, but you know. I don't talk about it a lot." He clears his throat and gazes out over the water. "She was in a car accident, driving with her friends. She was the only one who didn't make it."

Joy gazes at Ryder, his eyes downturned and thick lashed, his expression unreadable in the darkness. She scoots closer to him on the boulder. She can't get over the strangeness of it all—how she barely knew Ryder existed the first time around, and here he is now, opening up to her. A whole other reality is unfolding before her, a parallel world of experience that was here all along, she just didn't have any idea, any reason to look for it.

"Does it ever get easier?" she asks now, truly curious.

"In a certain way it does," Ryder admits. "I'll realize I've gone whole hours, or days, without even thinking about her. But then, forgetting sucks in a different way. That's what the song's about. It's like the person just keeps disappearing from your life. You thought she was already gone, but then memories start to fade, too, or your dad finally cleans out her old bedroom and donates a bunch of stuff, and with each thing, it's kind of like she's gone again and again, ya know? So I guess the answer is yes and no."

"Does it ever make you, well, mad?" Joy asks quietly. "I mean, how unfair it is."

"Hell yeah. It makes me mad all the time. That's the whole thing about life, though, right?"

"What is?"

"It's unfair. That you just have to accept things, take whatever you're dealt and work with what you got. There's a lot I wish I had done differently. I wish I'd been nicer to her when we were little, and stuff like that. I wish I hadn't burned off all her Barbies' hair. I wish I'd told her how much I looked up to her." His voice catches in his throat, and instinctively, Joy puts her hand on his arm. "But you get to a point where at least you're happy for the time you did have."

"I wish I could say something that would help," Joy says, her chest swollen with the weight of Ryder's confession.

"It's all right. I can't even believe I told you. But you're so . . . easy to talk to. And you're singing my song, which is pretty sweet," he says, turning to face her, his clouded expression softening into a smile. "I'm happy about *that*. I'm happy about this," he adds, gesturing at the space between the two of them. He leans back onto one hand, still studying her. "Has anyone ever told you your eyes are very intense? It's like you're not just looking at me, you're, like, I don't know—"

"—sucking you into my soul?" Joy suggests.

"I was gonna say vacuuming me into your vortex." They both laugh. "No, I mean you're actually present. Like, you actually

147

care. But you know, your phrasing works, too."

This close to him, she can see the tiniest bit of stubble along his otherwise smooth jaw and smell his rugged scent of sweat, dirt, and lake water. She feels a confused itch in her arms, caught somewhere between the desire to hug him and run her hands through his hair. She settles on nudging him with her shoulder.

"Come on, we should get back to our cabins. Gotta rest these pipes for tomorrow," she says, realizing as she does that she's tired—exhausted, really, maybe from the climb earlier that day, or maybe from something else: the dark secret, eating its way through her.

When Joy slowly creaks open the door to Bunk Blue Heron later that night, the lights have already been turned off and many of the girls appear to be asleep in their bunks. Just before she lets the door close, a tiny beam of moonlight sneaks in, flashing against Sam Puliver's retainer, its plastic case open in her cubby. It glints briefly in the dark like a metallic grin, and then is swallowed again in darkness.

Sarah Hawking is snoring softly, a comforting buzz, and a few campers on the other side of the cabin are still murmuring to one another in hushed tones. It's all quiet enough that Joy can hear the crickets outside, too, loudly masturbating, or whatever it is crickets do to make that chirping noise she once mistook for the electricity of stars.

She doesn't want anyone to wake up and notice her, to ask her where she's been. She doesn't want to be forced to tell, to reveal the secret of her shared day with Ryder. In some crazy part of her mind, she can't help fearing that by morning, she'll have realized none of this ever happened.

Hurriedly, quietly, Joy strips off her dirty rock-climbing clothes, throws on her pajamas, and dives under the covers of her top bunk.

But before she can even get settled, the crown of Zoe's blond head appears.

"I can't sleep," she whispers.

Joy sighs. Part of her really wants to throw the covers over her head and fall into a deep, blissful sleep, as dark and numbing as the lake itself.

But another part of her misses Zoe so much she can hardly remember why she pushed her away two years ago. And her evening with Ryder has only made that feeling—that missing—*more* intense. It's as though a tightly wound clock in her chest has started to come unstuck, winding backward, and with it, all her old emotions have been released.

With hardly another thought, Joy swings back her covers. "Come on, get in," she whispers back. "It's quieter on this side of the cabin."

Zoe climbs up the ladder and, somewhat awkwardly, slides in next to Joy.

Now that they're lying this close, Joy remembers how often they did this that last summer and how natural it was for them then. So much space lies between them now, like two refrigerator magnets that can't line up evenly without bouncing slightly apart due to some force within them.

They both settle onto their backs, looking up at the dark ceiling. Joy thinks of watching the clouds passing lazily overhead as she and Ryder sprawled out on the ledge of the climbing course earlier today. She can almost still see them, bright white against the blue.

"Did you hear about Hadley?" Zoe whispers after a minute. Joy shakes her head. "Apparently she gave up her V to Nate Howard after a band practice."

Joy smiles in the darkness. "I'm just surprised she has slept with *anything* other than her horn," she whispers. Zoe snorts. Joy knows it's mean, but it feels so good, so right, to be gossiping with Zoe again, whisper-laughing together. And at least Hadley's getting some. Joy has never been with anyone.

At least not yet.

Instantly, Ryder's face flashes into her mind.

She listens for a while to Zoe's breathing, wondering if she has drifted off yet and debating whether to force her to wake up and move, wondering if she should tell her about Ryder after all. Instead, Joy lies awake, letting the ceiling turn to swirls of infinite space the longer she stares, thinking about what Zoe said. Thinking about Hadley, and how you never really know anyone. Like Ryder, and the story of his dead sister.

Then she hears Zoe's voice, whispering drowsily in the darkness. "Joy?"

"Yeah?" Zoe's shoulder rests against her own, a familiar sensation, even after all this time.

"How come you left us?"

Joy can't answer right away. When she does, there's a hoarseness to her voice. "I don't know. Things were changing. I had to let them."

She expects Zoe to respond, but at the soft sound of snoring, she realizes her old friend has fallen asleep, her form tucked into Joy's side, while the night—mysterious and heavy—folds down around them both.

13

THURSDAY

Three days down. Two days left. Zoe wakes cramped from sharing Joy's tiny bunk bed and nearly falls out of it when her foot gets tangled in the sheets. She frees herself with a certain sadness. She remembers when she woke up more often in one of the other girls' bunks than her own, when they were her best solace against even the darkest, most claustrophobic nightmares.

Three days down. She can't get it out of her head. They've now spent three full nights at camp, in the past, and time is running out. Tonight is the talent show. Tomorrow it will be carnival night, reunion night, end of summer, and their plan to re-create the photo will either work or . . .

She shakes her head, willing away the doubts. She needs to focus. Today Zoe is determined to figure out what makes Ellis tick—and where her weaknesses are. With only one more day left before the tournament, Zoe's options are dwindling: either learn Ellis's strategy by heart, or convince her—even beg her—to back down. Since just thinking about begging makes Zoe cringe, her plan is to focus on the former. Ellis's technique *must* have a weakness. Zoe beat her once before.

She just has to remember how.

Which is why during lunch she heads over to the main offices and walks straight into the Cruz's private study, knowing that Bernadette Cruz is always roaming the campgrounds checking in on counselors, and can rarely actually be found at headquarters. Sure enough, the study is empty and Zoe relishes the welcome blast of air-conditioning as she quickly locates the campers' files, flips to Ellis Green, and jots down her address.

As a day student, Ellis participates in only the morning activity sessions, then heads home. Day students don't stay at camp for afternoon session or dinner, though they do often return in the evenings for special event nights—like the cruise, for instance, or the talent show. Definitely for reunion night.

This morning, Zoe learned from Indigo and Samantha that Ellis is receiving additional *private* lessons at her house on Monday and Thursday afternoons, about four miles from the campgrounds. *Bingo.*

What Zoe needs to do is study Ellis when she doesn't know she's being watched. Find out what her private trainer is teaching her, then somehow use it against her.

By around two o'clock, Zoe is making her way past the entrance to the campgrounds, trying her best to thumb a ride.

It's another incredibly hot day; the sun is blazing and the dust hovers above the gravel road, trapping in the heat. Zoe has never hitchhiked before, but she has always wanted to. Still, when an old Subaru finally pulls over to the shoulder and a middle-aged mom-type rolls down her window, the glamor of it vanishes and Zoe blushes.

"You all right, sweetheart?" the woman says, squinting at Zoe like she might sprout another head.

"I just need a ride to my friend's house," Zoe tells her.

Luckily, the woman shrugs and lets Zoe hop into the car. Within minutes, they arrive at the address Zoe scrawled down. This neighborhood is even fancier than Luciana's. The giant white house stands at the end of a tremendously long dirt driveway lined with skinny birches. Wide-winged yellow monarchs flutter lazily between the trees like something out of a fairy tale, making it almost seem like the leaves have come alive. She has the distinct impression that she's entering dreamland through an invisible, gauzy veil.

Zoe gets out of the car and ducks into the trees as she follows the long driveway toward the mansion—it *is* a mansion, there's no other word for it—wishing she'd thought out the rest of her plan in advance. It's possible they have their own fencing piste somewhere in the back—so she decides to sneak around the side of the property and try to locate Ellis without being spotted.

This plan goes well for about three minutes, before her cover is blown by loud barking coming from the screened-in front porch. Two Pomeranians are leaping up and down on their little legs, head-butting the screen and yapping at Zoe. She dodges toward the garage, hoping to find a place to hide, and comes to an abrupt halt as she rounds the corner.

There is Blake, Tali's crush, hauling a racket and can of tennis balls from a covered shed at the side of the garage.

Zoe gasps and takes a step backward. "What are *you* doing here?"

Blake tousles his dirty-blond pretty-boy hair with his free hand. "I *live* here," he says, staring at her with steely blue eyes— the same blue as Ellis's, Zoe realizes. And that's when she puts it together: Ellis must be Blake's little sister. It makes so much sense—they are both day campers with a reputation for being spoiled, privileged, and highly competitive. *Ugh.*

"The real question is, what are *you* doing here?" he says, squinting, with one side of his mouth turned up. She can't help but notice his pronounced dimples—Ellis has them, too. Zoe can sort of see why Tali thinks he's so cute. "Spying on me?"

Before she's able to quip back, a female voice pipes up from behind her. "I invited Zoe over." Zoe turns to see Ellis, decked out in her fencing gear, her helmet in hand. "We're practicing together today. Greg thinks I should work with a partner," she adds.

Blake raises an eyebrow. "All right, then. You girls have fun. Try not to let all that sword play wear you out." With a smirk, he saunters off to the tennis courts around the side of the garage.

"Come on," Ellis says, waving her forward. Zoe is too mortified to resist.

"Why'd you cover for me just then?" she asks, her mind racing.

Ellis turns around, walking backward. She grins—much fuller and even more mischievously than her brother. "You. Are. Slow," she drawls.

Zoe's not sure if it's an answer or a taunt, so she just shakes her head and takes the spare helmet and épée Ellis hands her, sliding it easily from its sheath, ready to engage. Her hopes of spying might have flown out the window the second the two yapping furballs on the porch outed her, but she's not going to miss another opportunity to practice with Ellis.

Entering an open-air deck with the borders of the piste drawn out on the wood, the girls begin to spar, as Ellis's coach, some glasses-wearing guy named Greg, shouts out instruction after instruction. They are pretty evenly matched, but Zoe is restless, despite a slight aching in her legs from yesterday's aborted climbing session. She wants to prove to Ellis that she's not intimidated. She wants Ellis to back off. And so she lunges at her, perhaps more aggressively than usual. Once again, Ellis neatly dodges and returns with a glide, throwing Zoe off balance.

Zoe could not be more flummoxed. How did this girl evade notice the first time around? How in the world did Zoe best her in the past? After another twenty minutes, Zoe is burned out, breathless, and totally fuming. Her cheeks blaze from the exertion, which is good because it serves to hide how mortified she feels. Every time she tries to surprise Ellis, Ellis reacts casually, like she knew the play was coming all along. And every time she tries her usual intimidation strategy, Ellis finds a way to turn it against her.

"Greg, I think we need a break," Ellis announces, and in one crisp movement, she has removed her helmet and gestured for Greg to head inside. "My mom left your check on the counter," she calls after him.

"See you next week, Miss Green," he says with a curt wave before ducking into the house, leaving the two girls alone on the sprawling lawn.

"I just don't get it," Zoe confesses, catching her breath at last. "It's not usually this hard for me."

Ellis cocks her head at Zoe and slowly approaches. "Want to know my secret?" she asks, her big eyes trained on Zoe with an unreadable expression.

Zoe feels a flicker of distrust, and another of intrigue. "Sure, what is it?"

"Drop your sword first," Ellis commands.

Automatically, Zoe sets down her épée and puts her hands on her hips, waiting for further instruction. Now that they're on a break, the sound of Blake's tennis practice seems louder in the background, echoing across the vast lawn: *pong, thwack, pong, thwack, pong, thwack.*

"Okay, now put out your hands like this," Ellis says, putting her hands up vertically, palms facing Zoe as though to indicate a stop.

Zoe mimics her, then steps back, startled, when Ellis lines her own hands up against Zoe's. "No, come back, this is the exercise," she says, looking a little annoyed.

"Sorry," Zoe mumbles, once again stepping closer to Ellis and lining up their hands.

"You think it's all about psyching out the other person, but it's not. It's actually about trust," Ellis explains.

It sounds a lot like New Age bullshit, but Zoe waits for more. "So now what?"

Ellis smirks. "You can't just rely on your strength. You can't win if you're holding back. You have to *lean in* toward your opponent. Put your actual weight into it. Most girls give up their footing too easily, but you're the opposite. You're a withholder. You're so focused on maintaining your stance that you don't truly engage. The two swords have to share the weight. The connection has to be *real*, you know? Here, let me show you. Lean toward me," she orders.

Zoe does as she has asked, and Ellis purposefully backs up. Zoe stumbles forward.

"See? If I don't engage, it's not really a fight at all, is it?" she points out. "There's not enough resistance, no clear next move. Now do it again."

This time when Zoe leans toward her, putting her weight into her hands, Ellis leans in as well, sharing the weight. They balance like that, their noses almost touching. Slowly, Ellis pushes a little harder, then a little less, and the two girls sway back and forth, almost like a dance—but one that would be thrown off instantly if either of them were to pull her hands away, leaving the other to fall onto her face.

"See?" Ellis says quietly, her words a whisper across Zoe's face. "Just be with it. In the moment. When you get it, it *feels* right."

Zoe feels a flash of excitement. She *is* getting it.

They pick up their épées again and begin to spar once more. This time, Zoe tests her weight, leaning in more, like Ellis taught her. At first, a wave of nervousness passes through her and she's certain she's going to lose her balance. But then she successfully pulls off a smooth glide, never losing contact with Ellis's weapon. And it starts to click into place . . . it starts to feel right, like Ellis said.

A jolt of adrenaline races through Zoe's veins—she rears, swings, and effectively knocks Ellis's sword from her hands. "Yes!" she hollers, relief flooding her entire body. She did it.

Ellis dusts her hands off on the sides of her shorts. "Not bad," she admits, and Zoe feels her entire face glowing both with triumph and the heat of the effort. "Keep it up and you're bound to win tomorrow."

Zoe nods, realizing that for the last few minutes, she completely forgot this was even about winning at all, about getting the medal, about escaping back to the present. For a second or two, she was just living in the moment.

Ellis leads Zoe toward the shed where all of her family's extensive athletic gear is stored, neatly arranged by sport and season. Zoe feels another flash of wistfulness—if only Calvin were here to joke about this with her.

"So, see you tonight?" Ellis asks as Zoe prepares to make her way back to camp.

Zoe turns and looks at Ellis curiously, once again—for what must be the millionth time this week—thrown off by her.

"You didn't hear?" Ellis explains. "My brother's throwing a rager after the talent show. Special guests only. Mostly private-school friends and tennis assholes. But you should come."

"Yeah, maybe," Zoe hedges. Another party. And yet another element of the summer that in no way matches what really happened the first time around. Has she already pushed the boundaries of history too far by coming here and confronting Ellis? "Thanks. For, um, everything."

She trudges back toward the long driveway.

"Don't forget your bikini," Ellis calls out after her. Zoe turns once more as Ellis gestures toward the gleaming pool beyond the tennis courts in the distance, where Blake's perfect form moves neatly through the air as he hits the ball with a satisfying *thwack*. Behind him, the pool seems to wink in the sun, turquoise and undulant in the slight breeze, almost taunting, and beyond that, a giant lawn mower has started up, slowly drowning out everything else with its hum.

Zoe just raises a hand, and Ellis smiles.

Why not *party tonight?* Even though it'll take her a full hour to get back to camp on foot, she's in a great mood now. With the progress she's made, Zoe knows she's got tomorrow's competition in the bag at last.

Besides, it's like Ellis said: She may as well start engaging, start living in the moment. You can't win if you're holding back.

14

"I think I have something that will work," Brianna Bradley says, eyeing Tali up and down, then surveying her chest with extra attention. "A *padded* something," she adds.

Brianna turns around and roots through one of her cubbies, pulling out various lacy thongs, demi-cup bras, and a few other items that even Tali has never worn, like a garter full of pink and white ribbons. "Why do you have *that*?" she blurts out.

Brianna turns to her, swishing her shoulders and pinning Tali with a stern gaze. "Tali. You of all people should realize that *anything* can happen at camp." She shrugs and turns back to her rifling. "I like to be prepared."

Finally she extricates a matching lime-green thong and bra, all lace, the tags on. "*Here* we go. I knew I still had this set. Bra was too small, plus I found out Mike doesn't like green, so . . . never been worn. Now," she says, putting her free hand on her hip. "What are *you* going to give *me*? And don't say hair product—I already got a Feddy full of them last week."

It's all Tali can do to keep from rolling her eyes. She knows from Facebook that in two years Brianna will have gotten addicted to self-tanners and takeout, and redubbed Oompa Loompa by her peers. Even as Brianna lords over her, wielding her power as one of the only nonvirgins in their bunk, Tali feels a pang of pity. *No one* deserves what Bri's got coming to her.

Tali offers up her watch—the one her dad bought for her last time he was in Paris—in exchange for the matching lingerie. It's worth it—she certainly doesn't have anything like it in *her* cubby.

After finding out about Blake's party from Zoe this afternoon, the idea formed rapidly in her mind: She'd skip dinner and head over to Blake's place early, offering to help him set up for his big bash tonight. It might be enough time that she can race back for the talent show, and then return for the actual party. This way, Tali will find some alone time with Blake before the party even starts, and hopefully make up for her humiliating overboard moment. She still can't remember the fall without cringing. No *wonder* Blake has barely looked at her except to wink and call out, "Staying dry, Bender?"

Of course, she also can't help but cringe remembering how he'd called her Tanya. Did he really not know her name? Or had she just been disoriented out there, thrashing in the water, and misheard?

Plus then there were his hands on her body, overeager, over-hasty . . . the memory makes her feel a tad sick to her stomach. But, it's still Blake Green, the hottest boy at camp. And whether she wants to admit it or not, this isn't just about a crush anymore. She *needs* him.

Or at least, she needs his underpants.

Hastily, hidden away in a shower stall, she changes into the pretty bra and underwear, slipping an almost-see-through white dress on over them, then stashes the tags in the Dumpsters by the main hall.

She is forced to scare one of the younger campers into lending her his bike. She's certainly not going to a hitch a ride down the road like Zoe claims she did earlier today—not in *this* outfit. That's how pretty girls disappear. Even Tali, who hates reading the news, knows that.

Now, on the too-short bike, Tali pedals along the gravel road, letting the late-afternoon wind ruffle the hem of her dress. It's got to be after four p.m., maybe even closer to five, but the sun is still blazing on, relentless. Tali pictures Blake's smile, and recalls once again the feel of his hands around her waist as he touched her on the boat two nights ago. . . . *Obviously* he wanted her. She can do this.

When she arrives at the address, she ditches the bike in the bushes by the edge of the woods and takes in the grandeur of his house. She isn't used to families richer than hers is—*was . . .* whichever. For a second she freezes, the call she had with her mom in Luce's kitchen ringing loudly in her ears. *Fraud. Investigation.* Though she hardly understood what her mother was trying to tell her, the details didn't matter—she got the basic point. Their assets are frozen. Her dad is in trouble. For years, he's been lying to them, corrupt. He's not the man they thought he was. . . . She's been so horrified by his deceit that she hasn't spent much time considering exactly how their lives are going to change. But it occurs to her now that *everything* is going to change. Her future is a big fat unknown, threatening to unravel her.

All she can do, she realizes, is cling to the unknown of *now*. Blake.

She reaches up compulsively to smooth out her hair, praying it looks okay, and swallows back the lump of fear that has formed in her throat. Then, setting her shoulders back and standing tall, she walks down the driveway, feeling the white dress swish around her legs.

She is about to knock on the front door to a chorus of yapping dogs when, beneath the high-pitched barking, she hears the siren call of the tennis ball—*pong, thwack, pong, thwack*. Blake.

Stepping back from the door, she makes her way around the side of the house instead, noticing the heady scent of freshly mown grass—so strong her nose starts to twitch. Finally, she catches a glimpse of Blake, his shoulder muscles moving fluidly as the ball machine shoots tennis ball after tennis ball at him and he easily sends them to the other side of the court. She approaches slowly, not wanting to interrupt his practice but still floating toward him helplessly, as though carried in his direction by an invisible tide.

By now the yapping dogs have quieted down, and she hears another sound—a low buzz, rumbling not too far away, almost like an overloud generator or some kind of motor. She's about to raise her voice and call out to Blake, when the source of the distant hum makes itself known—a big, heavy-duty lawn mower appears in her sightline, rounding the tennis courts at the far end, about to make a turn back toward the house.

And sitting on top of the lawn mower is Tow Boy.

With a flood of horror, she realizes that as soon as the mower rounds the corner of the courts, he'll see her, standing there in her sexy dress. Instinctively, she leaps to the side, toward the garage, which has a storage unit attached to it, containing rows and rows of fancy-looking athletic gear. As quickly as possible, she closes the door almost all the way shut. It's hot and dark inside the shed, but at least she's concealed.

How the *hell* did Tow Boy get a job mowing Blake's lawn? How many jobs does this frigging guy *have*? She knows the lifeguards switch off days, but *still*, her luck has never been worse. It's like he's following her or something. Briefly she thinks about the feel of his arms around her when he hauled her to the surface of the lake . . . how he lectured her about the rules of camp . . .

How he took off his shirt, revealing maddeningly ripped abs. Nudity. No one can resist it.

The engine of the lawn mower shuts off. Good. Tow Boy must be done. She'll just wait a minute or so, and the coast will be clear.

Quickly, she strips off her dress, excitement coursing through her body. This is *definitely* something the old Tali *never* would have done, way too self-conscious about her body. When Blake comes to the shed to return his racket, he'll find Tali ready and waiting. There's no way anything can stop them from hooking up now. It has become a point of pride—she's *got* to make this happen. She's not sure she'll be able to withstand failing again.

She's so distracted that it takes her a second to realize something has changed—she no longer hears the *pong, thwack* of the tennis ball. This is it. He's done with practice.

Suddenly, she's awash with nervousness and wishes she had something to wipe her sweaty palms on. She grabs onto something—possibly a ski pole—and does her best to strike a casually seductive pose, resting her cheek against her arm like she's just relaxing in here, ready for whatever. She hears an exchange of low voices and footsteps just outside the door of the shed, and through the crack of light where it's still open an inch she sees a shadow fall across the bright green grass.

The handle of the shed door creaks, and then it swings open, and standing there before her, in all his tall, glorious, muscular height, tennis racket hanging from his hand, the sun blazing around him like a full-body halo, is . . .

Tow Boy.

Tali screams.

Without thinking, she pushes past him. Her blood races to her head so quickly she worries she's about to pass out, but she doesn't care; she dashes toward the bushes at the corner of the front lawn where she left the kid's stolen bike, hearing Tow Boy call out after her. She can't even tell what he's saying, whether he's laughing at her. He *must* be laughing at her.

Why why WHY? Where did Blake *go?* Tali doesn't know whether to feel embarrassed or furious. She pushes hard on the pedals of the bike, riding as fast as she can, wishing she could ride through the woods but knowing the terrain is way too thick with trees, praying no one drives past and sees her like this . . . riding a child's bike. In a bright green *thong.* She'll probably get arrested.

She keeps replaying what just happened: Tow Boy came to the door. Tow Boy saw her. Tow Boy saw her basically *naked.*

A car drives by, honking. Someone shouts at her.

Fuck fuck fuck fuck fuck.

Tali bangs the palm of her hand against the handlebars, which causes the bike to wobble dangerously in the gravel. *Shit.* The last thing she needs right now is to bite it on the side of the road and return to camp both half-naked *and* injured.

She tries to recall Tow Boy's face in her mind as she pushed past him but can't. Was he grinning? Shocked? Disgusted, horrified, amused? She must have seemed like an insane, half-naked alien, shoving into him, darting past him, in her practically neon undies.

She sees the Camp Okahatchee entrance up ahead and makes a sharp left turn into it, her legs starting to ache from pedaling so fast . . . just as the loud wail of the dinner horn breaks into the evening air.

Wooo-ooooh! it cries like a foghorn.

And then, as though physically attached to the sound itself, dozens, if not hundreds, of campers, stream out of cabins, some in lines, some in chaotic clumps, making their way to the dining hall.

Tali tries to hit the brakes violently, causing her bike to almost fall again. *Oh great.* Already, a group of boys has turned to look at her, pointing and laughing.

In what seems like half a second, tons of other campers are screaming, shouting, whistling, laughing, and calling to her. It's so surreal, Tali can't think. She just keeps pedaling—determined to keep riding to safety, somewhere at the edge of the woods where no one can see her.

Like some sort of coordinated, choreographed flash mob, the crowd separates all at once, enough to let her through.

And then, something weird happens.

It starts with Crazy Casey. She races out of the arts and crafts center cheering, then whips off her own top and runs after Tali in only her bra and shorts. Tali is astonished to see a few more girls join in. They're not just laughing, they're cheering, too, hollering but not in a mean way . . . in an excited away. Like Tali is their hero.

A couple of counselors notice the commotion and start shouting, "Enough!" One is waving her arms and another blows his whistle at her. The wild desire to laugh bubbles up inside her. Then it bursts open, and she *is* laughing. She's laughing and crying and screaming. "Wahoo!" she shouts, raising a fist into the air, not even caring anymore *what* these people think. It's way too late for that. It's too late for sex appeal, too late for dignity, too late for *worrying*.

She has ridden straight down to the sand. And so she leaps off the bike, ditching it in the sand, and races the rest of the way to the edge of the lake. Then she throws herself into it, knowing full well that basically all of Camp OK just got a full view of her perky ass.

She flies into the water, then comes up for air, realizing she's still laughing. Water streams off her body. The lake is refreshingly cool against her skin, which is hot from the bike ride and the intense waves of embarrassment. She turns around. About twenty or twenty-five girls are splashing around in the lake, too.

And the counselors are *not* happy about it.

She stands to her full height in the water, powerful now, like the Pied Piper of Streaking. She did this. She caused this. She just led a *movement*, a protest of some kind. A bunch of counselors have gathered at the shore, furiously blowing into their whistles and shouting, and yet all around her girls are diving, stripping, laughing, splashing, and screaming. Boys have gathered, too, cheering them on. It's inexplicable. It's intoxicating.

Through the kaleidoscope of naked arms and legs, of rainbow-colored bras and underwear, she sees the Cruz, standing on the shore with her hands on her hips. She freezes. The Cruz catches her eye and glares.

Tali stands there for a second, wondering what to do. She looks around and sees Zoe and Joy in the water with her, also in just their bras, smiling and laughing.

Zoe splashes Joy, who screams, wading over to Tali and grabbing her shoulders from behind.

"Hide me!" Joy shouts, laughing still.

Zoe tumbles over to them, landing a giant splash in Tali's face.

"Back off, Albright!" Tali announces, whirling a big splash of water back on Zoe, whose hair is plastered all over her face like some sort of sea monster.

Zoe screams and then leaps on her, and soon, the three of them are tumbling backward into the water in a giant heap of squeals and shouts and arms and legs.

In that moment, Tali really is fifteen again. Who cares if she has changed history irrevocably? Over her last two years in Liberty, it was like she won the popularity lottery, and she has had to be super careful not to screw it up by saying, doing, or even thinking the wrong thing. Now that she's back in time, she has nothing to lose. It doesn't *matter* what anyone thinks.

She leaps up and falls back into the water again, making a huge splash, smiling at the sky. She has never felt so free.

15

"The court's clear. He shoots!" Rob Gurns says, standing in perfect form for a shot at a basket.

Luce looks up just in time to see his wadded-up popcorn bag sailing in a high arc through the early-evening sky, right toward her head.

"Ew!" she screams, dropping the garbage bag she's been holding open and dodging to the side to avoid getting hit in the face with the trash.

"Air ball," Rob says with a shrug, going back to collecting more litter strewn across the sand. He's so tall, his body looks something like a question mark as he bends over the ground looking for forgotten garbage. With his warm complexion and twin dimples, Rob should be cute, but there's something wild-eyed and goofy about his face, and his arms and legs always seem to be moving in contradictory directions like a giant octopus.

"Look, neither of us is happy to be here, okay, Rob? The

faster we get this done, the sooner we can go in for dinner." It's all Luce can do to keep her voice steady. She's annoyed, tired, depressed, and on the verge of a meltdown. While the other campers were leaping wildly, half-clothed, into the swimming area of the lake, including her three best friends, she and Rob have been collecting trash on the opposite shore for what feels like hours. Today's punishment is even worse than yesterday's, when she had to spend the afternoon helping Kelsey from Bunk Coyote peel gum off picnic tables.

She saw Tali's antics from afar an hour ago and wonders if her mother will see fit to dole out punishments for her, too. It looked like so many of the campers had gotten involved that there was probably no way the Cruz could make *all* of them face the consequences. Besides, they might have been streaking, but none of them was the Cruz's daughter. None of *them* was expected to be perfect.

"What're you doing time for, anyway?" Rob asks, slacking off again on his duties by kicking a lost Nerf ball.

"None of your business." She scrunches her face, watching as he retrieves the ball, which looks like it's been half-eaten by vultures, and pokes his thumb into a hole in its yellow foam. "And this *isn't* 'doing time.'"

She knows she's being huffy, but who cares? Rob Gurns is a basketball player, an all-around slacker, and fruit of the loins of not just one but two Okahatchee alums. He's been at camp as many summers as Luce has, and she's steadfastly stayed out of his way for just as long.

"We're out here by the lake cleaning up other people's shit. That's doing time," Rob insists, ripping the Nerf ball into two mangled halves.

"Well, I guess *you* would know," Luce snaps bitterly. "You're always in trouble for something, right?"

"Yeah," Rob sighs. "But it's such a deliciously delightful, herbally stimulating something. Just can't help myself."

Luce puts the garbage bag back down again. It's getting heavy. They've been out here for almost three hours, collecting everything from used food containers to empty sunscreen bottles. She can't believe what a wreck the lakeshore is. But that's nothing compared to what a wreck *Luce* is. After getting caught in just her underwear two nights ago with Andrew, she never thought she'd hear the end of it from her mom. She can't help but think she's getting *extra* punished.

First, there was the humiliation of *how* they were caught: the midnight "moon walk" for the under-tens. Second, the unfairness of the punishments—all Andrew had to do was scrub down the tennis courts. But third, and far worse, was the look on her mother's face. Luce can't take it when her mom looks at her like that, and she has been trying to avoid her since.

Usually, Luce is the one who can be counted on—to make sure Julian and Silas have had their dinner and finished their homework, to give Amelia her medication before bed, to leave the light on for Dad. And not just at home, either: if it weren't for Luce, there would *be* no SAT-prep course at Brewster, the Trivia Team would be no match for the Massachusetts Mathletes, and the National Merit Scholars would have no local spokesperson. *Luce* is the number-one problem solver, the girl who gets things *done.*

Now here she is, that same girl everyone relies on, that girl who *never* screws up, doing community service with Camp OK's most notorious pot dealer, with utterly no hope of ever laying her hands on the merit badge.

Tonight is the fateful talent show, where Joy has to be voted Miss Okahatchee. And then tomorrow is the end-of-summer carnival and reunion. After tonight there's only one day left to make sure they have everything they need for the photo booth. Twenty-four hours to make it back to the present, back to their *real* lives. And then, if their plan doesn't work . . . well, it's going to be two more years of doing everything exactly right— applying to Princeton all over again. Getting straight As. The tutoring, the babysitting, the committee leading, the student organizing, the plans, the rules, the—

"So let me guess," Rob says, interrupting her thoughts. "You broke into the kitchens at night and scarfed all of the chili dogs?"

"Ew," Luce says.

Rob shrugs. "Tell me, then. Imagination's worth a thousand words."

"That's not the phrase," Luce mutters.

"Huh?"

"It's a *picture.* A picture's worth a thousand words. Anyway, it's nothing. I was just, um, out past curfew."

Rob turns his face toward her. "Alone?"

"With Andrew," she admits, her face flaming.

"Ah. Got it," he says, and even though he's clearly assuming wrong, she lets it go.

"Okay, let's cut west," she says with a sigh. "We still need to cover the area by the volleyball—"

"Why do you *care* so much?" Rob asks, cutting her off. He's looking at her like she's a science experiment—some chemical that could either explode or dissolve when placed into a substance.

"What do you mean?" Luce can feel her face heating up. "I'm just trying to clean up the beach, like we're supposed to."

"Do you always do everything you're supposed to? Forget it. Don't answer. I know you do." He turns his back to her.

"You don't even know me," Luce says, fighting down the urge to slap him.

"I know you're the Cruz's daughter. Total good-girl type. Nerd. *Cute,* but still a nerd," he says, adding up the facts as though he hasn't completely insulted her. "Anyway," he goes on, locating another mangled ball, tossing it into the air, and catching it. "It's human nature to screw up. So just chill out already."

Luce huffs out the breath she's been holding. "Even *you* wouldn't be chill if you knew what I have to deal with," she says angrily, quietly, balling her hands into fists and then flexing them again.

"Oh yeah?" He still hasn't turned around. He lets the ball drop, then fumbles in his pocket and—she can't frigging believe it—actually *pulls out a joint*, lights it, and begins smoking. "Go on. Try me."

Luce just stands there, uncertain. Should she report him? Finish cleaning up alone? Go back before the dining hall closes and give up for the night? Instead she says: "You wouldn't get it."

"Ah. So it's girl stuff."

"*No*, actually, it isn't. It's . . . it's way more complicated than that." She squints out over the lake, which has gone dark in the waning evening, the mountains swallowing the sunlight with one final shrug.

"Dude, what could be that complicated?" he asks, letting the smoke out of his slack-jawed mouth, like he can't even be bothered to purse his lips around it. "Come on, Cruz. What's got you so wound up?"

"*Wound up?*" Suddenly Luce is intensely, uncontrollably enraged. She throws her garbage bag into the sand, not even caring that some of the trash billows out of the top. "Oh, I'm not *wound up*, Rob. I'm freaking *furious*, okay? First you accuse me of caring too much, when really, ya know what? I'm the *only* one who cares. I *have* to care. When I don't, when I let go, everything falls apart. Does that seem fair to you? Do you think I *like* being stuck out here with *you*? I mean, I *never* break rules. Never. I'm supposed to be Little Miss Merit Badge. Everyone else is always skipping curfew and never getting caught, so what are the chances? Why me? Is the whole freaking universe against me right now? Because that's what it seems like, Rob. I didn't *ask* for this. I didn't *ask* to be trapped back here in this horrible rehash of a life."

Realizing she's gone too far, Luce cuts off her own tirade. She shouldn't have said that stuff about the universe, about rehashing her life. But it's true, she *is* furious at the universe, or the unknown, or whatever it is, for throwing her back into the past without any say-so. She remembers how she used to go fishing with her dad, and they'd always have to toss the small ones back into the lake. That's what she feels like: some rejected little fish, not good enough, tossed back into the murk. A furious fish. A furious *fucking* fish, who everyone takes for granted—her boyfriend, her family, her friends, even Rob *fucking* Gurns.

Finally, she registers Rob's face—one of complete calm, as though he's just channel surfing, as though she didn't just fly off the handle and completely insult him in the process.

With a small heft of his long, awkward limbs, he moves closer to her. She stands there, numb, as he takes the joint out of his mouth—thinner and shorter than a cigarette—and wordlessly offers it to her.

She takes it automatically and holds it before her like a laboratory specimen.

"Don't inhale too deep," he says.

Luce stares at the rolled stub in her hand for a second longer. She's done being angry, done worrying, done *thinking*. She pinches the rolled paper between her thumb and index finger like she's seen Rob do, and tentatively puts it to her mouth. As she breathes in, she has the sensation of inhaling the overpowering scent of her aunt Alice's matcha green tea while simultaneously choking on an ashtray. Her chest seizes and she begins coughing hard.

Rob pats her on the back roughly. "Okay, now try again," he says, his voice strangely soothing. It feels good to just take orders from someone else, to not be the one running the show. This is Rob's game now, his territory, and she can sense his authority taking over. "This time," he adds, "go gentler, let it fill your mouth."

She does what he says, mechanically, with precision, as though practicing playing the clarinet. This time it goes a bit better, and he coaches her on how to let the smoke back out of her mouth slowly; she still coughs but not as harshly as before.

Rob retrieves the joint from her and takes another hit, then says, "You're a swimmer, right?"

Luce is startled—surprised that he knows this fact, when, even after almost ten summers of camp together, she knows so little about *him*. "Um, yeah. I am." She wonders what else he knows about her.

"Okay, so it's kinda like swimming. You breathe in, you hold, you release gradually. It's pretty comfortable once you get the hang of it. Here, try again."

He hands it back and she takes another hit, then imagines herself going under, delving into the tranquil turquoise of the Brewster athletic pool, the reassurance of water pressing in all around her, filling her ears and drowning out the whistles and shouts of the spectators above. Drowning out everything, until it's just Luce and the water, and the constant push forward.

"Nice," he comments as she releases the smoke. "Like a pro."

In the middle of breathing out, Luce laughs. She didn't expect to laugh, but there's something so absurd about being told she did a good job by *Rob Gurns*, of all people. King of fuckups. Master of failing. She hands the joint back to him.

"So what's this Red Badge of Courage that's gotten your panties all tangled up?" he asks, and sits down on the sand, stretching his long legs out in front of him.

Luce does the same, with a long sigh, not even caring that he said *panties*, a word she usually can't stand. By now it's gone from dusk to darkness and cool wind from the mountains wraps around her, the same wind that's gently rippling the lake's surface. But she isn't cold. The warmth of the weed is winding through her, making her feel like she's floating just a centimeter above the ground.

She shakes her head, twisting the cheesy plastic purple ring around her finger—the one she's been wearing ever since Andrew won it for her on the cruise. The one he gave to her, promising to be good to her forever. Its painted-on smiley face almost seems ironic to her, like a taunt.

Finally she says, "Jade Marino has been promised the merit badge this summer, but I wanted it—I *needed* it. I still do." She takes another slow breath—*in, hold, release. In, hold, release.* "I've always won it: three summers in a row. But this summer, for some reason, everything's gone differently." She explains it all as though it's a story about someone else, not her. "And it's not even about actual *merit*. It's sort of, like, a promise I made to someone else. I can't really tell you why it's important, but it is."

Rob juts up his lower lip in thought. "So what you're saying is, it's the *having* it, not the *meaning* of it, that you're after."

"Exactly," Luce responds as he hands the joint back to her. Some of the tension restricting her chest releases. It feels good to tell someone.

"In that case, there're other ways you could go about getting your hands on that puppy," Rob says.

Luce turns to him. "What do you mean?"

"I mean, why don't we just steal the thing?"

Luce gasps, causing herself to choke on smoke.

Rob starts laughing.

Luce gives him a hard look through her coughing, which turns into laughter as well.

They both lie back against the sand, giggles rippling easily out of them like water. Before Luce knows it, she's snorting. She can't even remember the last time she laughed in such a relaxed, effortless way.

"If it weren't so absurd," Luce says between snorts, "I would say that's actually a really good idea, Rob."

"If it weren't so absurd, it wouldn't *be* a good idea." Rob sits up, takes the butt of the joint and puts it out, burying it in the sand. She feels light-headed as he leans over, grabs her hands, and pulls her back to her feet.

Before Luce really knows what's happening, she's following Rob through the musky, darkened woods with their trash bags in hand, snickering. The trees and branches form an obstacle course and Luce dodges them, keeping her eyes on the white of

Rob's T-shirt, barely noticing a scratch here or a near-tumble over roots there.

"Slow down!" she whisper-shouts. "I'm supposed to be heading to the talent show! It's gotta be starting soon."

Rob turns around. "Are we on a mission or not?"

She feels a ripple of dread now. "Wait. Crap. Are we gonna get caught? I can't get in trouble again. Forget it. This was a terrible idea, Rob. I need to go. I need to get to—"

"Shhhhh." He puts his hand to his lips. "You're getting paranoid. It's just the pot. Come on, follow me."

She does. Sooner than she expected, the back of the main office building emerges through the inky night, lit from within by the after-hours emergency lights.

"To the right," she commands. "My mom keeps all the trophies and badges in the prize shed." Saying it aloud confirms what they're really up to, but for some reason she doesn't care. The acceptance speeches are scheduled for tomorrow afternoon, and that's when the badges will actually be doled out. If Luce steals the merit badge, her mother will be forced to hand Jade a different honor, and Luce can then sneak off with her friends later that evening, get inside that photo booth, and make it back to the present. Then none of this will matter. It will all be erased.

Or none of this will work, and she'll be stuck living her life over again, stuck on what she's now realizing is a miserable repetition of expectations and assignments and tasks and awards and hard work and lots and lots of winning badges just to win badges. She tries to shut off the spiraling thoughts. Like Rob said, it's probably the marijuana making her paranoid.

They deposit their trash bags into the big green Dumpster, and Rob accidentally lets the lid clang shut afterward. They both cringe at the sound, but no one shows up to scold them. Luce waves Rob over to the back of the main offices next, where she gestures for him to crouch down. She peers through her mother's office window.

Bernadette Cruz is fastidious in her neatness—the room is spare, with two matching leather chairs, a set of filing cabinets, a bookcase, and a series of ribbons and medals won by Luce. For a brief second, she feels a wave of not quite sadness . . . something more like *distance*. As much time as she's spent inside that very office, she has the odd feeling that she's peering in on someone else's life. The room is dimly lit, the computer's screen saver casting an eerie blue glow as pictures of Luce, her two brothers, and their little sister pop up on it like shuffled cards. There's one of the twins in braces and hockey uniforms, one of Amelia in the helmet she used to have to wear before her surgery, one of Luce and her dad hugging after Luce completed a swimming competition, coming in third place. She remembers how she had to fake a smile while swallowing her anger and frustration about failing to secure first place, even though she'd beaten her record.

Rob taps Luce on her shoulder and she squats back down. "She's gone. Come on." They crawl across the grass to the shed and Luce points to a high window, the same one that Tali used to boost Zoe up into when they were kids stealing from Bernadette's spare-candy stash. Luce always refused to be directly involved, though once they were safely stowed away in the Stevens she was happy to partake of an equal share of the hard-won goods.

"Boost me up," she commands in a whisper.

Rob botches the first try. Luce falls into Rob's chest awkwardly.

He snickers. "Sorry, dude, I wasn't ready." He holds out his hands again.

She grabs his shoulders, and puts one foot into his hands, holding on as he easily hoists her up to the window. It's smaller than she remembers. She pushes the glass pane upward and thrusts the upper half of her body through. Her bottom half proves a bit trickier, and she wavers there for a second, feeling like a total idiot with her butt hanging out in the night air, trying not to dissolve into laughter again. Then she grabs onto a sturdy metal shelf and heaves herself farther into the darkened shed, managing to get one leg through and then the other, climbing down the shelves.

She stands there waiting for the objects inside the crowded shed to take form as her eyes adjust. It smells of must and plastic and, faintly, Skittles. All sounds from outside seem muffled by the thick darkness within.

Gradually she is able to see that the metal shelves are lined with plastic Container Store bins, each labeled with an age group, a cabin, an activity, an accolade. Luce can barely make out the writing on the labels, even up close, with only the light from the moon through the window to read them by, but she manages to locate the three bins designated for the badges, alphabetically ordered. In the bin labeled K through R, she is shocked to find not just one but several copies of each badge. There are about twenty-five kinship badges in a row at the front of the box. Her head feels thick, her eyes slow, her hands clumsy. Something about this box makes Luce's stomach drop. It's not like she ever thought winning the badge was all that special, but still . . . Seeing them all lumped together like that, unceremoniously, makes the whole thing seem like a joke. Meaningless.

She stares at the stack of badges in her hands in the darkness, not sure what to do or how to feel. Just then, the beam of a headlight flashes through the window, reflecting off the metal bars of the shelving, and she hears a car pulling onto the gravel right next to the shed.

Someone's *here*. *Shit*.

Stuffing a badge into her pocket, she begins climbing back up the shelves to the window, heart hammering so loudly she's sure it can be heard all the way at the boys' cabins. When she peers out, she sees Rob's back, darting away into the night. She could swear he's still snickering.

Double shit.

Of course Rob would ditch her. He probably thinks this is absofrigginglutely hilarious.

From this vantage point, she can see a figure getting out of the car, which is parked only about seven or eight feet from where she's hiding. The person emerges—a woman in a black dress. Luce's mother. Weird. She must have gotten dolled up for the talent show. Which reminds Luce that she needs to hurry and get out of here. She can't miss the talent show. She needs to be there for Joy.

But she can't tear her eyes from her mother, whose thick, wavy hair is tied in a low, elegant knot at the back of her neck. Luce is struck by how *pretty* her mom looks. She's wearing the diamond earrings Luce's dad got her on their fifteenth anniversary, and they sparkle just slightly in the moonlight. What's she doing back at the office after hours?

Then someone steps out of the passenger side. A man, wearing khaki shorts and a collared short-sleeved shirt that shows off his biceps. Mr. Wilkinson, the sailing instructor. The one who forbade Tali and Blake and his friends from swimming in the lake for the rest of the summer.

Luce lowers herself down by one shelf so that her eyes barely hover over the edge of the window. The last thing she needs is her mother noticing movement in the shed and coming over here to investigate.

Luckily, her mother seems distracted. She's in the middle of a conversation with Mr. W. Luce's mom throws her head back, laughing. Luce had no idea they were so chummy, though her mother gets along with most of the staff pretty well.

Now her mom is picking a piece of lint off Mr. W's collar, or straightening it, or . . . or grabbing it and pulling him closer to her. And kissing him.

Bernadette Cruz is kissing Thom Wilkinson.

Luce's mother, her *married* mother, infamously strict

disciplinarian and revered camp director . . . is *making out with the hot sailing teacher.*

She hardly realizes she has let go of the shelving with a loud gasp until she's landing hard on her elbows and knees on the floor of the shed.

Without thinking, filled with a sudden, powerful nausea, Luce bursts through the door, gasping like a fish on a line, running, blind. She runs, runs, runs, not caring if her mother saw her. She can't breathe, but she can't stop running, either. Past the back corner of the offices, past the dining hall, past the soft halo of the older girls' lit cabins.

She knows she's got to make it to the talent show. It's the only fact keeping her mind from unraveling. But as she runs, a chill races down the back of her neck. She can't tell if she's hot or cold, only that she feels like she's been punched in the gut. She veers back toward the woods, and as soon as she reaches the first tree, she leans into it, heaving, unsure whether she's going to throw up or faint. She hears the distant sound of applause erupting from the rec hall, where the talent show must have already started, and feels a pang of loneliness—awash in the intensity of being completely, incontrovertibly solitary in this world. *Solace, solicit, solitary. Comfort, ask, alone.*

The world spins fast around her: trees, trees, darkness, cabins, grass, lake, more trees.

Her perfect mom. Her perfect mom. Her perfect mom.

A cheater. A liar. A fraud.

16

"But it's clear, oh so clear,
You'll never be here
Because every day, a little more
You disappear, you disappear, you disappear."

Silence wraps Joy in its thick blanket, too warm, stifling. The footlights are so glaring, she can hardly differentiate the faces of her fellow campers in the audience. During the song, she was grateful for those lights—they let her feel like it was just her and Ryder, singing alone on the boulder as the sun set, like yesterday. She completely forgot to worry about what her voice must seem like outside of her head, whether it was too whiny or too high-pitched; she was not worrying about whether she'd get the lyrics right or what the other kids were thinking.

Everything fell away, and she felt *right*.

But now the song is over, and the terror comes flooding back in: *Did they screw up? Did they sound okay? Is everyone trying not to laugh at her? Did she look like an idiot?*

And then there's a loud rush of noise—applause. People are clapping. Some of them are even standing—not just the ones who squeezed in behind the back row after the chairs ran out. Suzanne Simonson, head of Bunk Chipmunk, is wiping tears from her eyes. Even Jeremy Farber puts two fingers into his mouth and whistles—and for once his whistle doesn't make Joy's skin crawl. In the crowd, she spots Tali, Zoe, and Luce—who snuck in late—clapping.

Ryder stands up and swivels his guitar strap so that the instrument is out of his way. Then he leans over and helps Joy out of her chair, and she realizes she's beaming like him. They turn toward the audience again and take a bow, then Ryder pulls her off the platform and through the door to the "green room," which is really just the rec hall supply room, lined with makeshift vanities and mirrors propped against the wall, lit with clamp lights. She catches a brief glimpse of their reflection in one of the mirrors— he's about six inches taller than her, and she fits nicely under his shoulder. *We make a cute couple,* she thinks, and then is startled by the thought. They look *normal*. Like any other couple.

After all the pain and anger of the last couple of years, after all the loneliness, she stopped believing that she'd ever have that. Have *this*.

As soon as the door closes behind them, Ryder is enfolding her in a giant bear hug. She lets him press their bodies together, her face against his hard chest, and she breathes in his smell. He's wearing some old band shirt and it's surprisingly soft against her cheek.

"We rocked it," he says.

"I know," she says, pulling back so she can look at him, feeling the giant, geeky smile stretching across her face. "We did."

They watch the rest of the talent show from the wings, along with some of the other performers; they laugh together when Dave Krauss and Mike Lawrence perform a comedic skit imitating Okahatchee's counselors, and they clap along during an adorable tumbling routine performed by the little girls from Bunk Robin's Egg.

Joy loses herself in the night—the feeling of endlessness, like it's a single snapshot from a long photo strip of more nights just like this one—and is startled when she hears her name called during the awards announcement. Someone from Bunk Bear Cub has already won first place in the talent show for her incredible Hula-Hoop dance, and Hadley Gross won second, like always, for her French horn solo. A few runners-up were announced, but Joy lost track as Ryder wrapped his arm around her. So why is her name being called now?

Ryder drags her back onstage to another round of applause. With a rush of clarity, she understands what's happening: she's being given the Miss Okahatchee tiara. The faux-metal crown's sharp combs scratch her scalp as Suzanne Simonson places it on her head.

Quickly Joy scans the crowd again for her friends. She was so wrapped up in the performance with Ryder she literally forgot what was at stake. She spots Zoe, who gives her a thumbs-up, while Luce and Tali clap.

"Wh-why me? Why do I get it?" Joy finds herself blurting as Suzy shakes her hand to more applause.

"Why you?" the counselor repeats. "Because, girl—your voice made all of us cry out there! You deserve it!"

The audience begins to filter out. Joy follows the crowd, for some reason unable to speak, unable to talk to Ryder, unable even to be proud. All she feels is numb confusion.

She just won Miss Okahatchee.

Just like last time.

Only not like last time at all.

Suddenly Zoe throws her arms around Joy.

"You did it!" Zoe shouts. "Holy shit, I was so nervous. But when I heard you sing I knew you had it in the bag. I'm so proud of you."

Joy tries to smile, but it's as though her mind has left her body.

"*Finally,*" Tali says in an urgent but hushed tone, shaking Joy's arm. "We're making progress!"

Joy stares at her.

"Aren't you excited? We're one step closer to going home!" Zoe tugs at her T-shirt.

Luce, unusually quiet, scrunches her forehead and puts a hand on Joy's shoulder. "Hey, are you okay?" Her own eyes look red, and normally Joy's reaction would be to ask *her* the same question.

But not now.

No. Joy can feel the word burning inside her, but she can't say it aloud. She's not okay.

And she knows, suddenly, with total certainty: She's not going home.

She's not going back.

She's heaving by the time she reaches the boulder by the lake, past the footbridge, where she and Ryder sat practicing "Disappear" just last night. Was that really only one night ago? It seems like she's known him forever.

But what does forever mean, anyway?

Her throat feels hot and sticky. In the darkness, the boulder looms up before her quite suddenly, shapely and mysterious, like an ancient rhinoceros fast asleep. She climbs its back, then stands on the side facing the lake, only about a foot from where the lip of the rock touches the water. Tonight the moon is eclipsed by clouds, and the lake, sloshing with secrets, licks at the shore as though it's thirsty for more.

But she's not telling hers. Not yet. Maybe never.

Joy rips the tiara off her head and throws it as far as she can into the waves. It's so flimsy, it doesn't even make a splash—it's just swallowed, whole. Gone. There's a small taste of relief, some space opening up at the back of her throat at last, her mind starting to clear like a good high—another thing she never used to know about.

And then she hears footsteps behind her. "Hey."

It's Ryder. He has followed her. She can see he's not angry, just bewildered.

"Why the hell did you do that?" he asks.

Why? Because she can't go back. Because no matter how much you try, you cannot change the future. You cannot change. Not *really*. That's the problem with optimism, with hope. You end up disappointed.

She feels like a complete idiot for even thinking it was possible to break out, to start fresh, to undo the damage of the last two years, to think she had some power to cut her own path through this universe, that living differently, being braver, would alter her fate forever. But there's no such thing as forever; she knows that.

He takes another step toward her on the boulder, and she repositions her footing. "Hey," he says, and then softer, "is everything cool with you? What happened? Was it the song? Was it . . . me?"

His concern is so genuine it actually makes her laugh. "Sorry, Ryder. It's not the song. The song's perfect. It's just me. I didn't deserve the crown."

"What are you *talking* about? You were amazing!" he says, rubbing her arms. She hadn't realized she was shivering. His face is partly hidden in the misty night, his eyes two dark stars, burning almost invisibly.

She backs up, even though her whole body wants to stay. "You shouldn't get close to me."

"Why not?" he asks, meeting her eyes. She's never met anyone who can hold her gaze with such confidence.

"I'm . . . dangerous," she answers, for lack of a better way to put it. Really, she's a volcano. She's Vesuvius. Three million people . . . three million idiots live around that place, just waiting for an explosion, just waiting to be painted in ash, just waiting for disaster. How did they not see it coming?

How can Doug Ryder not understand that they're doomed?

Because he doesn't know the truth. No one does.

He steps even closer to her. "I'm not afraid."

She feels like a rubber band, stretched taut—she has no idea which direction she'll fly once released.

"Maybe *you* should be afraid of *me*," he says, getting even closer, so their noses are almost touching—too close.

"Oh, really?" Her heart aches. Her whole body aches. His hands are skimming her shoulders, making a new kind of shiver. "Why's that?"

"Here's why," he says softly . . . and then pushes her.

She shrieks and tumbles backward right into the lake. It's shallow here and she comes up laughing, spluttering water, then grabs his ankle and yanks him in, too.

Now she's in his arms, in the water, and she can feel his breath against her wet cheek. All it would take is to lean in, just a little. . . .

His kiss feels like it has been coming forever, and yet she's still surprised by it, his lips warm and soft and urgent against hers. She lets herself go, gives in to it, gives in to *him*, even if it is wrong, even if it is doomed.

He leans back just a fraction, his bottom lip still touching her top lip, then kisses her eyebrow, her cheek, then her mouth again, pulling her toward him so that their bodies are completely aligned. He lifts her slightly out of the water. She wraps her arms around his shoulders and he lifts higher, so her hips are pressed against his abs. His hands grip her waist strongly, like he knows what he's doing—like he's been waiting to do this for a while.

He trails his kisses down her neck. He kisses the soft spot just between her shoulder and collarbone. "You're shaking," he says, slowly putting her down.

"I'm fine," she says, though it's more like a sigh.

"You're freezing," he says.

"I'm hot," she says, giggling, happiness rising inside of her like a bubble. "I'm boiling, see?" Spontaneously, she pulls her drenched shirt off over her head.

He draws her toward him again, touching her all over, kissing her everywhere. Her skin feels cold and hot, sticky and smooth, tingly and static, like her body carries an electric charge. She fumbles to take his shirt off, too, drawing it over his torso, laughing as the shirt gets stuck coming over his head, feeling wild and a little dizzy. Is this even real? But then it's almost like her hands have a mind of their own, tracing his chest and shoulders, as though desire itself is a directional force, a compass needle that always knows north.

Now he's tugging at her shorts, which are so sodden with lake water that they cling to her thighs, until she's in only her underwear, and then he's carrying her, carrying her, over to the mossy shore by the mini waterfall, which is really more of a five-foot-high trickle, and he's laying her down on the mossy shore and they're kissing more and touching more and their bodies are speaking to each other in a language Joy had no idea she even knew. Her nerves feel like they're on fire, like they'll burn right through her skin, like they'll singe *his*.

"Joy," he whispers.

Her name, like long-awaited punctuation in a run-on sentence, a sentence that wants to keep going forever. In this moment, she *does* believe in forever. The Joy who didn't believe just moments before is a stranger to her now. She's floating. She's all rhythm and touch and heat. She curls into him, feeling sweat or possibly tears on her face, or a light mist from the waterfall spraying off the rocks.

She has no real clue how they both ended up naked, how any of it happens—she doesn't know anything at all. She kisses him again. He smells like the lake. He puts his arm around her to keep her from shivering, which she didn't think was possible after being so hot.

"This sounds crazy," he whispers. "But do you believe in love at first sight?" Then he laughs a short, sheepish laugh.

Joy smiles, burying her face into his chest. "I don't know," she answers honestly. She suddenly feels so *young*. Usually she feels mature, old, like nothing can surprise her. But in this moment, she's realizing maybe she hasn't lived at all before now. Maybe her life is just beginning, from this point on.

Some of the clouds have parted and a few stars are faintly visible over them. The lake is quietly whispering near their feet, and

Joy knows at least one of its secrets, but that just makes her realize the infinite ones she'll never know.

Ryder rolls slightly more onto his back. "I think that's the Big Dipper," he says, pointing. "I've never actually noticed it before. I'm terrible at that stuff."

She laughs, looking up at the series of stars forming what looks like the bottom half of an octagon. "Yup, that's it."

"Seems like it's gotta be, I don't know, proof of something," he says, tracing his fingers down her arm, writing unreadable cursive on her skin.

She looks up at the sky again, at those tiny pinpricks of distant fire, burning out there in cold, black space, forming their pretty, arbitrary shapes.

"Hey, what time is it?" she asks.

He fumbles for the phone in his jeans, long discarded. "Eleven forty-five."

She sits up, an idea occurring to her. "Then there's still time to catch Blake's party."

Ryder laughs again. "You're a little bit insane, aren't you?"

She turns to him, then grabs his hands and pulls them both up to their feet. It feels awkward, standing like that, naked, with someone she was just . . . intimate with. She's almost dizzy with the knowledge of it. She pushes that aside. "I don't want to miss anything."

He shrugs. "Okay. I guess I'm game. Life's short, right?"

Joy stares at him for a beat, his tall body naked in the faint starlight. There's something completely absurd about it. But then again, there's something completely and wildly absurd about *all* of this. "I couldn't agree more," she replies.

"Should we get some dry clothes first?" he suggests.

"That's probably a good idea," she answers. "But you realize we're going to have to streak all the way to the cabins to get them, right?"

"Then let's get a move on." He gathers their sopping wet clothes in one arm, then grabs her hand and together they run, completely nude, back over the footbridge, through the woods, like some insane version of Adam and Eve. She's beaming so hard her face hurts, her heart so happy and full it feels like her chest could burst open.

This is life, she thinks, giddy with the realization. *This is love. This is* it.

17

From afar, the lights from the party appear to rise up and burn into low-hanging clouds, smoking the sky. An electronic beat throbs through the humid night air. As Zoe, Tali, and Luce walk through the dewy darkness of the Greens' front lawn toward the lit-up mansion, Zoe can't help but feel like she's about to enter an alternate reality.

She's once again approaching dreamland.

She feels good. She feels *ready* for something. Ready for tomorrow's tournament—she's been drilling ever since she left here this afternoon.

Ready for something else, too . . . ready to be surprised, maybe.

Zoe and Tali wait impatiently as Luce double-checks to make sure the golf cart they stole from camp is sufficiently hidden behind a set of trees. From this distance, Luce looks even tinier than usual, and it occurs to Zoe that she has barely seen her without Andrew's arm draped around her shoulders. It's refreshing to have Luce alone, though she can't help but wonder why Luce didn't invite Andrew.

As for Joy—she fled after the talent show, and they're still wondering if she's going to make an appearance at the party or not. Zoe knows she should probably be worried about Joy, but instead she just feels light-headed, unfocused. Tomorrow is their last day. . . .

"Hey," Tali bursts out, causing Zoe to do a double take.

"What?"

"Oh, nothing," Tali says, looking fidgety and itchy.

She wonders what happened to put Tali in such a strange mood. Over dinner, Zoe tried to ask Tali about her impromptu streaking session and Tali just shrugged, saying she couldn't find Blake and got locked out of the house while she was changing. But she knows Tali's not telling her the whole story.

"No, what were you gonna say?"

Tali swallows and shifts her weight, keeping her gaze focused on Luce in the distance. "Oh, I was just gonna say I'm sorry about . . . I mean, it sucks how we stopped hanging out. We still go to the same school. We see each other every day."

Zoe cocks an eyebrow. "I don't think they allow people like me at your lunch table, if you know what I mean."

Tali turns to her then. "No, I don't know what you mean. Why are you always putting up these, I don't know, false dividers between us?"

"False dividers? Tali, the kids you hang out with, the popular crowd? Ashlynn and Tim and Mike and whoever else . . . I'm sorry, but they're assholes and they're mean to anyone who's *not* part of their little inner circle. I'm not exactly dying to cross over to the other side."

"That's always been your problem," Tali huffs.

"What?"

"Being so opinionated. Judgmental. You always assume everyone's out to get you. Ashlynn and all those other people— my *friends*—they're fun! And *they* don't ditch me without any explanation."

Now it's Zoe's turn to scoff. "I'm sorry, you're saying *I* ditched *you*? Yeah, right."

Tali shakes her head. "You guys were *always* leaving me out. Even when we were friends."

Zoe can feel her jaw practically drop off her face. "What are you even talking about? That's ridiculous!"

"Is it?" Tali asks, her eyes dark.

For a second, Zoe stops feeling angry and just feels . . . *bad*. Bad for Tali—which is a new one for her. Tali is the one who got popular and left her behind. It's *not* the other way around.

Is it?

Tali turns away. "Whatever. I'm not getting into it. The past is the past."

Luce returns then, wiping her hands on her shorts. "I think we're good. Though at this point, if we get caught—" She throws her hands up in the air as if to say, *I give up.* Zoe is equally per-plexed by Luce tonight. She almost missed the entire talent show, arriving only seconds before Joy's performance with her eyes all red like she'd been crying, and when Zoe tried to ask her what was wrong, she shrugged and whispered simply, "Just getting a heavy dose of reality tonight."

Zoe wasn't sure if she meant her punishment—cleaning up garbage around the lake—or something else.

And then of course, there's Joy, missing in action since she ran from the talent show with the coveted Miss Okahatchee crown on her head.

For two years, Zoe had been content to allow them all to grow apart; it had seemed an inevitable part of growing up. But now she can feel the invisible barrier between them like it's an actual, tangible *thing*, a substance, a fog. If only the sun would rise and burn it all away so she could see her friends again—really see them.

A scream pierces through the music now, followed by laughter, and the girls turn back to face the mansion. Zoe gulps.

As soon as they open the door, they're enveloped in sound and haze. The music's so loud it feels like an external heartbeat. Dozens of beautiful, unrecognizable people filter past her wearing everything from sequined dresses to bikinis. By comparison, Zoe's standard summer uniform of cutoffs and a man's T-shirt over a bathing suit looks totally out of place, but it doesn't matter—she slips into the stream of people invisibly, savoring the power of anonymity, yet also kind of liking being part of something so big, so wild.

A girl with thick liner and huge fake eyelashes steps in front of her and winks. Then she stands there with a hand on her hip and says, "Well?"

"Well what?" Zoe says, and then realizes the girl is wearing all black and white—she's a *waitress*—and she's holding a tray of shots in shot glasses made of actual glass. They twinkle with something pale green sloshing inside. Bravely, Zoe grabs one and downs it, feeling the foreign liquid tingle and burn inside her. When she turns to give the empty glass back and check on her friends, the waitress has already disappeared, fairylike. So have Luce and Tali—carried away by the party's current. She finds an empty space on a mantel and puts the glass down, then catches her reflection in the mirror. Flat blond hair. Wide-spaced blue eyes. Boring all-American-looking face. Spontaneously, she grabs her hair, scrunches and swishes it around until it looks like she's been riding cross-country on the back of a motorcycle. Better. Wilder.

The living room is almost the size of the entire downstairs of Zoe's house in Liberty. She sees now that there's a full bar next to one of the brass-studded leather couches—a real bar, made out of mahogany or something else dark and glossy.

She forces her way through the packed crowd, following the tickle of breeze that's coming from the far doorway. Through it, she enters a dining room lined with huge windows, then a giant kitchen with a sitting area that opens out through a screen door into the backyard. She can see it's only one of several exits to the expansive property that lies behind the house.

There are people everywhere—sprawled out on the lawns,

dancing on the tennis courts, playing in the pool, laughing on balconies, and spilling out of the game room and wine cellar below the deck. Zoe can only assume most of them are Ellis and Blake's high school friends, though she recognizes one or two other campers in the mix as well who must have similarly braved sneaking out past curfew and found rides here. Zoe scans the crowd before it occurs to her that she's looking for Ellis. After all, Ellis is the one who invited her, and besides Tali and Luce, she's one of the few people she knows here, even if she *is* Zoe's competition.

But she can't spot her.

No surprise—that's how Ellis is, Zoe's beginning to realize. Elusive. There and then not there. It's what makes her so skilled with a sword in hand. She flits around so much, like a butterfly, that it's hard not to want to pin her down to get a better look.

Zoe resolves to get herself a proper drink instead, and pushes her way into a long, winding line by one of the bars . . . right behind Russ Allen. She'd recognize that stupid lumpy backpack anywhere.

Shit.

"Albright!" he says, catching her before she can flee. With his buzz cut and broad shoulders, he's not *terrible* looking. Her taste isn't that bad. He's just . . . awkward.

"Russ!" she says back. "What are you, um, doing here?"

"Partying, obviously," he says. "And hoping to run into *you*, of course."

"Of course."

He smiles, clearly getting his hopes up. "So, do you, like, wanna go somewhere?"

"Right *now*?" Zoe asks. How disinterested does she need to be for him to get the hint? "Russ, I just *got* here."

"Later, then?" he asks, and she hates the desperate squeak in his voice.

"No, Russ. Never." The dismissal flies out of her mouth automatically, and she's amazed how much easier it is this time around. After Cal, she's got rejection down pat. "I'm sorry," Zoe adds quickly. "It's just that I'm, ah, dating someone else. Currently."

He crinkles his eyebrows. "Are you sure?"

They move forward in the line. "Am I *sure*? Yeah, Russ, I'm sure." It's all Zoe can do not to roll her eyes. She's trying to make this easier on him and instead he's questioning her lie. *Of course* it's a lie. She's trying to be nice!

"Okay, well, I can get you a drink at least," Russ says, seeming deflated.

Zoe shrugs. "Okay."

By now they're almost at the bar. Once he hands her a vodka tonic, she turns to head off into the party without him, but he grabs her shoulder. "Zoe."

"Yeah?"

"Whoever it is, they're lucky."

He lets her go, but his comment has unsettled her, and no matter how hard she concentrates as she allows the crowd to absorb her back into its pulse, she's unable to pinpoint why.

Several hours, several beverages, and several "emergency" primping sessions with Tali later, Zoe finds Luce being carried on the shoulders of some burly-looking dude who has *got* to be at least a college freshman. *Jesus.* Whatever that "dose of reality" she took earlier was, it's got a powerful hold on Luce now—and so does all that pink punch she's been downing since they arrived.

"Come down!" Zoe screams up at her. The burly dude ignores her, pushing through the thick crowd of dancers and slapping another guy five.

"I'm fiiiiiine, Zo!" Luce shouts down at her, swaying to the music, clearly very drunk.

"Dude, what are you, her babysitter?" the guy slurs, accidentally dropping a beer bottle. They both watch it shatter on the ground as though in slow motion.

"I'm her *friend*," Zoe states desperately.

All of a sudden Luce squeals. "Joy baby!" she shouts. "You're here!"

Luce clambers clumsily down off the guy's shoulders as Joy approaches, with Doug Ryder not far behind her. Joy appears to be wet, as though she's been swimming. Her cheeks glow rosy pink.

Before Zoe can check to see if Luce is okay, she and Joy are dancing—bouncing up and down and wildly waving their arms. Both have a huge smile on their faces, and Zoe effortlessly joins in—it's not a decision, really, more like riding in on a tide. Tali appears in their midst. Doug Ryder might still be there, too, and

Russ Allen. Zoe isn't even sure. It's mayhem. A song comes on that they all know the words to, and now they're jumping, shouting the lyrics at the tops of their lungs.

What could be minutes but must be hours pass by in a dimly lit blur of dancing, singing, laughing. Zoe looks up at her arms, at the haze-filled sky beyond, feeling the bass pump through her body as though it's part of her blood. The night air is cool against her sweaty skin. She could keep dancing forever—the planet has stopped spinning and time no longer exists. Everything falls away—her stress about the tournament tomorrow, missing Cal, avoiding Russ, her suspicions that Tali's keeping secrets, her worry that something's up with Luce, questions about why Joy ran off earlier . . . all gone.

It's neither the past nor the future—everything that has happened before now mashes up to everything that will happen one day, and she feels endless: young and ancient at the same time, like she's always existed, like she's shining brilliantly. She feels beautiful.

But just as quickly, she's coming down, sliding out of the party-induced high, looking around her at the spinning faces and writhing bodies. Teeth flashing in the strobe light. Arms waving like a field of tall, wild grass. She's hot. She's thirsty.

"I'm getting water!" she shouts.

The other girls keep bouncing and swiveling and spinning. Joy gives her a grin and a nod. She tries to get Luce to focus. "Do you want one, too?" Zoe asks.

Luce just shakes her head, stumbling slightly into a stranger dancing behind her, then laughing and pushing her glossy black bangs out of her eyes.

Zoe winds through the dense mob, relishing the refreshing gulp of air when she gets to the outskirts of the dance floor. She's almost tempted to dive straight into the pool. Two couples are playing chicken, splashing everywhere. Zoe heads to the indoor bar instead, where there's likely a shorter line.

She enters the house through the door next to the deck—the one that leads straight into a "wine cellar," and then up a few stairs, through the game room, and then into some sort of library or study where, sure enough, there's a nearly half-stocked bar with no one at it. Zoe can't help but wonder what it would be like to grow up in a house this big—did Blake and Ellis ever get lost in it? All the furniture seems to shine like the leather or wood has been recently polished, much of it featuring tufts and darts and brass studs, subtle touches that make it seem even more expensive.

"Psst!"

Zoe spins around.

It's Ellis—her hair pulled tight from her face, emphasizing her cheekbones, and that sly grin creeping onto her face, then disappearing just as fast. She's wearing ripped shorts a lot like Zoe's, with a loose button-down (Blake's school shirt, maybe?) tied in a casual knot over her belly button, the white halter strap of a bikini showing at the neck.

"The punch is one of Blake's nasty concoctions," Ellis informs Zoe in a warning voice, reaching around the bar, then squatting down so she's out of view. Zoe hears bottles clinking. "We have something better back here, I'm pretty sure. Aha. Here we go." She stands up with a bottle of whiskey in her hand and proceeds to pour them each a glass with ice cubes.

"Thanks," Zoe says, taking hers, both curious about where Ellis has been and vaguely resentful. *You're the one who invited me here in the first place,* she thinks. But quickly the feeling passes—Ellis probably invited a ton of friends.

She takes a sip, and the liquor burns her throat, but she tries her best not to cringe.

"Smooth, right?" Ellis says, taking a much more confident sip, then swirling the ice in her glass like an expert. The whiskey catches the light, winking.

"Um, yeah, sure," Zoe says. She clears her throat. "Thanks again for inviting me over. My friends and I are having a great time. Good DJ."

"I figured you wouldn't have anything better to do at camp," she says, with a puzzling look of amusement, her dimples showing.

"True," Zoe says, taking another, slightly braver sip. Heat from the alcohol sinks through her. "So," she announces, raising her glass. "To a fair tournament tomorrow."

Ellis nods. "And to unexpected wins," she adds cryptically.

They toast, and then Ellis downs her drink like it's a shot.

Zoe tips back her glass, too, almost choking on the stinging, intense liquor. It leaves the taste of honey and ashes on her tongue. She feels dizzy as she hands the glass back to Ellis, their fingers grazing lightly, and for some reason Zoe imagines they're opening up a bout—Ellis's initial contact is always light and easy, she's noticed, almost gentle: a tap to say *Let's get started* before she's fully into the match.

"Feels good, doesn't it?" Ellis nudges Zoe with her shoulder, like they've just shared an inside joke. And then Ellis runs her hand up Zoe's arm, spins her so that her back is to the bar, and kisses her.

There's a brief second where Zoe's mind shuffles itself back into place—Ellis is kissing her. Soft lips. Curious tongue. Slow and suggestive.

Zoe yanks back, a little too violently, elbowing the pitcher of remaining punch and overturning it. Red liquid spills over the glossy bar top and drips off the edge, splattering across Zoe's shirt and shorts. "Whoa. What . . . what are you doing?" she blurts out, confused about what to focus on—her stained clothes or Ellis's curious, foxlike face, or the fact that a girl just kissed her. *Ellis* kissed her. What the hell?

Ellis shrugs. "Having fun. It's no big deal."

Zoe stares at Ellis. The floor spins beneath her. *It's no big deal.* Is this how all ridiculously rich kids act? They make out with whoever they want, boy or girl, whenever they feel like it?

"I mean no one even knows we're in here," Ellis adds, playing with her ponytail. "Oh, come on, Zoe, don't be ridiculous about it."

Zoe shakes her head, overcome with the mixed urge to slap Ellis, to laugh, to run. But she doesn't do any of those things . . . because part of her is completely intrigued. It's like Ellis has no rules—on the field or off. She just . . . does whatever she wants.

Free.

"Hey," Ellis says. "You have punch literally all over you. Let me at least give you something else to change into, 'kay?"

Zoe follows Ellis's ponytail, feeling like she's a hound on a hunt, tracking a strange creature that refuses to be caught. Just when she thought she had Ellis figured out, the girl managed to surprise her again, to unnerve her completely.

Ellis's words weave through Zoe's mind: *Just having fun.* The thought braids together with the lingering warmth of the whiskey and that unquenchable desire Zoe feels around Ellis to *win*, to best her at something.

They enter an upstairs bathroom—it's one of those connector bathrooms, with one door opening to Ellis's bedroom and a second door that leads into Blake's room, which Zoe can guess by the boyish plaid comforter and all the tennis posters. Ellis closes the adjoining door to her brother's room with an apologetic, *Boys are disgusting* look, and digs out some stain stick from underneath the sink. "Here you go," she says, then backs into her room and starts going through her clothes.

Zoe turns on the sink faucet to let the hot water steam up, then slowly peels off her shirt—she's wearing her bathing suit underneath, so it isn't that big a deal, but the shorts are stained so they'll have to come off, too. She starts rubbing stain stick on the bright red spots before putting the shorts into the sink to soak, feeling weirdly exposed in her black two-piece, despite having worn it all the time for the last few days. She remembers how she used to live in this thing for the whole summer. Now it strikes her as pathetically utilitarian and uncool.

"Nothing clean. You know what?" Ellis calls from her room. "You can wear what I have on and I'll change."

She walks into the bathroom again wearing only her white bikini, and hands Zoe her jean shorts and button-down shirt. As Zoe takes the balled-up clothes, which smell like Ellis's citrusy perfume, a rush comes over her. *It's my turn* she thinks, without knowing exactly what that means. She drops the clothes on the counter and puts her hand on Ellis's shoulder.

Ellis pauses, staring at her. Caught. Zoe's the one in charge now. She does what Ellis taught her earlier this afternoon, and leans in. Ellis's lips part and they kiss, lightly. Their mouths do a warm, soft, easy dance, coming closer and then moving apart, with little breaths in between. Ellis licks Zoe's lower lip. She can feel Ellis's taut body up against hers—they're almost the exact same size, both thin but rippled with long lean muscles. Ellis's bare stomach touches her own, and it sends a shiver of uncertainty through her.

What is she doing?

But at the same time . . . it's *fun*. In fact, it's way better than most of the fumbling make-out sessions Zoe has had in the past with boys who were clod-like, overly aggressive, or awkward. With Ellis it feels easy. It feels right.

And maybe it *isn't* that big of a deal, not really. Just one crazy night. One party.

Ellis's knees bump into Zoe's as she shifts her weight, but she doesn't seem to notice—they keep kissing, almost like it's a challenge to see who will give up first. Waves of heat and electricity race through Zoe's body. Her toes tingle. Her lips burn. Her hips come forward slightly and Ellis grabs them with both hands—unsurprisingly strong, even though her hands are delicate and small. Zoe gasps and Ellis smiles, which Zoe can feel against her face, like an invitation.

It feels like the perfect bout, one that could go on forever because they're perfectly matched, move for move, touch for touch.

And then everything happens in a confused blur: the bathroom mirrors now seem like funhouse mirrors and there's a whoosh of cold air as Ellis leaps away from her with a tiny, almost inaudible squeal. Zoe spins around, barely recognizing the clicking sound of a turning knob. The door that leads to Ellis's bedroom is swinging wide open, and Ellis is in the shower, hidden behind its thick white curtain, and Zoe is fumbling with the loose strap of her bikini top, and *Tali* is standing there with a look of complete shock and horror on her face.

"Zo?" Tali spits out. "What are *you* doing in here?" Her eyes go to Blake's bedroom door. "Have you—are you . . ." Her mouth tightens to a thin line. "Where's Blake?"

And then, practically in slow motion and before Zoe can say a word, Blake's bedroom door opens.

"I'm right here," he says, smiling easily, sauntering into the bathroom, shirtless. "You need something, Bender?"

Tali stares. Zoe is frozen, horrified, knowing exactly how this must look—praying Ellis will emerge and explain this all away, yet at the same time thankful that she hasn't—that no one has to know what happened in here moments before.

"It's not what you think," Zoe finally manages to say.

But Tali just storms away.

Blake looks Zoe up and down. "Nice bikini," he says, with a cocky grin. "Does your friend always scare so easily?" he asks.

"Leave me alone," Zoe blurts, running out of the bathroom, through Ellis's bedroom, and into the hall. She grabs Tali's shoulder, forcing her to turn and face her.

Her eyes look wet. "I think you owe me a fucking explanation," Tali states, her voice shaking.

Zoe struggles to find the words. How *is* she going to explain this? "It's not . . . it's not what it looks—"

Tali throws a hand up into the air like a stop sign. "Really, Zoe? I don't need to hear clichés from you, of all people."

"Why do you even *care* so much?" Zoe bursts out, arms up, exasperated. "I thought he was just a boy toy to you, anyway! You've already hooked up with him, so what's the problem?"

Darkness clouds Tali's eyes and she clenches her fists. "No, I *didn't*." Her voice is low, husky, almost canine. "I *never* hooked up with him. And now, thanks to you, my chance is ruined!"

Zoe's head spins. It must be the whiskey . . . or that shot she took . . . or the punch. "But what about *last* time around?" she demands, her voice dropping to a harsh whisper.

"I was a *loser* back then," Tali blurts now, the confession clearly forcing its way out of her. "It never happened. Okay? Never. It was a lie. All along. So this *was* my only chance. But I guess none of that matters to you. You think I'm a cupcake, right? All frosting, or whatever? God forbid I should actually have feelings, actually *want* something for myself. Everyone assumes I have it figured out, that everything comes easy for me. No one knows how hard it is. No one cares."

Zoe hadn't thought this night could get any more shocking. What does Tali mean, they *never* hooked up? Is *everything* Zoe believed about the past a complete falsehood? "You're too good for him anyway," Zoe says softly now, still trying to get her thoughts together.

Tali scoffs. "And you would know? You *knew* I liked him, and you went for him anyway. The only thing I can't understand is why *he* went for someone like *you*."

"Someone like *me*? What's that supposed to mean?" Zoe spits out.

"It means someone who is content to live on the periphery, never *trying*, never improving your life. In twenty years, Zoe? You're still going to be having burping contests with Cal, refusing to grow up. So forgive me if that's not what *I* want."

Zoe makes a noise somewhere between a choke and a laugh. "I can't believe you actually think that you're the mature one here. If you didn't have your head up your own ass all the time, you would know that hooking up with Blake is exactly the *last* thing on my personal itinerary." She feels her cheeks heating up with anger. "But you don't know that. You don't know what's going on with *any* of us, and yet you expect us to give a shit about your own petty drama—"

"Right, me and my *drama*. What about you? You think you're so honest," Tali goes on, cutting her off. "Good old Zoe, always putting her foot in her mouth, saying whatever she thinks. The real truth is, you are the one who let this friendship die. You are the one who didn't want to move on, move forward. You're content to stay stuck. Joy had the right idea. Some of us know how to move on. I'm certainly fucking moving on *now*. I don't need any of you. This is all bullshit." She shoves past Zoe, almost violently, running down the stairs like her life depends on it.

Zoe's so furious her ears feel like they're on fire. "Yeah, Tali. Run away! That's the answer!" she screams after her, too full of rage to even really take in what Tali's saying. What does any of this have to do with moving on, anyway? What did she mean that Zoe's stuck?

"Guys, come on," Joy says, emerging at the top of the stairs with an extremely drunk-looking Luciana in tow. "Everyone calm down, okay?"

But Zoe can't calm down. Not now. Not when Tali has once again decided to make this all about *her*. And bringing up Joy leaving—that was a real slap in the face, and she knew it.

But before Zoe can think what to do next, Luce is leaning over the railing, puking. Joy looks distraught, doing her best to hold Luce's hair back from her face.

"Help me," she says to Zoe. "We've got to get her home."

Zoe sighs. Joy's right. Tali can go stew, can go act like this is all Zoe's fault instead of her own. They don't see things eye to eye, that's for sure. Come to think of it, maybe they never did.

But what did Tali mean about her refusing to move on, to grow up?

She and Joy help lead Luce out toward the driveway, where Doug Ryder loads them into someone's car. The whole time, Zoe feels nauseated herself, sick with guilt, regretting that she never managed to get Luce more water. Regretting that she didn't have a chance to explain to Tali—even if Tali does hate her, she should know that this isn't Zoe's fault.

But more than anything else, she regrets Ellis.

18

FRIDAY

Most Improved. Now that is some serious irony. Luce's forehead pounds, an inner jackhammer drilling away at her nerves as she flips the stolen badge over and over in her hands. The *wrong* stolen badge. Not that it even matters—what's the point in getting back to the future now? How's she going to face it, knowing what was really going on in the past?

She sits down on the grass near cabin 43, where Andrew told her to meet him today, and drops her head into her hands, closing her eyes. When she slipped out the door of the Blue Heron cabin this morning, the other three girls were still sleeping—Tali facing the wall, Zoe splayed out with her sheets half off the bed, and Joy looking oddly peaceful and fragile.

Luce stares again at the badge in her hands. She remembers who got the Most Improved badge two summers ago: Kendall

Meyers, a pre–fourth grade boy who went from complete awkwardness to archery master that summer. He also apparently finally stopped wetting his bunk bed, which, his bunkmates told everyone, was the *real* reason he was awarded the honor for most improved. Everyone knows it's a backhanded compliment—it implies you sucked before, despite what Luce's mother always says about how everyone's a winner at something.

Luce's mother.

Are *any* of her famous words of wisdom really true? Or has she been faking it all? Images of Bernadette Cruz in her black dress last night, in her glimmering earrings, leaning in toward Mr. Wilkinson, *kissing* Mr. W, easy, natural, like that wasn't even the first time, swirl through Luce's memory like a sickening carousel. Luce never liked carousels as a kid: around and around, and no one ever gets ahead.

She's been such a fool. For believing her mother. For believing anything at face value. Life *is* a carousel—just when you think you're up, you're down.

And what's the end goal? She never stopped to think about it. How many medals or good grades or honors or nominations are enough, the right amount so you can finally stop and take a look around?

She remembers what Rob said to her yesterday while they were getting stoned—it's the *having* of it, not the *meaning* of it. With a terrible thud of dread very deep in her stomach, Luce realizes that maybe everything in her life has been like that, has been more about the having than the meaning.

"Hey, you."

Luce sits upright. It's Andrew.

Even though her stomach is empty from the events of late last night—or early this morning?—she once again feels a swell of nausea, as though her body wants to purge *everything*. Why did she think going to Blake's party was a good idea? Luce should know better. But Luce, apparently, doesn't know better, doesn't know much at all. Luce barely even knows *Luce* anymore.

"Whoa. Where did you *go* last night? You look terrible," he states. When she simply stares at him miserably, he adds, "I mean, terrible for *you*, which is still awesome by most standards. Obviously. But . . . you do look like you've met a ghost."

"*Seen.*"

"What?"

"*Seen* a ghost, not met. Anyway I have, sort of," she says, wishing it were easier to explain. He cares about her, maybe more than anyone else. But is he merely a part of the carousel, too? Did they grow up together over the last two years, or has she simply gone round and round and round with him, pretending it's all leading somewhere? "Sorry, it's just that I've kind of found myself in the middle of a puzzle that I really can't solve. I need . . . I need to think." She rubs her eyes with her hands, wishing she could erase her whole face.

He takes her hands from her cheeks and holds them. "Are you still upset about getting in trouble the other night? Talk to me. Maybe I can help. I'm a really good problem solver, as you probably know. If only your mom had a badge for *that*, right?" He grins.

But the mention of her mom, and badges, is too much, and Luce feels her face crumple. She takes a deep, staggering breath. She needs to keep it together. Crying never gets a person anywhere. That's what her mother always used to tell her when she'd fall off her bike and skin her knee, or spill her juice at dinner, or get a B on a test, and tears would threaten to spill. It was like her mom was there in an instant, instructing her to hold it in, to get herself together and move on, to do better next time. Persevere.

Periphery, perpetuate, persevere. On the edge, cause to continue, persist in the face of difficulty.

"Luce," Andrew says, more gently. "Come on. Talk to me."

She shakes her head, but it all starts to tumble out of her anyway—everything she saw. Her mom. Mr. Wilkinson. The kiss.

Andrew squats beside her, listening, his eyebrows knitted in concern. She knows she's babbling, but she can't stop.

"I mean, it's disgusting," she adds. "I don't even know how to feel. I can't look her in the eye. How can I ever face her now? How am I supposed to fix this?"

Andrew tilts his head slightly, a funny look on his face. "It isn't your problem to fix, Luce."

She feels a surge of anger so strong, it's electric. "I knew you wouldn't get it," she says coldly. "Everything you *do* is perfect. It's always the same with you. But if I don't fix this, no one will. Our whole family will fall apart. Don't you see? I have to do *something.*"

Instead of offering a suggestion, Andrew stands up, looking

slightly hurt. "What does that mean—'it's always the same with you'?"

"That's not what I meant . . ."

"No really, I want to know what you were trying to say."

She stands up, feeling like her skin is stretched too tight across her body. Itchy. Stuck. "You're just—you don't change! You're always just . . . you."

"And that's a bad thing?" He scratches his head and she can see now that he's trying to contain his anger.

"This isn't *about* you anyway, it's about my mother," Luce says, feeling her cheeks flush with defiance.

"Well, it sounds a lot like you're taking it out on *me*. I'm just trying to help, Luce." He shakes his head and pushes on the door of the cabin.

Apparently it's unlocked because the door swings right open and he walks inside.

"Where are you going?" Luce calls after him, taking a second to wonder why he told her to meet him here in the first place. The haunted cabin. None of the older campers *really* thinks it's haunted, that's just how they refer to it, and ever since a plumbing issue two summers ago, it has gone unused, giving it an abandoned feeling.

"Forget it," he says, his voice muffled by the musty darkness of the cabin.

There's a moment of silence. It's as though he has disappeared into the cabin's depths.

"Andrew?"

He doesn't answer.

She goes in after him. It's muskier within, smelling of old cedar. As her eyes adjust, she sees a trapdoor near the back of the room, with a cord dangling from it, and a three-rung ladder unfolded from above. A chair has been placed underneath the ladder. She can hear rustling overhead, and steps onto the chair, then pulls herself onto the ladder.

"Andrew, what's going *on*?" she shouts, emerging onto the roof of the haunted cabin. The words die in her throat as she looks around. A picnic has already been laid out—a bottle of wine, scattered wildflowers, and a cooler.

Luce just stands there, gaping, as Andrew refolds a blanket he had laid out.

"Wait, stop," she says to him. "You set all this up?"

He turns to face her. "Yup."

"Why?"

"I thought it would be a nice surprise," he says, a note of remaining bitterness in his voice. "But I guess my timing was off."

"But how—how did you even get all this stuff?"

"My brother drove from Boston to drop it off," he says.

Beyond him, the lake can be seen, looking shiny and silver against the cloudy sky. Rain will probably come soon, but for now, the view from here looks misty, peaceful, beautiful.

"I just thought, I don't know, that I would try to cheer you up."

Luce shakes her head. With the gray light glowing behind

him, Andrew looks so young to her. He doesn't have the pathetic makings of upper lip and chin scruff she knows he'll have in the future—his face is smooth, sweet, open, innocent somehow.

"I'm sorry," Luce whispers. It's all she can think to say. And it's true—she's sorry for not appreciating him, for being so caught up in her own crap that she missed this side of Andrew. Is this a *new* side to him, or has he always had it in him to be spontaneous?

All this time, she assumed Andrew was the one who made things steady, reliable, and yes, sometimes overly predictable between them. But now she wonders if maybe it was *her* all along.

He shrugs, holding the blanket awkwardly. She can see he's mortified, and still a little upset. "Whatever. It's not a big deal."

She forces herself to smile, choking back her frustration and confusion about her mom. She walks over and takes the blanket from his arms, re-spreading it across the roof. "Come on. Let me see what you brought." She gestures to the cooler.

"I figured you might want this instead," he says, pouring some Gatorade into one of the wineglasses.

She sits down next to him on the roof as they unwrap the lunch he packed. She can't muster conversation—her confession about her mother has left her dry and empty—but at least she can take a few bites of a sandwich.

"So," he says after a couple of minutes of silence. "I just want you to know, that whatever you really saw last night, it's not, I mean, it doesn't . . . I don't want you to think all men suck. Because I really like you. I'm . . . falling for you. I know it's kinda soon to say that, but, yeah. I am."

"I like you a lot, too," she says, wanting to tell him she loves him, but that she's loved him for two whole years and is still falling more in love with him right now.

"Good. Because if we stay together, I promise I'll be really good to you. Like until you can't stand me anymore."

She smiles at him, but her chest hurts. She knows she's upset about her mom, that it has nothing to do with Andrew, and yet there's still a taste of sadness on her tongue.

"Do you believe me?" he asks.

Despite herself, she laughs, a small, awkward burst. "Yes. Yes, I definitely do."

"But you're still miserable."

"Well, Mr. Wilkinson has . . . *seduced* my mother, so I guess I'm a little distracted."

"Whoa, there. You don't really know what's going on between them. Maybe it wasn't what you thought. Or maybe it was only a one-time thing, a fluke."

"A *fluke?*" Luce practically spits out her Gatorade.

"I'm just saying you don't have proof that it's anything more."

"Fine, you're right. Then let's get some more proof," she says, standing up, a streak of her *own* spontaneity returning, like it did on their night of Strip Twenty Questions on the tennis courts. "Do you have paper?" she asks, pointing at his backpack.

Andrew retrieves a red spiral notebook. "Yeah, why?"

She takes it from him and rips out a page, then writes in block letters: MEET ME IN CABIN 43 AT 2:00. She signs the note with

Mr. Wilkinson's initials—T.W.

"Because I'm going to set a trap. It's my mother's chance to face him in private and tell him she's not interested, that she made a mistake last night, that she never meant for the kiss to happen. If she shows up and doesn't tell him to get lost, we know she wants him."

Luce takes a big gulp of Gatorade, looking up at the sky. The clouds are darkening. The rain will be coming soon, she can tell. And so will the truth.

19

All around Tali, kids are shouting to one another. Laughter fills the cafeteria. People race past her, through the giant dining hall doors, and out into the misty, muggy air. The great lawn's parched late-summer grass looks greener in the gray light of the coming storm, and Tali feels like she's at the center of an ever-moving kaleidoscope, beautiful but hectic, impossible to follow, impossible to find a pattern.

She can't keep reliving last night's fight over and over again. There's nothing to be done about it now. Her friends don't get her, and maybe she doesn't get them, either. She's scheduled for an afternoon session doing *something*—sailing, maybe?—but she can't think straight. Her head has been full of cotton all morning, and not just from last night's vodka shots.

All she wants to do is dive into the lake. She knows she's not allowed, but maybe a swim will wake her up, revive her, and she'll be able to come up with a new plan. There's more than one way to skin a cat, and there's got to be more than one way to de-pants a boy. Even a boy who botched her name and tried to bang her friend. *Ugh.* How could she have been so *wrong*? Sure, he apologized about the Tanya thing at the party—apparently that's his cousin's name. (Gross.) But then to turn around and immedi-ately go after Zoe? She can't believe she didn't see his true colors sooner. She must've been blinded by his smile.

No, she was blinded by the idea of winning. Of proving something.

All those summers of returning to Okahatchee over and over again, she never once felt such intense, irreparable *aloneness.* Some of the campers pushing past her and jostling one another in the field have been attending Camp OK for just as long as she has, and yet, aside from her tight circle of friends, she hasn't gotten to know them. Not really. She doesn't know what their favorite candy is, or their greatest fears, or what their parents do, or whether their parents are even around. If they come from good families, ones who care. If they're happy. They may as well be strangers.

Maybe you can never really know another person. First her father. And then her friends. All of the constants in her life, erased.

She turns around and pushes herself back out into the thick gray air. In a state of numbness she cuts across the damp grass toward her cabin. *Where is Joy?* Even though she doesn't want to speak to her friends, she can't help the thought. Joy is the only person she's ever known who could fix this feeling, who could make her centered again.

She just wants life to go back to normal. Back to the present. But even if she did make it back, what would she be coming back *to*? What she needs is a clean slate. Her dad may have lost his job, or worse—they may lose all of their money. But even if the present is going to be a horror show, at least it's a chance to start over. She's done it before—remade herself completely—and she can do it again.

Or can she?

Inside Bunk Blue Heron, it's sweltering and dim. She has the urge to call her mom, to warn her about what the future is going to bring for them. She fishes out her cell and the number for their hotel. But something stops her from dialing.

Instead, she peels out of her clothes in the quiet of the bunk and slips into a bathing suit. To avoid getting caught for swimming when she's on the forbidden list, Tali heads straight to the little spit of beach outside the prescribed swimming area, near the staff cabins, which look more like row houses. At this hour, the counselors should all be busy running afternoon activity sessions, and the lake should be empty. The idea of plunging in, eyes closed, letting the soft water wrap itself around her and drown out the rest of the world, propels her forward.

She steps out of her flip-flops when she gets to the sandy portion of beach around the side of the last row house cabin, cabin 43—the empty one—and approaches the lip of the water, wading in to her ankles.

And then someone surfaces from the lake in a loud whoosh, and she gasps.

Great. Not again.

Tow Boy.

She feels her whole body flush with embarrassment, and she freezes—but it's too late to turn around. He's already seen her.

Water drips from his broad shoulders as he stands to his full height. His chest glimmers with water droplets, like his body is made out of crystal. A slow grin spreads across his face.

"Looks like you walked straight into the hands of the enemy," he says, coming toward her.

She crosses her arms over her chest. "What are you talking about?"

"You aren't supposed to have lake privileges," he says matter-of-factly.

Tali's baffled. She wants to reprimand him, but she's so *tired* and she can feel the stockpile of tears just waiting to spill out at the slightest trigger. "Why?" she asks finally. "Why me?"

He shrugs his big, muscular shoulders. "As I recall, you were the one caught drinking on the cruise and fell overboard, so . . ."

"No, I mean why do you keep *picking* on me? I don't even *know* you," she says, her voice shakier than she expected, "and yet everywhere I go, there you are, scolding me, teasing me, laughing at me, giving me a hard time, treating me like I'm a child. I wish everyone would just leave me *alone* already." She swivels away from him and starts marching back across the sand, fast, feeling her face about to give, her voice about to crack. She's not about to have a breakdown in front of Mister Pick-up.

She's almost at the first row house when she hears splashing behind her and then the sound of breathing as Tow Boy catches up to her and grabs her arm.

She gasps and turns back around. "Let *go* of me!"

"Sorry, sorry," he says, dropping her arm. "I just . . . you're right. You don't know me. I'm Shane," he says. "And look, I'm sorry if I've given you a hard time. I don't think you're a child. At all. I just figure—you know." He shrugs, and to Tali's surprise, red begins to creep over his cheeks. "It's always better to keep girls like you at bay."

"Girls like me?" Tali raises an eyebrow. He better not be on the brink of launching into another tirade about how she's a spoiled brat. Not now. Not when her entire world is lying around her feet in shards.

"You know you're a complete red flag," he says, almost sheepish.

"A *red flag*?" Tali repeats, crossing her arms. Even when he's apologizing, he's a total dick.

"Oh, come on. Look at you," he says, gesturing helplessly. And as he does, something in her stomach somersaults. "You're gorgeous," he mutters. "Totally the kind of girl I could go crazy for. And I'm not about to lose my head. Or my job."

The last part of what he has said fades out, and all Tali hears, on repeat, is "the kind of girl I could go crazy for." *Go crazy for. Go crazy for. Go crazy for.*

Oh, holy *everything*. Tali feels like she's been socked in the gut. Completely winded. This tall, incredibly hot, chiseled, often maddening guy who listens to the Lost Tigers and notices when she's crying even when no one else notices, standing in front of her with his bare chest dripping with lake water, just told her she's gorgeous.

That he could go crazy over her.

Shane clears his throat. "However, now that you've made it clear you detest me, it should be *slightly* easier for me to keep my hands off you."

Tali's jaw flops open. "I . . . I . . . I don't detest you," she finally manages. Inside, her brain is screaming. *Does* she detest him? Of course not. *Of course* not. It's the opposite. She has been so determined to prove she can get with Blake, prove she can change the past, when *Shane* has been right in front of her, quite literally, all along.

"You don't?" He smiles, and it sends another wave of tingles down her chest and through her belly, making her knees wiggle imperceptibly.

"I don't detest you at all," she says. The words come out as barely a whisper.

She feels completely ridiculous. And stupid. And blind. Torn between laughing and crying.

He grabs her wrist again, but gently this time, pulling her closer to him.

"Good," he whispers. "Because I don't detest you at all either."

"Really?"

"Really."

She steps back just slightly. "But you should. You should hate me. I've been nothing but bitchy toward you. I was preoccupied, I was—"

"Lucky for you, I can take a lot of flack. I have four older sisters, so . . ." Shane shrugs, and suddenly he doesn't seem arrogant at all anymore. He seems . . . cute. Sweet. Maybe even a little innocent. "Besides . . . ," he adds, trailing off.

"What?" she asks, feeling like her voice has fallen down a well and she can barely pull out the word.

They lock eyes, and his are the exact shade of green the pines around the lake turn before a storm. "Nothing, it's just—I can tell you're more than some crazy bike-stealing nudist."

She can't help it. She bursts out laughing.

"Seriously. It takes a certain kind of confidence to start a revolution, and that's kind of what you did yesterday."

"Well, I'm glad you see me as more of a revolutionary than an escapee from the local asylum."

"How do you see *me*?" he asks, and the *way* he asks her sends tingles all across her skin.

"You're kind," she says, surprising herself. "Clever. Brave. Thoughtful. You have good taste in music. Good taste in girls, too." He smiles. "Also you're a tiny bit obnoxious." His eyebrows shoot up. "But only enough to match *me*," she adds with a grin.

He pulls her even closer and she lets herself fall into the magnetic energy between them, tilting her head up the tiniest bit without even realizing she's doing it. His lips touch hers, brushing softly against them like he's uncertain. She parts her lips slightly, and they begin kissing, slow and long, and he moans softly, pulling her tighter against him. She gives in helplessly, feeling waves of vertigo wash through her as he kisses her again, deeper this time.

When he moves back for a breath, she gasps.

"Hold on," he says, his jaw twitching slightly, his lips wet in the misty air. His chest is heaving, as though from effort. "We . . . I shouldn't. I really *could* get fired, Tali. I never meant for this to happen. We need to wait, we need to—"

"Shane," she says. "Just give it up, okay? I never meant for *any* of this to happen either, but guess what?"

"What?" he asks, his green eyes twinkling like splashed water as he looks into hers.

"It's happening," she says, no longer nervous or embarrassed. She just feels . . . relaxed. Comfortable. Right.

She takes his hand and leads him around the corner of Cabin 43, pushing open the front door. To her surprise, it gives easily, and then they're inside, falling onto the standard-issue, cot-sized bed, which doesn't even have sheets on it, but she doesn't care. He rolls onto his back, pulling her on top of him.

Out of nowhere, he laughs.

"What? What is it?" she asks, painfully self-conscious all over again now, basically straddling this boy she's fallen for so fast, wearing only her black bikini, her hair probably frizzing out like crazy from the humidity.

"It's just . . . I was thinking about how I saw you in that shed in your . . . *you* know."

Ah, yes. The bright green bra and thong. As if she could ever forget. She blushes, praying he doesn't demand to know what she was doing in there, dressed that way.

"I assumed that was about as lucky as I was going to get this summer."

She laughs but feels a flicker of concern. "So you're saying you think you're about to *get lucky* right now?"

His face gets serious as he reaches up to trace her jaw, then her shoulder and down her arm. "I'm saying I'm already lucky."

Relief floods through her. "Me, too," she says, kissing him again. "I didn't even know you *worked* here till a few days ago," she says, truly baffled. There's so much she's been blind to.

He flips her over gently, so she's on her back, and leans next to her, propped on one elbow. "Well, it's my first summer here. I'm saving up for school." In between kisses, he tells her about the community college where he finished his freshman year, and how he's hoping to transfer to a bigger university this January. He hadn't planned to come back, but now, he admits, he's fallen in love with Okahatchee. "It's beautiful here," he says.

He traces his hand along her stomach, and she's shivery all over again.

"There's a lot to love about this place," she responds, remembering that it's true—seeing Okahatchee from his eyes: The regal mountains surrounding the lake, whose surface is always changing depending on the weather. The lake that's always present even if you can't see it, its scent hovering in the air, its waves nodding like a deep pulse of nostalgia and memories and happiness. The people, too, coming together every summer and then pulling apart at the end, over and over and over again. She'd almost forgotten the magic of this place.

And strangely, even though she's lying right next to Shane, for a few minutes all she can think about are her friends: Joy, Luce, Zoe. How she should be with them right now. How she can't separate the idea of this place from their friendship. It's like the location and the emotion are locked together. She smiles to herself, already imagining the looks of surprise on their faces when she tells them about Shane. *If* she tells them. No, *when*. She knows, with certainty, that their fight isn't the end. They'll make up. The four of them will be together again, if Tali has anything to say about it.

Hours later, Tali feels drunk from kissing, and touching, and just being *happy*. In between all the making out, they've talked, and laughed, and recounted the horrible things they said to each other over the last few days. And even though her body is burning with the desire to go further, she's grateful that Shane hasn't tried. Not once has he made the move to shove her bikini straps aside or push things past PG-13, like Blake did immediately on the boat. She shudders, remembering that.

But Shane's patient—almost like he knows this won't be his last chance.

She hopes it won't be.

She cuddles into him now, pressing her whole body against his, her hand in his hair—something she's read about but never actually done before—and kisses him again, slowly and softly, lingering, breathing in his coconut-and-grass smell.

When she pulls back, a slight glimmer of nervousness returns. "Are you really . . . really so . . ."

"What?" he asks.

"You know, *good*."

He laughs. "Well, I don't know if I'm all *that* good."

But she doesn't laugh with him. The moment feels weighty suddenly, important. Crucial. "I just . . . ," she says, searching for the words. "I want to know if I can trust you."

Shane looks at her. "It's a funny thing, trust."

"Why?"

"You can't make it happen, you have to *let* it happen. Over time."

She feels slightly deflated. He's right, but it's not the answer she's looking for.

He sits up, slightly. "Listen, I—"

But she raises her hand to quiet him. "It's okay. It's just that I've been . . . disappointed. By a lot of people lately."

He touches her shoulder gently, like she's a rare feather and he doesn't want her to blow away. "Anyone in particular?"

She wants to tell him—about her dad. His lies. Even though she doesn't understand it all herself yet. But it's too soon. He's right—they don't know each other that well. It takes time. So instead, she simply sighs and nods. Tears gather at the back of her throat, threatening to come out again.

He lets his hand slowly coast down her arm, then tilts her chin so she's looking into his eyes. "Tali."

"Yeah?" Her voice sounds small.

"I won't hurt you," he whispers.

She looks into his eyes, and then they're kissing again, and the tears that almost overtook her seem to flood backward through her body, washing away her fears. She feels like he *is* saving her life, in a totally different way than when he rescued her in the lake. No—not saving her—giving her a reason to save herself.

She's so caught up in the moment, she barely notices the whoosh of air against her skin as the cabin's door is flung open.

"What the hell!" Tali bursts, pushing herself away from Shane hard, almost falling backward off the bed, as simultaneously Shane shouts, "Someone's *in* here!"

Tali gasps. It's Cruz—not in her camp uniform, for some reason, but it's undeniably her, looking like she just sucked a lemon wedge.

"What is this about?" The Cruz's face is mottled red. She looks *furious*. "Is this a joke to you, Miss Webber?"

Tali sees now that the camp director is clutching a crumpled note in her hand—almost as though someone *told* her to come find Tali and Shane here, which is impossible, since the cabin's been abandoned all summer, and Tali's fairly certain no one saw them kissing on the beach, either.

"It's my fault," Tali blurts out. "I mean, Shane told me this wasn't allowed, but I . . . I couldn't help myself. He wouldn't have gone along with it if I hadn't—"

"I'll have you know, young lady," the Cruz replies, waving the crumpled paper at her, "that this form of attention grabbing has just cost your friend his job, starting immediately. Your little prank may have succeeded in getting him fired"—at this, Shane's face blanches—"but *you're* not getting out of this unscathed. This stunt shows extremely poor character, and your parents will have to be notified."

"Prank?" Tali stutters. She has no idea what the Cruz is talking about.

The Cruz uncrumples the note in her hand and begins reading it aloud: "'Meet me in Cabin 43 at 2:00.—T.W.' So I suppose this is what you wanted, isn't it? A classic cry for help from a girl who has already done enough this summer to show she is not ready for the privileges that go along with independence."

All Tali can do is gape, confused.

Shane whips around to face her. "You set me *up*?" he rasps. Hurt and shock are written all over his face.

She shakes her head, unable to explain, unable to understand what's happening. "No," Tali gasps. "No, you don't understand."

"No, *you* don't understand," Shane says. Then, in a low voice: "You wanted me to leave you alone, huh?" He throws his head back, like he should have seen it, like he's been a fool. A fool to trust her. Because, like he said himself, they really *don't* know each other all that well. Not yet. "Well, congratulations," he says, practically spitting. "You just got your wish." He turns to the Cruz. "I'll have my bags packed by dinner," he says, his face cut from stone.

Without another look back at Tali, he's gone.

Tali's head spins and her chest feels like it's caught in a vise. She can't breathe. *Prank?* If anything, she's just been the butt of someone *else's* idea of a joke. How did this happen? And how could Shane believe she would do something so awful?

Exactly because this is what *everyone* assumes about her.

That she's spoiled. Shallow. Self-serving.

"I'll see you in my office once your family has been notified of the situation," the Cruz says coldly, evenly. Tali wraps her arms around her stomach, feeling like she might throw up. "They'll be the ones to decide whether you stay for the last day of camp or return home early." She turns to go.

"Wait!" Tali cries. "It's not what it looks like," she says frantically. "I swear. I didn't write that note. I have no idea who did. Please. Please don't fire Shane. He loves it here. He told me."

The Cruz turns to face her, arms crossed. "How I handle Shane is not any of your business, Tali." Her expression softens then. For a second, Tali can recognize Luce's features in her mother's face—the pretty, wide cheekbones, the delicate eyebrows—though of course Bernadette's face also bears the stamp of age. Fine wrinkles line her brow and form crinkles at the corners of her eyes, making her seem fiercer when she's angry, but kinder when she's disappointed, which is how she looks now. "The camp rule books are clear. I'm very sorry. My hands are tied."

The Cruz turns and stalks back to her office, and Tali melts into the ground outside the cabin; the damp grass and gravelly dirt tickle the backs of her bare thighs. She reaches up to her chest to touch the Taurus pendant that made her feel loved, made her sure she'd always come out on top of things. But the necklace must have fallen off—the pendant is gone. Just like all of her father's promises.

Just like Shane now, too.

Before she can fully take in what's just happened, she hears a rustling, and then Luce emerges from behind Cabin 43.

"Tali?"

"Luce?" Tali swipes at her face with an elbow, realizing only when she feels dampness that she's started to cry. "What are you doing here?"

Luce's tan face flushes. "I was, um . . ." She trails off, looking guilty.

Tali's heart nearly stops beating as realization settles into her brain. "Are you *spying* on me?" she demands. This is just the icing on the whole disgusting cake.

"What? No way!" Luce exclaims. "I was *waiting* for someone, actually. I had no idea *you* were going to show up and ruin everything."

"*Excuse* me?" Tali says, her voice bordering on a screech now. "*I* ruined everything?" Now her sadness and confusion is transforming into anger. Luce. Luce and her mom. It's their fault. All her earlier thoughts of reconciliation fly from her head. "What are you even *talking* about? Did you tattle on me or something? Run and tell your mommy I was being a bad girl? Is that your idea of a good time? Haven't you ever seen anyone screw up before? Oh wait, of course not—you're Little Miss Perfect."

Luce backs up like she's been slapped. "Maybe if you ever paid attention to anyone else," she says quietly, "you would see that you're actually not the only one with problems." Her voice wavers, and Tali realizes that Luce is on the verge of tears, too. "But I guess that's too much to ask," Luce finishes, practically spitting.

She turns and heads off into the woods, leaving Tali alone— with no friends, no boxers, and no way out.

20

There are things people don't tell you about having sex for the first time, about what it's *really* like. How, for an entire day, your inner thighs feel weird, but not like after rock climbing— a different kind of weird. How your entire body feels feverish, a little traumatized even. How there is a tiny bit of blood on your leg that you don't notice until later. And now that you've experienced *it*, it's almost like your body doesn't think any other activity is particularly interesting. All you can do is lie around, replaying the event in your head, reliving the touches, the kisses, all the awkward moments, all the breathtaking moments. *I had sex,* you keep thinking, like you just discovered the internet or that space is infinite yet contracting at the same time. . . .

Which is why Joy lies in her top-bunk bed, skipping every single one of her morning sessions.

Truthfully, it's not the only reason. There was also the punch she drank at Blake's party. And the dancing for hours.

And then there was the fight.

It turns out that Joy isn't the only one with secrets. Tali lied about her hookups with Blake. Some tiny part of Joy feels hurt and surprised that she didn't know. But what she still hasn't yet figured out is why *Zoe* went after Blake. Of all people, Joy knows Zoe is the least likely to pursue a guy who's already spoken for. When Joy and Zoe both had a crush on Michael Lawrence for two weeks the summer before sixth grade, Zoe graciously backed off so Joy could go with him on the midnight nature walk.

It doesn't make sense.

But then again, pretty much nothing that's happened in the last few days makes any sense at all.

And even below these other things—sex, a friendship splitting at the seams just when she thought they might have a chance of reconnecting, buried secrets coming to the surface—below all of that, is the final thing keeping Joy locked to her bunk bed, unable to move, unable to process, unable to figure out what's next:

Today is the last day.

Technically parents come to pick up campers tomorrow morning at 8 a.m. But today is the day of the carnival. Tonight is reunion night.

Tonight the photo booth will be back in place.

Tonight they're supposed to return to the future. *If* their plan even works.

And *that* thought is haunting Joy, raging through her veins, causing her to burn and toss in her sheets—because it's the very last thing she wants.

She's praying Zoe's whole idea is bonkers. She's praying that she still has those two years to relive. To do it all differently, better.

Sometime during lunch, Joy finally crawls out of bed and gets dressed. Life goes on, and you have to go on *with* it. And that means rolling out of your sweaty sheets, switching off your daydreams, stepping into your unwashed jeans—unshowered—grabbing your backpack, and facing the music.

She's terrified of seeing him again.

She *has* to see him again.

As Joy is approaching the dining hall, though, Zoe slams into her.

"Sorry, Joy, I'm just distracted," she babbles, shuffling her weight from side to side.

"Where are you off to?" Joy asks, overcome with an insatiable need for Zoe *not* to run off. "Have you eaten yet? Wanna go in and have lunch with me?" There's so much she wants to catch up about—what happened last night between her and Ryder . . . what may or may not have happened last night between Zoe and Blake . . . the fight with Tali. She just wants to sit with her friend and hash it all out like they would have done, once upon a time.

Zoe bites her lip. "I ate already. Hey . . . you wouldn't happen to know where Blake is, would you?" She pauses, and clearly reads the surprise in Joy's eyes. "I mean, it's . . . not what you think. He's perpetuating the rumor about us and I need to set him straight." Her face is deadly serious. "*Nothing* happened."

"I believe you," Joy says, realizing in that moment that she absolutely does. Whatever her reasons, Zoe isn't telling the whole truth. But she's telling the truth about Blake. And maybe it's best that Zoe handle the problem on her own, as much as Joy would like to help, would like to be let in on her secrets.

After all, Joy has secrets of her own—ones she doesn't ever plan to tell Zoe. Her whole body aches thinking about it.

"Have you tried the boys' bunks?" she offers. "I know he lives off campus, but I think Ryder mentioned that he sometimes hangs out there anyway."

Relief washes across Zoe's face. "Great idea. Thanks." She starts to leave but pauses, turns, and puts her hands on Joy's shoulders. Then she leans in and hugs her. "Thanks for believing me."

For one wild second, Joy thinks she's going to cry. Instead, she just lets her friend wrap her in her arms, breathing in her familiar smell of chamomile and sunscreen.

And then she lets her go.

Disoriented, Joy turns back toward the dining hall. She really should get a bite to eat. Now that she's up and out of her bunk, she feels faint.

But then Doug Ryder materializes before her, his hair like a lit flame in the gray air, his smile goofy and lopsided. Joy takes his hand and pulls him behind the dining hall, and they're kissing before she even realizes what's happening.

Taking a breath, she steps back. "Hey."

"Hey," he says, his face almost the color of his hair.

"So . . . ," she begins, at a loss for what you're supposed to say to the person you recently gave your virginity to.

Clearly he's on the same wordless page. "So," he concludes. He smiles again. "I've been looking for you. Do you want to help me with the scavenger hunt? I'm supposed to be in charge, but honestly I've been a little bit . . . preoccupied the last couple of days."

Joy swallows. "Are we supposed to, I don't know, talk about last night first or something?"

Immediately, Ryder's face gets serious, his freckles crunching together in the middle of his forehead like he's been delivered a pop quiz in math. "Oh, yeah, definitely. We can talk about it." His eyes dart across her face, probably looking for some sign that everything's okay between them. "So . . . what do you want to say?"

Joy can feel the blush spreading from her toes to her cheeks, warming her from the inside, even as a faint rain begins to fall. "I don't know. But . . . I'm happy. Are you?"

Ryder ducks so he can meet her eyes. "Are you kidding? Yes. I'm happy. I'm really happy. The stuff I said last night? I'm not sure anything made sense, but I meant it." He rakes his fingers through his hair. "I meant all of it. That is, if *you* wanted me to mean it. I mean, if you . . . I mean . . . I like you a lot."

Joy smiles. Maybe she's gotten used to the absurdity of everything that's happened in recent days, because she believes him. She really does. "I like you, too," she says, though she can barely pronounce the words through her grin.

They kiss some more in the lightly falling rain until Joy pulls away, a little breathless. Another thing they don't tell you about the first time you have sex? When you start kissing again, it's really, *really* hard not to just do the whole sex thing all over again, right then and there, regardless of the circumstances. Like, even if pre–fourth graders are walking past you in the distance, carrying vaguely offensive, brightly colored, handmade tomahawks, slightly wilted from the rainfall, on their way to Arts and Crafts.

"So, Big Dipper." She tugs on this T-shirt. "Tell me about this scavenger hunt." Life goes on, and so do ancient, notoriously forbidden (but secretly probably counselor-sanctioned) traditions such as the end-of-summer scavenger hunt.

Ryder starts laying out the details and making a list of what everyone will need to find and the elaborate puns and clues that the participants have to solve first in order to figure out what the objects even are. He instructs Joy on how to leave the clues scattered throughout the woods. They agree to split up so he can spread the word for everyone to meet at five o'clock by the flagpole.

After one more long, deliberate kiss, she clutches her list and marches off in the opposite direction.

Joy carries her objects into the woods—Coach Miller's baseball mitt ("the best catch at camp"), Farber's whistle ("the most evil foul-caller"), and the Cruz's clipboard ("the one thing Cruz can't live without"). Under the canopy of trees, the drizzle is loud against the leaves but doesn't reach her face. She feels protected and takes a deep breath, inhaling the familiar, piney musk of the woods. Maybe everything that's happened was meant to be.

Despite the rain, it's hot out. And that's not just her day-after-sex fever talking. It's *really* hot. Pre-storm muggy, the humidity causing her jeans and tank top to cling to her skin uncomfortably. She wishes she'd thought to bring a Gatorade. Or eat breakfast and lunch, for that matter.

The afternoon is pouring by her—already, it must be after three. She wishes she could stop time, freeze it in place. *It's a wonder we're not all dizzy from it,* she thinks, *riding on this planet that's tumbling rapidly through space in its slightly uneven orbit, on and on.*

She *does* feel a little dizzy, actually.

Maybe she should go back. A drink of water would be a good idea. Besides, the skies are probably about to open and drop a serious downpour on her. Even now, the low growl of thunder moves through the trees. Her stomach rumbles as if in response. She's running on empty. She got too carried away with Doug and didn't think about the fact that she'd skipped two meals, that she was feeling a bit weak and groggy, that she should probably rehydrate after last night's party.

She pushes through a clearing, into a new patch of trees. She's pretty sure the lake is to her left—she could swear she can hear it lapping quietly, reassuringly, a constant presence defining everything else around it. She decides to veer that way, so after she's done placing the final two clues she can cut straight up toward the dining hall.

Recognizing one of the many dirt paths that wind through the forest, rutted at the center where years and years of bicycle wheels have passed through, Joy makes her way onto it, following its gradual curve to the left. It's not the path that leads up to Red Cliffs; it's another one. She's pretty sure it's the one that winds all the way back toward the volleyball area. She keeps following it, feeling dizzier as she goes. The air is thick, so thick it's not easy to suck it into her lungs. The secret that has been lurking inside her chest starts to weigh on her, making her breathing labored.

The old Joy's small, pathetic voice comes back to her now, sounding scared. Scared of *everything*. Always worried. But this is *new* Joy, and she refuses to be paranoid or insecure or anything that's going to hold her back. Here she is at the heart of Camp Okahatchee's best tradition, at the heart of the summer and everything she loves.

She stops walking to hide a baseball mitt in a pile of twigs, then looks up at the dark gray sky between the leaves and branches overhead. She can see the long shadow cast by the mountains in the distance. Only the shadows aren't where they usually fall. She can't tell if it's an illusion or if she's actually turned around, heading *farther* from the lake instead of closer to it.

She stops, listening. That gentle lapping sound . . . she can't hear it.

Okay, time to turn around. She must be going the wrong way. The best idea is to follow the path back the way she came. It must funnel out onto the campgrounds; they all do.

She still has to bury the clipboard and stow Farber's whistle somewhere, but her head feels hot and her ears are pounding. She *really* needs a damn Gatorade. She picks up her pace and starts to jog, tossing the whistle up into the branches of a nearby tree. Roots and leaves crunch beneath her sneakers as she traces her way back down the path, through the woods, feeling sweat prickle against her neck, but there's not enough wind to cool her down. She squints through the mist as she runs. This better be the right way.

The path seems never-ending, and she leaps over a pile of horse dung, realizing she had it all wrong. This is one of the paths used for the riding school two miles down the road. *Crap*. She *knew* she was lost.

There's nothing to do but head off-trail again, back through the bushes. Branches scrape at her arms. Her backpack bangs heavily against her back. One of its straps snags on a tree branch. She stops to disentangle it but is too annoyed. She lets it drop. There's nothing really important in there. She needs, more than anything, to get back to Ryder, back to her friends, back to the safety of the campgrounds.

She runs faster now, thrashing, feeling that old friend—panic—taking over. Her body's on empty. Empty. Empty. She slows down slightly and finally stops to lean against a tree, feeling the individual ridges of the bark against her hand like braille, telling an age-old story she doesn't know the ending of. She looks up. She's *not* going to pass out. Not here.

But the sky spins. Her head feels light, like a balloon. She blinks once. Twice. There are stars. Maybe one of the dippers, but distorted, floating across her vision. And then she's sliding, and falling, and sinking into the black.

21

The rain—just a spray of mist—leaves the taste of salt and aluminum on Luce's lips as she and Andrew trudge across the wet field and into the sodden sand. She marches with determination, Andrew following silently a few paces behind, to the far side of the lake, where the Okahatchee sailboats are docked at a wide, flat pier.

Since her attempt to test her mom failed—thanks to Tali—it's time to take matters into her own hands. She hopes the sky, now tinged a deep purple, isn't about to unleash its looming wrath.

Part of her thinks Andrew is right—she should just leave the whole thing alone. It's her mom's business. But it's too late. It's already in motion, and she can't unlearn what she knows. As much as she'd like to, she can't forget what she saw. She can't eradicate the truth.

Eradicate, erratic . . . shit. She can't remember the third word in the grouping. She shakes her head, trying to clear the fog within it, but still she feels numb and light.

It's quiet on this side of the lake, eerie. Most of the other campers are tucked away inside bunks, or the crafts shed, or the dining hall. A layer of mist sits on the water like a powder puff, and the tied-back sails poke through it at their slanted angles, bobbing slightly, sometimes disappearing altogether into the thick white.

Andrew squeezes Luce's shoulder while she's paused in front of the low wooden door. She takes a deep breath and pushes it open.

They find Thom Wilkinson bent over a desk in his office. Past him, there's a window facing the lake, the pre-storm fog so dense the view doesn't look real, resembling instead the Rothko of deep plum paint fading into ivory that Luce recently took off her wall to pack for Princeton.

He looks up, hearing the door creak as she enters the room. Andrew hangs back in the shadows of the doorway.

"Luciana," Mr. Wilkinson says, clearing his throat and sticking a pencil over his ear, tucked slightly under his wavy, some-salt-but-mostly-still-pepper hair. He *does* sort of look like George Clooney, like some of the girls always say, but squarer and squatter. His button-like nose seems too small for his face.

It strikes her that she must look dramatic, with her glossy black hair damp and clinging to her face, her gray J.Crew V-neck torn slightly, she realizes now, from her quick escape from the storage unit yesterday—after her shower this morning she'd been too tired to pick out anything new to wear.

Her body's buzzing, like the time she touched an electric fence at a horse farm when she was seven. "I know what you've been doing," she states, almost robotically. It's what she's rehearsed in her head the whole way over.

He cocks his head at her, like she's grown a second set of ears.

"And it needs to stop," she adds. "Leave my family alone."

All the color goes out of Thom's face. He puts one hand on the back of his chair to steady himself as he stands up. "Luciana—"

Luce hastily steps backward, away from him. "No. I don't want to hear it. I don't want to know anything. I just want it to be over. Whatever is going on between you and my mom. If you don't promise to stop, I'm going to tell, and you'll be forced to leave your job here." She's surprised how certain her voice sounds.

He gapes at her for a second, looking exactly like a caught trout.

Then he seems to gather his wits and his eyes become sharper, more focused. And she knows, in that moment, that everything she suspected is correct. He *did* have an affair with her mother. Is perhaps, in his mind, *still* having an affair with her. A rush of nerves and anger rise through her and she's certain she'll throw up.

"Listen, Luce," he says, with a nervous look at Andrew, then back at her. "You really don't have any idea what you're talking about. I would suggest you head back to your cabin and cool down before—"

"Before . . . before what?" she says, her voice coming out like a squeal. "Before you admit the truth?"

This seems to get under his skin. She's never seen Mr. W angry before. His cheeks flame. "I really don't have time for this nonsense. Were you the one who sent that note? I knew it wasn't— How did you even—"

"I *saw* you." Luce's voice freezes in the air between them, forming invisible icicles.

"Luciana, this is not . . ." He runs a hand through his hair, and then seems to soften, to give up a little, like a sail when there's just not enough wind to hold the course. "Listen, what happened . . . between . . . between your mom and me . . . it has *nothing* to do with you. It isn't your business at all."

"Not my business? It could destroy my entire family, but you think it's not my *business*?"

"Enough!" It's like the lid popping off a boiling pot. Mr. Wilkinson sweeps his hand across his desk, sending a bunch of papers and pens and a stapler tumbling onto the floor. "It was a fucking mistake!"

Luce flinches—she's never heard an authority figure curse like that. Somehow it shakes her deeply. "A *mistake*?" Her skin flashes hot as a burning sensation travels down her spine. "A mistake is a wrong answer on a test. Cheating with a married woman? With someone's *mom*? That's not a mistake; that's low; it's messed up; it's . . . it's disgusting." She swallows hard.

He shakes his head. "It wasn't planned, Luciana. You just . . ." He brushes his hand uncomfortably through his hair again, this time dislodging the pencil he clearly forgot was behind his ear.

It clatters to the floor, but he doesn't seem to care. He looks like he's wilting. "You simply can't plan for everything."

"So that's it? That's all you have to say?" Luce demands, trying to keep her voice steady.

He looks down. "I'm sorry you got caught up in this, Luciana. I truly am sorry." He shakes his head, looking at all the items that have scattered on his office floor. "About the whole thing."

Andrew clears his throat from behind her. "Luce," he says low, nearly a whisper. "We should just go. He apologized. It's over."

"It's *not* over, Andrew. Are you kidding me?" she asks, swiveling to look between both the man and the boy, overcome with the sense that they're conspiring against her, forming some sort of male pact of solidarity. "*Sorry* doesn't just make it go away," she informs them both. "I'm going to have to deal with this—my *family* is going to have to deal with this—for the rest of our lives."

Andrew squirms. "Eventually you'll have to let it go, Luce," he says softly. "It's like he said: You can't plan for everything."

She stares at him—at the face whose every contour she could draw from memory; that's how long they've known each other. This boy she has *loved* for so long. "So you're taking *his* side?" she says, her voice breaking. She doesn't even care if she seems hysterical—if the normally sane, über-organized, clean-cut Luce has become a raging, uncontrollable beast. Maybe it's about time people realize what it's like when Luce pulls anchor.

"It's not about sides, Luce. I'm just—"

"It *is* about sides." Her pulse is pounding in her ears. "It's about right and wrong. Don't you get it?" She doesn't even know who she's talking to anymore, Wilkinson or Andrew. "Without sides, without rules, the whole world falls apart. *Everything falls apart.*"

"Luce—" Andrew tries to reach for her, but she pushes past him, no longer able to breathe in the stifling office.

Andrew calls out to her, but she swivels around. "*Don't* follow me. I don't want to talk to you."

She marches away, sucking in a deep breath, trying not to cry. Her fingers tingle as though she's actually disappearing into the fog. It disguises the campus landmarks—tall firs loom all around her, shadow figures from a childhood dream.

The peeling red paint on the old wooden sidings of the cabins seems to flicker, like the whole world is a still-wet canvas. Reality is dissolving around her, and she's sure that if she reached out to touch anything—the damp, drooping volleyball nets or the striped bark of the skinny ash tree by the footbridge—her hand would float right through to the other side, or she'd find she had no hands, no body, no foothold. She'd find she was floating, like a ghost returning to a long-forgotten former life.

The world feels *too* silent, too eerie. Her pulse picks up, a panicky thrumming in her chest and wrists. Like she's entered into the middle of a ticking time bomb—how can she possibly disable it? She needs a pen and pad. She needs a list, *dammit*.

Infidelity, she thinks. Then, *Options:*
Confession → divorce
Denial → forced to pick sides or live a lie

She swallows hard, blinking rapidly. Her thoughts come at her in fragments, in action steps.

Affected parties: Me, Amelia, the twins, Dad, Mr. W, Mr. W's family (?)

Her breath comes short. *Think. Think!* Who else would be affected by her mother's transgression? Was it possible her mother would retire early or be forced to quit? *All of Camp Okahatchee,* she adds to the mental list.

Luce heads straight to her mother's office, pulled there by an invisible gravitational force. But her mother isn't there. It's possible she's already setting up for carnival night, coordinating the arrival of the rides and the food vendors and the old photo booth—confirming and then triple-checking the tent setup on the Great Lawn and micromanaging everything, even down to the placement of the garbage bins. Marching around with that clipboard and that illusion of order, of rightness.

How is Luce going to return to the present, now that she knows it was all a lie?

Luce slides the key from under the entryway mat where her mother leaves it in case of emergencies—Bernadette Cruz is prepared for anything. Like mother, like daughter . . .

The thought rises to her head, makes her feel hot and dizzy with anger. Wrong. Everything's wrong.

She pushes into the quiet office, her hands shaking as she floats through her mother's sacred place, its stillness a cruel joke. It's like her mother's gaze is everywhere, stern, telling her that crying is a sign of weakness. Why is it so quiet? Why is it so still?

Her body moves on its own, and she's standing in front of the bookcase, where a picture of her with her brothers, her sister, and both parents sits prominently displayed. It's in her hands. It's flying. It's shattering on the floor of the office.

Books follow it. A figurine. It makes a satisfying clunk on the wooden floor. More, she needs more. Nothing is right. It's all a lie. Everything. Every bit of it. The neat stack of papers on the desk. *Fuck* the papers. Fuck the glass jar of pens. That breaks on the way down, too. She's filled with heat, with purpose.

She grabs for the phone. "Call me sometime!" she screams irrationally, at no one, throwing the entire contraption at the wall, where it cracks the paint.

There are no tears. There's no pause. She's swiveling around, looking for her next victim. She's not a person anymore—she's not Luciana Cruz—she's the Terminator, or some character from one of Zoe's sci-fi novels, charging through the world, bent on inhuman destruction. She grabs the desk lamp, feels its weight in her hands as her arm muscles flex. This one will hurt.

In an instant, she launches it at the window.

"Whoa, whoa!" someone is shouting, grabbing her, but it's too late. The window shatters. Everything's broken. Everything's shattered. Nothing is perfect.

It's Tali, wrapping herself around Luce from behind.

"Stop it, Luce! What are you doing?" Tali demands.

"You don't understand!" Luce screams back, struggling. But Tali is strong. "Let go of me!" She can't be contained. She can't be stopped.

"Luce. Come on. It's okay," Tali chants. "It's okay, Lu. I promise. It's okay."

Her body is still vibrating, but suddenly she's crumpling into Tali's arms, and they're both on the floor. Tali leans against the desk, her arms still around Luce, who feels herself shaking violently. It won't stop. Luce still isn't facing her. She can't face her. Her breathing is ragged and harsh. She presses her cheek against the cool metal back of the desk, trying to take in air.

God. What has she done? Has she lost her mind?

Maybe.

It seems like an eternity passes.

Tali shifts. "I shouldn't have said you were spying on me," she says quietly.

Luce sighs, on the verge of laughing for some reason. She moves so both of their backs are against the desk, their knees folded up.

"It's fine," Luce says. "Really."

"What *were* you doing there?" Tali asks gently. Not *Why the hell were you just destroying your mother's office?* Or *Since when have you gone batshit crazy?*

Luce sighs again, finding her voice. "I was waiting . . . for my mom."

"Ah," Tali nods, even though she can't possibly get it. She looks around the room—the array of pens and paper and books. The picture frame with its crushed, mangled glass. "So I take it whatever happened, it's, um, still unresolved."

Now Luce *does* laugh. A shaky, deranged sound pouring out

258

of her. "You could say that," she says, wiping the corners of her eyes.

She turns to her old friend—her only anchor at the moment. If Tali hadn't shown up, who knows what would have happened, what Luce would have done next? "Why did you come here?" she asks.

Tali bites her lower lip. "I had to talk to your mom about what happened with Shane . . ." Her lip starts twitching then, like it did the night Luce walked in on her arguing with her own mother on her cell phone in her kitchen . . . the night of the camp reunion. Exactly two years into the future from today. She looks up, her eyes the exact color of maple syrup. "Someone set me up. Shitty prank. Probably Rebecca. I think she hates me." Then she adds, so quietly Luce almost doesn't hear her: "I think a lot of people hate me."

Luce sits bolt upright, filled with a new clarity. *This* is one problem she *can* fix, one mess she can clean up. "I wrote the note," she says. "*I'm* the reason my mom came to Cabin 43."

Shock and outrage flicker like lightning across Tali's face, but before she has a chance to respond, Luce goes on: "But I didn't *mean* for her to catch you. I had no idea you'd be there. How would I have known?"

Tali squints. "You signed the note with my initials."

"They're . . . someone else's initials . . . too," Luce admits. Her throat feels thick, and the words have a difficult time coming up and out.

"Whose?"

"Mr. Wilkinson's." Luce practically chokes on his name.

Tali's brow crinkles. "I don't get it."

"Believe me, I don't either," Luce says. A relieved breath ratchets through her chest and she knows: she's going to tell.

And then the story comes, all the gory details, even more than what she told Andrew. Not just the image of the kiss, seared into her brain, but also her fury and powerlessness, as though everywhere she turns there's another wall of fog, impenetrable, refusing to let her through, refusing to reveal an answer. She even explains how she planned to entrap her mom at Cabin 43 and confront her there.

Tali listens but doesn't react right away or immediately reach around to give Luce a hug, like Andrew did. Instead, her brows knit together and she nods slowly, taking it all in.

When Luce finishes talking, Tali simply leans back into her club chair. "I wish you'd talked to me, Lulu." Luce looks up quickly, startled by the old nickname. Tali goes on. "Look, parents are . . . they're unpredictable. It's a simple fact that they will disappoint you. It's like, their purpose in life."

Luce looks down, blinking quickly. Now that she's confessed everything, it's like the words have left a void inside of her. She feels deflated. "Tali," she starts.

"Yeah?"

"I overheard. Part of it, anyway. That call with your mom. What happened? I should have asked sooner, I just—"

Tali's body tightens next to hers, like she's bracing herself. "It's my dad."

Luce's heart is racing. Tali and her dad are *thick*. Her dad is her hero. She's his baby. He's been to every tumbling match. He's *there* for her, whenever he can be. Way more than Luce's parents are for her, even though they never travel far, while Tali's dad is always flying around the country and the globe.

Tali clears her throat. "He's been lying to our family my whole life. He's a fraud. His company is under investigation by the government. I don't even get what that *means*, but it's bad." Then after a pause, she adds, "I know it means he's not who I thought he was. And that he has, quite possibly, destroyed my life."

Now it's Luce's turn to wrap her arms around Tali's shoulders.

For a full minute or two, they're silent. Luce is filled with wave after wave of guilt. She overheard the phone conversation on reunion night. She knew Tali's family was in trouble this whole time, but she didn't say anything. She was too concerned with making it out of the past and back to the present. Back to *her* present.

Earlier, she accused Tali of being selfish. But maybe she's the one who's selfish.

Tali heaves a halting sigh. "The funny thing is," she says, "I'm not even certain I have any present worth returning to, ya know? But after everything that's happened in the last couple of days, I'm not sure I want to stick around here, either."

"I know exactly how you feel," Luce says, standing again. Then, after another pause, "So . . . the lifeguard. Do you actually . . . like him?"

Tali looks up, and to Luce's surprise, there's a small smile on her face. She nods. "That's the crazy thing. I do." But then the smile evaporates. "Unfortunately, he hates me now. I can't say I blame him. There's no way to fix it. Unless," she adds, "you've got another plan to travel back in time."

Luce snorts. "I couldn't even get the merit badge." She cracks a smile. "I did get Most Improved, though."

Tali raises an eyebrow.

"Don't even get me started," Luce says. "I actually kind of *stole* it, but I stole the wrong one."

Now it's Tali's turn to snort. Then she drops her head in her hands and starts to laugh, which makes Luce laugh—at the hopelessness of it, the absurdity. Soon, they're both hysterical, cackling in the middle of her mother's office.

"Ohhhhhh, man," Luce finally says, when she can draw a breath. "What are we going to do now?"

Tali stands up, wiping tears from her eyes with a thumb. "We're going on a scavenger hunt," she says. "It's our last night at camp, and no matter what happens, we're doing this thing together."

For once, Luce is relieved to have someone else take over and lead the way. She looks around her mother's office, briefly wondering if she should clean up, if there's some way to undo all of this, but Tali's pulling her hand now.

They slam the office door behind them, and Luce turns to Tali. "Let's do this," she says.

22

Even with the rain now falling heavily down on them, there's an impressive showing at the flagpole—the designated meeting spot for the scavenger hunt—when Tali arrives, her arm linked in Luce's, both of them sharing a sweatshirt as feeble covering. She feels lighter somehow, despite the rain—and despite the thoughts of Shane that keep cycling through her mind: the disappointed look in his eyes, thinking she betrayed him. It's got to be the fact that finally, after all this time, she is linked to Luce again—not just physically but in some other, more profound way. It's not just that they bonded over their parents sucking so bad either—though they did—it's something else. It's like Tali has rediscovered Luce *now*. Whichever version of her this is. A girl who needs Tali, and cares about her, and sees her for who she really is. And so her heart feels a tiny bit less heavy. Because despite everything, there's this: *hope.*

A second chance.

People are crowded around, sharing umbrellas and tarps, some simply letting the rain soak their clothes.

The staff carries on with preparations for Carnival Night, trying to erect a giant tent despite the weather. Which means no one has attempted to disband the scavenger hunt.

Tali's fingers flutter across her exposed collarbone for the Taurus pendant, then she remembers she lost it. She can't see Joy or Zoe in the crowd.

She's desperate to apologize to Zoe. She shouldn't have freaked about the fact that Zoe hooked up with Blake. She owes her an apology. It's the least she can do. More than that, she wants to *understand*. Especially since she found out what a gross player he really is. She needs to hear Zoe's side of the story. It hits her that she hasn't thought enough about what really is going on with Zoe, and now more than anything she feels like that's a loss. She wants in again—back into the friendship they used to have. Zoe and Luce were right—she *has* been selfish.

Joy was right, too. She needs to tell her so.

For the first time since all of this began, it hits Tali how much she took Joy for granted. And when Joy disappeared from their lives, Tali pushed the hurt away, refusing to feel ditched, instead just chalking it up to everyone growing up and growing apart. She didn't spend too much time thinking about it—hadn't wanted to.

But now she does. She wants to do it all differently.

She wants to know what happened to make their friendship unglue.

More than anything, she wants to know why Joy left.

"All right," Doug Ryder barks out, trying to get everyone's attention.

He hands out copies of the list of twenty-five clues: the best catch at camp, the most evil foul-caller, the one thing the Cruz can't live without, the horniest noisemaker, Indigo's hole, Simon Says, Foot-Spunk, White Flag of Surrender . . . and the list goes on. They have to split into five teams of five, and then figure out what the clues mean. Whichever team gathers the most items on the list wins.

Tali and Luce end up on a team with Hadley, Uma, and Sam Puliver.

"I know one of these," Hadley says, her face fuming. "Horni-est noisemaker."

Uma gasps. "Your horn?"

Hadley nods. "It's been missing from my bunk since after-noon session. We need to find that *first*."

"Okay, but we still need to go for quantity," Sam points out, then shuts up under Hadley's stern glare.

Before Tali and Luce make it into the trees with the other girls, Ryder calls out to them. They stop and turn, and he jogs over, handing them a spare umbrella.

"Here, use this."

"Thanks," Luce says.

Tali assumes he'll turn away again, but he lingers for a second, his face flushed.

"Also . . . I was wondering. Have you guys seen Joy?" he

asks. "She was helping me set up earlier, but then we split up, and now I'm not sure where she went," he says, scuffing the toe of his sneakers in the damp ground. "I'm kind of starting to get worried."

Tali raises an eyebrow and looks at Luce. She knows they're both thinking the same thing: *Does he like Joy? Does Joy like him?* She smiles. "I'm sure she's fine," she reassures him. "She's probably just planning some extra surprise." As they walk off, she adds with a mutter, "Boys are such puppies."

Luce giggles, and for another fleeting moment, Tali feels just as close to her as she once did. Like together they can conquer anything.

More than an hour later, Tali's team has procured four items: Hadley's horn (they found it in the old birdbath behind the rec hall), Indigo's Hula-Hoop (this was "Indigo's hole"), as well as a guitar pick ("Something Ryder has fingered a lot"), and the official camp rule book ("Simon Says"). It's a good start but not nearly enough to win. They ran into a team of boys who had a cafeteria tray, a big foam pool noodle, Farber's whistle, Brianna's favorite zebra-striped push-up bra, *and* the water ski that Dave Krauss infamously broke when he ran into the pier.

After a brief huddle, they decide it will be faster if they all split up. Hadley pairs off with Uma, planning to return her horn safely to their cabin first. Sam Puliver goes off on her own.

"Let's separate and look for these three," Luce says, pointing out the final items on the list.

"Aye, aye, captain," Tali says, marching in the direction she *thinks* is south, toward the stables.

Not long after, she hears giggling and ducks behind a tree. As she peers around the rough bark, she catches a glimpse of something ivory: it's a piece of cottony fabric, stuck to a baseball bat, looking not at all unlike a *white flag of surrender*. It's hidden somewhat beneath a pile of twigs, but that has to be it.

The flag and accompanying pile of twigs are propped against a rock down a short slope from where she's standing. Tali sprints for it, slipping and sliding a bit in the mud, the rain making it hard to see.

Just as she's closing in on the flag, however, another figure darts out of the woods—a figure with cropped, bleached-blond hair. *Rebecca*: the girl who was acting like Blake was her personal possession during the bonfire on Tali's first night back in the past.

Rebecca reaches the flag at the same time Tali does, and they both grab for it.

Oh. Hell. No. Rebecca may be sly, but Tali is determined. She yanks at the fabric, which, she now realizes, is a pair of boxers. And then she gasps. The boxers aren't just plain white—they're white with Batman symbols on them.

She recognizes these boxers.

"What the fuck?" she blurts out. "These are Blake's."

Rebecca takes advantage of Tali's momentary shock and grabs them from her. "You didn't hear?"

Tali leaps forward to wrestle the boxers out of Rebecca's

hands. The baseball bat is still attached to one end and it drags through the mud, tripping Tali. Both girls fall onto the ground. "Hear *what*?" Tali says, gritting her teeth as she tugs on the boxers.

Rebecca huffs, struggling. "He hooked up with Hadley at his party. She stole them."

"Wait, *Hadley*? Hadley Gross?" Tali lets go for a second and props herself up. "I thought he hooked up with Zoe."

Rebecca sits up. There are brown leaf crumbs in her hair. "Ya know what? Take them. They're probably crawling with herpes anyway."

Tali scrunches her brow and stares at Rebecca for a second. "Here," she says, getting an idea. She grabs the boxers at the seams and begins tearing them in half. Then she hands the half still tied to the baseball bat to Rebecca. She doesn't really need the flag. Winning the scavenger hunt isn't the important thing.

Winning *Blake* was never the important thing either, she realizes.

It's time to focus on getting back to the present.

Rebecca looks into Tali's eyes. Rain falls between and around them, tapping the leaves on the trees and on the ground. She sighs. "Thanks."

And then Tali is off and running to find Luce, the boxers in hand.

When she finds Luce, her friend is bent over something on the ground in a small clearing. "What is it?" she asks, approaching.

Luce looks up at her, holding a clipboard. "The one thing the

Cruz can't live without. This makes six."

"That's great!" Tali comes over to pull her to her feet, but Luce stops her.

"Yeah, but . . . look." She gestures toward a drenched backpack at her feet.

Tali squats down next to her, turning it over in her hands. "Is it a clue, do you think?" Tali asks.

Luce shrugs. "I don't know." She unzips it and takes out Joy's sweatshirt, an empty Nalgene, a flashlight, a bottle of pills, a notebook, and a dead cell phone.

"What are those pills for?" Tali asks.

Luce holds up the bottle and shakes it. "Not sure. The label is faded. Long, doctory words. Trust me, if I don't know what they mean, no one does."

Tali's own puzzlement grows deeper, driving lines of concentration into her forehead. They can hear shouting through the woods, and the echo of distant laughter. Other teams.

"I don't get it. Maybe she just lost her bag? But that seems weird."

"It doesn't fit any of the clues on the list, though," Tali says, trying to ignore the eerie sensation worming its way through her gut, the certainty that something isn't right.

Fear flashes across Luce's face. "What if something bad happened?"

"Like what?" Tali tries to act like she wasn't thinking the same thing. "We're, like, a quarter mile from camp. We'd know if she'd gotten hurt."

"Why don't we bring it with us, just in case," Luce suggests. "Besides, we can use the flashlight."

Tali reaches out and grabs it. She flicks it on and they begin making their way back toward the flagpole to meet their team. For a while, the only sound is the rain pattering against the leaves of the trees overhead. Nothing, Tali realizes, is as it seems. All this time she thought Rebecca was her competition, when maybe she could have been an ally. All this time she thought Blake was the ultimate guy, the ultimate win. Instead, she can see so clearly now that he's a loser.

What else has she gotten completely backward? For a moment, she feels breathless, like her own personality has been flipped inside out. She feels exposed, and wrong. So wrong. About all of it. This summer. Her life as she knew it. Her friends. Even Joy.

In the flashlight's beam everything flickers silvery as it bobs and weaves through the rain, tickling something deep in the back of Tali's mind, some mystery she can't quite articulate. She thinks of Joy's urgency when she called them all together for the reunion five days ago—or two years from now. She thinks of Joy's face as she hung up the phone outside their bunk on the first night. She recalls how Joy ran off with the Miss Okahatchee tiara right after winning it. She pictures Joy dancing with abandon at Blake's party, right in the center of the outdoor dance floor, her arms in the air, her face ecstatic and Zen and pretty in the strobe lights . . . and something else, too. There was something in her eyes last night, wasn't there? Or a feeling, maybe that's all it was, just a feeling that passed between Joy and Tali, but Tali had been too distracted by her attempts to corner Blake to really think about it until now.

Tali stops in her tracks. "Luce," she says.

Luce turns, rain falling on her face, soaking her clothes. "Yeah?"

"What's Joy hiding?" she says, surprised by her own words.

Luce shakes her head. Her normally golden-tan skin, courtesy of her father's Filipino heritage, looks wan in the gray light of the storm. "I have no idea," she says.

But the scared look in her dark eyes tells Tali she's right—Joy *has* been keeping a secret from them, and Luce has sensed it, too. The woods have become dark and gaping around them, and the voices of the other teams farther away.

"Come on," she says, grabbing Luce's hand, rain slicking across her skin, giving her the chills. "Let's get out of here."

23

Fencing tournaments are not that long but Zoe already feels exhausted by the time the moderator calls "Fifteen–twelve!" on her third bout.

Well, *shit*. Zoe got lucky on her first two bouts. They'd been easy. The first was against Indigo Perez, and Zoe reached fifteen touches before the three minutes were even up, basically slaying Indigo. No surprise there. In the second, neither of them got to fifteen—the opponent, this one from Meadowlark, was terrific at deflection—but Zoe still stayed several touches ahead the whole time, confident in her win.

But she just finished her third bout out of five—another Meadowlark stranger—in the best-of-five tournament, and it was a whopping fail. She knows why: The party. The kiss. The argument. The lie.

Ellis.

Patelski has Zoe and Ellis in two different brackets, since

they're two of his top performers. This means she knows she'll be competing against Ellis in round five.

Zoe's one-minute rest period comes to an end and it's time to begin bout four, with another person from Meadowlark. The Meadowlark girls are all prissy fighters—technically proficient, but they don't play to win. Their fencing style is more like performance art: perfect posture, graceful movement, beautiful arcs, and clean lines . . . but no drive. No imagination.

She moves through the fourth bout cautious and steady, like she's parting water. The rest of the gym fades away—the glare of the bright lights against the sterile white walls, the squeak of sneakers over the polished pine flooring, the clang of épées. She channels the power of the brewing storm outside, creating an imaginary web around the Meadowlark girl, ensnaring her in her own defense. She wins. Whether to applause or actual thunder beyond the high windows, or both, she can't tell. Blood thrums in her ears.

The final rest period slips by in a breath, and before she knows it, she's face-to-face with Ellis. Through the mesh mask, she could swear she sees Ellis wink. Zoe feels a familiar surge of twin emotions—determination and defiance. Like that time there was way too long a line at a Robyn concert, so she and Cal found discarded bracelets in the Dumpster nearby and snuck in through a back door, dodging two bouncers and snickering in the darkness. Or the time Joey Reynolds called her a dyke on the steps of the high school freshman year, and she told him to fuck off, shoving him against the main door, in front of a teacher and everything.

Or the time her mom left for three days—just drove away with no explanation and no word about whether she'd come back—and Zoe didn't cry, she didn't panic, she simply got on her bike and rode to the grocery store to stock up on macaroni and other food she knew how to cook herself.

When it *really* matters, Zoe doesn't cave.

And so, she leans in now.

The timer sounds and their bout begins. Immediately, Zoe gets three touches, almost back to back. To her surprise, *Ellis* is the one who seems distracted.

At least at first. But she seems to snap out of it, and returns with renewed force. Zoe stops trying to think, lets her body just move. She and Ellis have practiced together enough that she can *feel* what's happening between them, the call and response.

Back and forth they go, touch after touch. Zoe's in a daze when the timer sounds again, impossibly soon.

"Fifteen–fifteen," the moderator announces. "Priority toss."

The timer is stopped, and they break with twenty-five seconds left to the bout. Zoe shifts her mask, trying to get in a deep breath. She hadn't realized she was sweating, but her skin is on fire now, and her muscles throb, full of power. Priority means tiebreaker. The moderator comes over and tosses the coin. It lands in Ellis's favor. She has priority. That means the timer's reset and it's Ellis's win, unless Zoe can score one last hit in the next minute.

They get into stance. The timer sounds again. For a full five seconds, neither of them moves, and something deep in Zoe's heart freezes.

Then she lunges.

Ellis dodges and comes back at her, but Zoe deflects and leaps back.

Forty-seven seconds left on the new time.

They circle, each taking an empty thrust.

Thirty-eight seconds.

Thirty-seven.

Thirty-six.

Zoe breathes deep and a hunger swells up inside her, insatiable. She steps, spins, and lands a touch—harder than she intended. Ellis stumbles. The timer dings.

The touch was legit. Which means the bout's over.

A rush of electricity zings down Zoe's spine. She has won.

The medal ceremony is short and sweet. Everyone's sweaty and wants to change. Ellis gets silver. Two Meadowlarkers share the bronze. Patelski seems satisfied. Zoe feels numb and grim. She was so focused on victory, she didn't think about what would come after.

They line up to shake hands with the Meadowlarkers. She shivers. Now that she's got the medal, she's going to find out once and for all whether they can get back to the present—tonight.

And before *that* she's got to confront Ellis. It may be her last chance.

She's not sure what she's more nervous about—talking to Ellis, the thought of possibly not making it back to the present if the photo doesn't work the way she insisted it will, or the thought of having to leave if it *does* work.

Standing in line, she takes off her mask and, one by one, shakes the hands of the Meadowlark team. One of the girls Zoe beat nods at her again and congratulates her. Zoe nods back, as the adrenaline of the day races out of her. They get to the end of the line and head to the locker rooms.

Ellis leans in toward Zoe, so close her lips actually brush Zoe's ear. "I see you took my advice," she says.

Her words tickle against Zoe's neck, and Zoe steps away, sucking in a breath. "Can we talk after this?" she blurts.

Ellis raises an eyebrow. "Sure. Want a ride back to camp?" she offers.

Zoe nods. "That'd be great."

She changes in a hurry, then ends up waiting fifteen minutes for Ellis to finish getting ready. She lets Coach Patelski know she'll be getting a ride back and doesn't need the bus. He obviously figures gold and silver are off to celebrate, and he simply claps her on the back. "Nice job, Albright" is all he says.

A hint of expensive perfume trails Ellis when she finally emerges from the steamy locker room, her hair damp from a shower. It's the first time Zoe has seen her with her hair down. She has the strange urge to touch it.

Ellis looks even prettier than usual, in a crisp pair of shorts with gold nautical buttons at the front and a sheer tank tucked into them, showing off the outline of a lacy white bra underneath. "Come on," she says.

Outside, the sky is thick and heavy, and a gentle rain is falling.

The parking lot pavement shines silvery gray. They duck toward the convertible—its roof is on. Inside the car, Ellis's floral scent is even stronger, covering everything. Zoe's sure her own skin will soon smell like Ellis's. The rain patters lightly against the windshield.

"Nice win," Ellis tosses over her right shoulder as she starts the engine and pulls out of the parking spot. "I told ya you had it in you."

"I already knew I had it in me," Zoe says defensively, picking invisible lint off the knee of her leggings. The words come out automatically—she's not trying to be a brat, but it's true. After all, she *already* won it once, two years ago. But of course, Ellis doesn't know that, doesn't know that she's the primary reason for Zoe's doubts over the last few days.

"So what'd you want to talk about?" Ellis asks with a side grin. She leans across Zoe's lap, and Zoe startles, letting go of her knees.

But Ellis simply pops open the glove compartment and grabs a tube of lip gloss. She sits upright again, applying the gloss carefully as she drives.

"Well," Zoe starts, clearing her throat. This is much harder, *much* more awkward than she expected it to be. "I actually wanted to talk about, um, last night. What happened at the party."

Ellis says nothing, so Zoe pushes on. "What happened upstairs. Between us."

Ellis turns toward her, a goofy smile on her face. Then she looks back at the road. "I believe the technical term is we made out."

Once again Zoe feels thrown off, unnerved. She will *not* be the butt of this girl's jokes. "I know we made out," she says, trying to sound cool and casual instead of exasperated. "I just meant . . . like, why me?"

Ellis shrugs. "You didn't want to?"

"That's not what I'm saying. Was there, like, something about me?"

Ellis sighs, putting on her right blinker. "Zoe. Zoe, Zoe, Zoe. You think too much. Like I told you, it was just for fun. No one has to know. No one *should* know. It's not their business," she says, pulling over onto a dirt road.

"What are we doing? Where are we?" Zoe asks, realizing they've taken a detour.

"I want to show you something," Ellis says.

They get out and begin running through the light rain down the dirt road. Zoe can make out a giant house at the end. "Is this a driveway?"

"Maybe!" Ellis calls, running ahead. Before she gets to the house, she veers to the left and disappears around a fence.

Zoe runs after her, and finds Ellis standing in a gazebo on the far end of a gorgeous piece of property, facing Lake Tabaldak. She catches her breath, approaching Ellis to see what she's looking at.

Ellis points. "See that? Just past that bend in the big lake? That's Okahatchee. I like coming here. The owners are never home. And everything looks so small from here. Doesn't it?"

Zoe stares through the rain for a second in silence. Camp *does* look small, just a tiny cluster of brown and red peaked rooftops amid the trees, even though it's only a little ways downhill from here. You can't even see the actual lake, which is minuscule compared to Lake Tabaldak.

But what comes out of her mouth is, "I think there's been a, um, misunderstanding between us. I . . . I have a boyfriend." It might be a small lie, but it's in service of a greater truth.

Ellis smiles. "Me, too."

"You . . . *what*?"

"John. We've been together for a year and a half."

"And you . . . I mean obviously you like *him*," Zoe clarifies. She doesn't add, *and not me.*

Ellis sits down on the bench that lines the inside of the gazebo. "I think I do. He's great. But let's not talk about John. He's in Spain. And he's okay with whatever I want to do. He likes how free-spirited I am." She says the last bit with air quotes.

Zoe is dizzy with all this new information. She doesn't know what to make of it, so she simply sits down next to Ellis, feeling like a spun top. For some reason, a paper she wrote on *Macbeth* for senior English pops into her head. She'd gone on for five whole pages about the lines: "Stars, hide your fires./Let not light see my black and deep desires." She'd written paragraph after paragraph about how Shakespeare was trying to show Macbeth's moral conscience with those lines, how people could do bad things *knowing* they were wrong but wanting them too badly to stop themselves. How the whole theme of the play is desire and shame. It's weird, though—Ellis seems, well . . . shameless.

She listens to the rain beat against the wooden columns and roof. "So what *can* we talk about?"

Ellis leans back, her golden tanned legs stretching out toward the center. She turns to face Zoe. "Do we have to talk at all?" she says quietly. "There are much more fun things we could be doing."

Zoe doesn't respond, but her nerves instantly ignite. What is the right response? What does she actually *want*?

Ellis sits up again, looking around. "No one can see us in here."

She reaches up and touches Zoe's cheek, turning her so that they're facing each other. She trails her hand down to Zoe's neck and leaves it there, resting it lightly at the base of her head, underneath her hairline, as she leans in and kisses her, softly, on the lips.

It's happening . . . *again.* Zoe can't quite believe it. Her whole intention had been to get some clarity from Ellis—who knows, maybe even an apology.

Instead, they're kissing.

Still, Zoe feels the knot in her stomach untying itself, tight and tangled at first, but gradually looser, making it easier to breathe, easier to not freak out. *She's so good at this.* That's all Zoe can think as she melts forward, not flinching as Ellis's hand finds its way down to her waist. She kisses Ellis back, starting to explore more—pulling away enough to make Ellis lean in for it; then Ellis does the same and Zoe leans in. She's once again reminded of their fencing bout.

But this is less precise. It's different. The rules change as they go.

Zoe tries to swivel to get a better angle—just one more, and then they'll stop, then she'll figure this out, explain that it's wrong.

She bangs her right elbow against the column. Ellis snickers, leaning into her and grabbing both of Zoe's knees; her laughter brushes across Zoe's cheek.

"This bench is too small," Zoe says in a laugh-whisper.

As if in unison, they both sink to the floor of the gazebo, easily sliding off the edge of the bench and onto their knees, then lying on the floor. The rain beats down harder now on the roof. They kiss more, touching each other's faces. Ellis puts her hand on Zoe's waist again, her fingers finding their way underneath Zoe's loose T-shirt. Electricity flies up Zoe's body and she arches slightly, wishing she knew what to do with her own hands. But it's as though they know more than she does. Her right hand guides itself into Ellis's flowing, soft hair, still damp from her shower and from running through the rain. It's like her hand wants—no, *needs*—to get tangled in there.

Ellis responds by rolling on top of her, writhing against her. Zoe can't believe how mad she was at Ellis only moments before, and now she wants this to keep happening, on and on. It's like she has found her perfect match.

A blaze of lightning flashes in the not-so-far distance, putting Zoe on alert, as though they've just been caught on camera. It's enough for Ellis to pull herself off Zoe, rolling next to her again.

She laughs, and Zoe suddenly feels left out of the joke.

"What's so funny?" she asks, still catching her breath.

"Nothing," Ellis says, her voice high and soft. "You're just kind of a natural at this."

Instantly, the knot re-forms in Zoe's gut. The wild truth of the situation occurs to her now, as swift and bright as a lightning bolt: This isn't Ellis's first time. With a girl. Like this.

Far from it. She knows exactly what she's doing.

And what she's doing is using Zoe. Because it must be obvious Zoe doesn't want this.

It *is* obvious.

Isn't it?

For some reason, Tali's words during their fight float back to Zoe. *Content to stay stuck.* Something is illuminated, deep inside Zoe's chest now—harsh and sudden as the lightning—something she's been tamping down for a long time, plugging up like a persistent leak. A secret knowledge writhing within her that has wanted to breathe, to break the surface, for so long.

Ellis is talking, saying something else she apparently finds funny, but now all Zoe hears is Joy's voice. Joy from when they were both thirteen, just graduating middle school. At a sleepover party at Joy's house. Everyone had gone around saying the name of the boy they had a crush on. And Zoe insisted she didn't have one. But she *did* spend a lot of time staring at Joy's family's foreign exchange student, a tall, pretty blond girl named Katie, from Switzerland or Norway or somewhere. She was older, and effortlessly beautiful. Confident, too, even though she barely knew the other girls. Katie had an avid crush on a boy named Orlando at the high school; he liked to wear floppy hats and his brother was a big-time jazz musician or something. Katie played their newest album on repeat. And when Katie went into the room she was sharing with Joy to change into her pajamas, she left the door open, like they all always did—no one made a big deal about it. They were always getting dressed around one another. But for some reason, for Zoe, this was different. Katie was like an exotic animal, something fascinating and transfixing in the way she moved and dressed and spoke. Zoe watched Katie take off her clothes, swallowing repeatedly, her throat inexplicably dry. Later that night, Joy and Zoe were alone. The other girls had gone outside to tell ghost stories, and Joy and Zoe were looking for extra flashlights in Joy's kitchen. Joy turned to her then, when no one was around. "If there's anything you want to tell me, Zoe, you can, ya know," she said. "I promise I won't judge you or anything."

Her words were innocent and kind—typical Joy—but to Zoe they felt like the time Luce's little brothers attacked her with punches. But worse, she also felt exposed, endangered, like she was standing naked in the middle of a highway.

"I don't know what you're talking about, Joy," she said then. And whatever small flower of truth had been blooming inside her withered.

Over the last few years, Zoe has added more and more dirt to the pile, burying the voice of truth inside her.

And now, here it is.

"What's the matter?" Ellis is saying.

Everything, Zoe thinks. *You. This. The kiss.*

But she knows. She knows it isn't just this. It isn't just the kiss. It isn't just Ellis.

She pushes herself up off the floor of the gazebo and begins to run.

"Zoe!" Ellis shouts, but the rain drowns her out.

Zoe heads for the sloped part of the woods that leads downhill toward camp. She runs hard, her muscles still alive and vibrating from the tournament. The gold medal bounces against her chest bone like an angry metronome, counting her steps as she runs farther and farther away from that gazebo, away from herself.

I do not want to like her, she insists in her mind, picturing Ellis's odd, fox-like grin, then dismissing it. *She's spoiled and horrible. I definitely don't like her. And I don't want to BE like her.*

The thoughts repeat rhythmically: *I don't want to like her. I don't want to BE like her. I don't want to like her. I don't want to BE like her.* The inner chanting strangely calms her as she races downhill and the entrance to Camp Okahatchee comes into view in the distance. *I don't want to like her. I don't want to BE like her.* The rain blurs her eyes, but she keeps running.

I don't want to like her. I don't want to BE like her.

Finally, heaving, out of breath, and surrounded by trees, Zoe can run no farther. She looks up at the swaying branches of the evergreens, gray like the sky, dappled with the rain pouring down on them. She touches her face. Is she crying or is it just the rain?

She drops her hand and stands there, getting soaked, blinking into the rain, staring and staring at the sky, waiting for an answer.

Finally, the answer comes:

I DO like her.

And then, a distant echo: *I AM like her.*

The certainty thuds deep down into Zoe's chest, and she sways, almost dizzy, backing up as though if she could only rewind her life, retrace her steps, she might come to a different conclusion.

She swivels around in the density of the woods, panic seizing her, that old nightmare of being buried alive creeping over her now, reaching around her neck, choking her.

She staggers through the thick trees, rain pummeling her, and that's when she stumbles upon it:

A body.

Shaking and shivering on the forest floor.

Joy.

24

It's dark. No rain falls, but her body is wet, her clothes clinging to her uncomfortably. The trees wink in her peripheral vision; they seem to be chattering in worried tones. Hands gather around her. She's being lifted.

Joy blinks, her vision clearing. She's looking into the faces of her three best friends. Tali's dark skin and even darker eyes blend into the night around them. Zoe's shirt falls from her shoulder, which seems to glow, a small moon. Luce looks pale and frazzled. More than that, she looks *young*. Like a scared kid. Both Tali and Zoe hook their arms underneath Joy's armpits, dragging her forward through the woods, while Luce is saying something urgently, holding up Joy's backpack, gesticulating with her hands, asking questions.

Where is she? And that's when it comes back to her: She fainted. However long ago that was. *Shit*. It had been so hot, she remembers—too hot. But now the air has cooled off, and she realizes she's shivering. Her legs feel weak.

"What *happened*?" Luce is demanding. "Joy, *tell* us!"

"Guys, I'm fine," Joy manages, finding her voice. "Really. I just . . . I passed out. It's a hangover."

Under her breath, Zoe mutters, "I've never seen a hangover *that* bad."

"Where's Ryder? Who won the scavenger hunt?" Joy asks, knowing her voice sounds weak, but not caring.

The three girls look at her with exasperation.

"We don't *know*," Tali states flatly. "We got sidetracked reviving you and dragging you off the forest floor."

"Seriously," Joy says, her throat scratchy. She knows they're mad. And maybe they should be. But she's so tired. She doesn't want to fight. It's the last night of camp, and all they want to do is argue and disagree and worry. "Please, stop. You guys can let go of me. I knew I should've had a Gatorade."

"A Gatorade?" Zoe practically shouts. "Joy, we're taking you to the infirmary. You're *sick*."

"No," Joy says, trying to drag her feet to a stop. The other girls struggle to keep her on the path. "How come you guys won't listen to me?" She manages to wrestle free of them and stands back, as the dizziness clears from her head like a wave receding from shore. "Look. See? I can walk on my own now. It's *fine*."

"Why are you being like this?" Luce demands. "You *passed out*, Joy. And now you're acting like nothing happened."

Joy sighs. "Because nothing *did* happen, I promise. Nothing.

I only fainted because I was dehydrated. And I completely forgot to have breakfast and lunch. It happens to everyone. You don't need to take care of me. It's the last night of camp. I just want to enjoy it."

Zoe rubs her forehead. "I don't know . . ."

"Are you *sure*, Joy?" Luce says.

Tali throws her hands in the air. "You guys, she's clearly not okay. Joy, you need to get checked out. You could have mono or the flu or something."

Joy shakes her head. "I hate the Wellness Cabin! Come on, I promise you I'm fine. See?" She grabs Tali's hand and places it on her forehead. "Just cold from the rain."

Tali looks at her skeptically but shakes her head—obviously relenting.

"So who won the scavenger hunt?" she asks, hoping to redirect their attention.

Zoe shrugs—she seems to be avoiding eye contact with all of them. Joy can sense that the tension between her and Tali has not yet been resolved—they are standing as far apart from each other as they can. "I missed the game . . . I was busy at the tournament." Zoe holds up her gold medal, looking proud, and something else, too. Something Joy can't quite pinpoint.

Luce sighs. "We stopped counting items when we found *you*," she says. "You're the important thing."

Tali pulls a ripped piece of fabric out of her pocket and displays it to the rest of them. "At least I got these, though." The material is mostly white, but with little cartoon drawings of Batman on it. Blake's boxers. Or half of them, anyway—enough to cover a single butt cheek, probably. "This thing—this crazy plan . . . maybe it'll really work."

They emerge together from the woods, and Joy can see the moon now, through the parted clouds. The fields are glittering and wet, but at least the storm has passed. She takes a deep breath. Out of the forest, it doesn't seem so late out, so bleak. Dinging singsong noises trickle over to them from the Great Lawn, where she can make out the white cream-puff peaks of the big tent. Red, blue, and purple lights bounce off the remaining clouds.

The reunion night carnival has begun.

"Um, guys?" Zoe says, pointing into the crowd of people hovering by the nearest tent. "Did someone call camp pharma-ceuticals?"

Joy follows her gaze to see Rob Gurns jogging toward them. Sure enough, he seems to be waving at them, though she can't imagine what he wants with their crew.

"Hey, Luce," Rob says as he approaches.

The others gape slightly.

He holds out his closed fist, with a mysterious, lopsided grin on his face. Joy could swear that Luce is blushing as she takes whatever small object he has just handed her. "Hope you don't mind my bailing the other night—my record really can't take another hit. Maybe this will make up for it."

Luce begins to say something, but Rob holds up a hand to silence her.

"Don't read into it. It's just—like you said—the having of it, not the meaning of it. Or whatever." He nods to the other three girls, giving Tali a random salute, then jogs away.

"What was that about?" Tali asks.

Zoe steps closer to Luce. "Did he just hand you a bag of pot or something?"

"The merit badge," Luce whispers, holding it up so they can see. "He stole it for me."

Tali folds her arms. "Why?"

Luce shrugs. "Long story. I guess he kind of owed me one."

Zoe looks at all their faces. "So does this mean we actually have all four of the objects now?"

Everyone looks at Joy, wearing mingled expressions of excitement and hope. She can plainly see the medal around Zoe's neck, the boxers stuffed partway into Tali's pocket, and the merit badge still in Luce's palm.

She stands there, trying to figure out how to steer this, how to say the right thing. "Actually . . . ," she stalls, shaking her head as heat creeps into her cheeks; she's glad night's descending. "I, um, lost the tiara last night," she explains.

"You *lost* it?" Tali squawks. "What do you mean you lost it?"

Joy hugs herself. "I just did, okay?" she says quickly.

Zoe studies her face as if she doesn't quite believe her. "Maybe we can retrace your steps and find it," she offers.

"Well," Joy begins. "I, um, I ended up by the lake. Near that little waterfall," she says. "Past the footbridge. You know, not far from where the path leads up to the Red Cliffs." She speaks slowly, hesitantly. What happened last night—with Ryder. It was magic. It was surreal. It was something she's not sure how to describe, even to her friends.

"Doug Ryder and I . . . we . . ." And somehow, she manages to tell it all—well, *almost* all, leaving out just a few details to savor for herself. Their reactions—squeals, giggles, and exclamations of shock and awe—make her glad she told . . . despite the fact that subjects such as *did they use a condom* (obviously), and *was it everything she expected* (impossible to answer), are up at the top of the list of Most Mortifying Things to Talk About Even with Close Friends.

Tali pounds her on the back approvingly, and Joy sways slightly, a hint of her former light-headedness returning.

A look of concern flashes across Luce's face. "We should really hunt for that tiara, but first, I think we need to get you something to eat."

"I'm on it," Zoe says, seeming relieved to have a reason to back away for a moment. She disappears toward the glow of the giant tent, and only minutes later returns with a big stick of cotton candy, handing it to Joy as though offering a queen her staff.

"The sugar will help you feel less dizzy," Luce says with an approving nod.

The tuft of swirled pink, larger at the top and tapering in toward the rolled paper stick, reminds Joy oddly of the clouds she watched with Doug Ryder when they lay back against the dusty rocks at the top of Red Cliffs, only two days ago. She takes a bite, and its sweet stickiness fills her mouth: the flavor of happiness, childhood. It dissolves on her tongue, leaving a vague graininess until there's no mass left, just the taste of color itself, of vivid red . . . her mouth empty, her whole body high on memory.

They were wrong. She doesn't feel less dizzy. The memories take her over: Upturned board games and wild disputes over who won. Racing through the spray of sprinklers on the Great Lawn. Sharing candy in the Stevens. Like flashcards, they race through her mind. Tali, swiveling backward from her chair in French class to face Joy, who sat behind her for all of sixth grade, instructing her to always smile, no matter what happens. *Souris toujours.* Luce holding her hand, telling her to be brave when she was too scared to dive into the lake during swim lessons the summer before second grade. Zoe daring her to climb the big maple in her yard. The view from the tree, dappled in leafy shadow. All that cheesy crap from the past floods her head in a millisecond as the pink sugar melts and fades and disappears, leaving a subtle stain on her palms and lips.

Life is like cotton candy, she concludes. But she can't say it aloud, or they will think she is crazy.

"Guys," she announces instead. "I just realized something."

They turn their focus on her and she is once again their center, their gravity. They need her. And for one last time, that's all *she* needs.

"That time capsule I wanted to bury?"

They nod, Tali raising an eyebrow, Zoe tilting her head, and Luce crossing her arms tentatively.

"What a dumb idea," she blurts, surprised by the words.

"What are you talking about?" Luce asks, her face looking

just like it did the time Zoe dared her to eat a worm during the summer they were Bunk Foxes.

"It doesn't matter if kids of the future find our pictures and souvenirs," Joy explains. "That's *our* stuff. Those are *our* memories. Like . . . whoever comes after us? They'll make their own memories. They don't want to find *our* old crap. You know what I mean?"

"Uh-huh," Zoe responds. "Now gimme a bite of that." She grabs the stick of remaining cotton candy from Joy's hand.

Suddenly they're all fighting over the cotton candy and laughing. Tali suggests they go for a dive to find the lost tiara, and everyone agrees, so they start running, fully clothed, up the path to the tire swing, the cotton candy long forgotten, its pink fluff rolling in the mud in their wake.

Joy is running with her three best friends in the whole world, and it doesn't matter that they are heading back into the past and the future all at once, that if they retrieve the tiara they'll be that much closer to re-creating the photo and, possibly, going home. Nothing matters except now, and now, and now. Branches scratching their arms. Laughter stinging through the air. The lake whispering and waiting with open arms, an unreadable but welcoming pool of darkness.

Joy doesn't hesitate this time. Not like when she came up here by herself on the first night back in the past. When they reach the summit where the tire swing dangles listlessly, they don't even bother to stop. Tali, with her long legs, reaches the ledge first, and turns back to look at the others, pausing for only a moment.

Zoe arrives next and sticks her hand out to grab Joy's. Luce takes her other hand, and Tali's, and then they are linked.

A collective inhale.

A slight breeze ripples across the lake's hungry surface.

In unison, they leap.

Eight limbs flailing. Four bodies falling. The black iris of the lake staring up at them as they fly toward it, into its center.

The air wraps around Joy, whooshing in her ears, and time really does stop—or at least, it pauses—and she can see everything clearly: the mountains a deep charcoal smudge beneath the night clouds, the water inky and opaque below. The sky screams all around her, inside her. *I get it now,* she thinks, letting her fear wash through her and soar away on the wind, as she gives in, allowing herself to fall. Because it's all you can do. Let go. Fall.

Fly.

The impact is sharper and harsher than she expected: a slap against her skin—from her shoulders down the backs of her legs. It stings so much it distracts her from the cold.

Under the water, she flings her eyes open. As she surges toward the shoreline underneath the surface, she sees it: a distant glimmer. It has gotten dark out—it must be after eight o'clock—but the moon is huge and round and yellow, probing the water like a searchlight. The light bounces off the slimy, mossy, underwater rocks, illuminating something tinny and silver . . . the tiara. Unbelievably, it is still here, not too far from the mini waterfall.

Instinct takes over and Joy kicks at the fake silver crown, sending it tumbling deeper. She is running out of breath and needs to break the surface. Just as she begins thrusting herself upward, she sees a pair of golden arms and legs and a trail of long blond hair like pale seaweed flashing past her under the water, heading straight for the tiara. It's Zoe. Joy has no choice but to continue her journey up to the surface.

Funny how in just an instant your future can change.

Joy bursts into the air, gasping, her mind raging. *No no no.*

But it has happened. She can already see Zoe emerging nearby, holding the Miss Okahatchee crown in her fist triumphantly.

"Got it!" Zoe cries.

Tali and Luce's heads pop up not too far away, like curious seals.

"Hallelujah!" That's Luce, bouncing up and down excitedly.

"We've got all the pieces!" Zoe shouts. "This is *it!*"

"Nice work, Zo!" Tali calls out, her strong arms pulling her forward through the water.

They all gather around, slapping one another high fives in the shallow area where not more than twenty-four hours ago, Joy and Ryder were kissing, touching each other, groping in the starlight.

Joy shakes her head now, willing away the images—and the tingles they bring to her whole body. "And so we do," she says.

Now they are all solemn and frozen, like they've stumbled through the back door of a church in the middle of service.

"Is it time, then?" Luce says quietly, tiny droplets catching the moonlight on her shoulders, making them glow, even while her face is hidden in shadow.

Joy breathes in the smell of the lake for one last time—heady and minerally and full of the magic of the past, a thing she didn't realize existed, but she's sure of it now. The past *does* have a magic to it. You don't know it while you're living through it, but it's there, hovering around you and nudging you gently forward with its own mysterious will. There is no other way to explain the high Joy's experiencing right now, just from a scent, just from a moment.

She doesn't want to go, doesn't want to give in to the forward nudge—especially not with her three oldest and best friends together again, all gathered around looking at her with so much openness.

But they are ready. Which means *she* must be ready. All they're waiting for is her command.

"It's time," she says.

PART THREE
ALWAYS and FOREVER

"Life can only be understood backwards;
but it must be lived forwards."
—Søren Kierkegaard

25

Hair. If there is one thing that keeps Tali obsessed day and night, rain or shine, pre-storm and post-storm, that's it. Will it behave? Will it lie flat? Will anyone notice its peculiar antigravitational tendencies? Cool girls are supposed to have smooth hair, sleek yet pliant, like their personalities. Which is exactly why she is shocked to realize it has been a full forty-eight hours since her last attempt to tame her locks. The seventy-dollar anti-curl serum she once thought she could not live without lies on its side with the cap only half-closed, crusting at the edge, when she reaches into her cubby for a hair dryer.

Hair was only one of several topics of debate as the girls rushed back to Bunk Blue Heron from the lake that night in a whirl, passing by the glitter and music of the already-in-full-swing reunion night carnival, the tents glistening with raindrops, but the clouds now fully lifted and gone. Specifically, did it matter that their hair was wet but had been dry in the photo they are about to re-create? Other topics of debate included what the exact outfits they had worn that night consisted of, whether any of this was actually going to work in the first place, and whether they would get caught or stopped somehow before they had the chance to find out.

But here's the thing: life doesn't always hand you the answers. Sometimes the best you can do is make a decision and stick to it. Tali's dad always says that the best business decisions rely on intuition, after all. There isn't always a right move, just a move that *feels* right.

Then again, her dad is under investigation for fraud. So who knows if his advice will hold up. Tali, for one, is less than certain.

And thus it is with frantic energy and frayed nerves that the girls dry and style their hair and get dressed. The gentle wailing of Hadley's horn only adds to the manic feeling in the close quarters, but to Tali the familiarity of the music comes as a relief. . . . In fact, knowing it may be the last time she hears Hadley Gross play the French horn actually fills her with a surge of emotion, and she could practically kiss her—even if what Rebecca said is true, and *Hadley* was the one who was hooking up with Blake all summer.

As she buttons her jeans and steps into her trusty gladiator sandals, Tali notices Brianna Bradley—who has always made a tradition of skipping the carnival—observing them with arms folded across her chest, clearly wondering when reunion night became such a big deal, her eyes narrowed as if to say *Which one of you is getting laid, and what am I missing?*

You'll never guess, Tali thinks smugly. *We are heading forward in time. We're emissaries from the future. You didn't know?*

Finally they are ready. Or as ready as they will ever be. Zoe's newly won fencing medal hangs from her neck. She and Zoe still haven't exactly *reconciled* after their fight, but Zoe seems oddly subdued—not her usual chatty self. Tali feels somehow scared to apologize, like the wounds are still too fresh, like she'll somehow make it worse.

Meanwhile, Joy is wearing her lucky green cardigan, the Miss Okahatchee tiara, and an expression of complete uncertainty in her eyes, which briefly unnerves Tali. And Luce has on her favorite floral romper, which is both weirdly childish and, at the same time, fitting, with her badge pinned to the breast pocket. They look pretty much exactly as they did in that original photo strip, from what they all mutually recall.

Tali sucks in a breath as she glances around the cabin for one last (hopefully) time. Positioned cross-legged on her bottom bunk, Hadley raises an eyebrow at her but keeps playing. Mildewy towels litter the floor, scenting the air, but not enough to disguise Jade Marino's cigarette smoke. In a corner, Paige is bent over a stack of a few mislabeled Feddies, sorting through the leftover packages like Santa's little helper on Christmas Eve. Other than that, the cabin is empty, most of the Blue Herons having left to enjoy the festivities at least an hour ago.

"Come on, girls, it's now or never," Joy says.

Tali tries to release the tension in her shoulders as she follows her old friends toward the door, tucking the Batman boxer flag into her side so as not to draw suspicion. But a part of her is filled with sadness. She feels upturned, emptied, all the stardust of the past flying out of her pockets and away on the breeze.

She wonders if the other campers, along with the alums who have begun to show up for the festivities, can sense their nervousness as the four of them hurry through the crowd on the Great Lawn. She finds herself scanning everyone she passes and realizes she's searching for Shane. He must have left the campgrounds by now, though, and the thought sends a stab of regret through her. She can't stop picturing his hands, his kisses, his kind eyes, his laugh. Their amazing conversation. How well they seemed to fit together despite the initial surprise of it—not that it was really surprising at all, come to think of it. The most surprising part was how utterly idiotic Tali had been up to that point. Her heart rate picks up, thinking about how furious he was when he stormed out of the cabin. She's *still* an idiot.

Zoe taps on Tali's shoulder, snapping her out of her memories and pulling her back from the other two girls. "Tal," she says with urgency in her voice. "I just want to say sorry, for, you know, what happened at the party. Everyone thinks I . . . well, that Blake and I—" Zoe's face turns beet red.

Tali swallows. She can see how sorry Zoe is from the pinched expression on her face. It makes Tali feel pinched, too, somewhere deep inside. "Whatever happened, it doesn't matter to me anymore." She means it. She just hopes Zoe *knows* she means it.

"But really," Zoe insists. "It matters to *me*. I wanted you to know that's not what happened. And I shouldn't have called you self-absorbed."

Tali looks at Zoe and can't help herself. She laughs. "Zo, I *am* a little self-absorbed. At least, I know that I have been recently. And I want to fix that. I want to be better . . . be a better . . ." For some reason the word stops on her tongue.

But it's as though Zoe can read her mind. She nods, her eyes brimming with tears. "I want to be a better friend, too."

Tali's throat starts to close up, but she's not going to cry, not when there's so much at stake for this photo. "So what *did* happen that night, anyway?" she asks.

Zoe's face blanches and she swallows. "It was just a coincidence that Blake showed up when he did. I wasn't making out with him, I was making out with . . . someone else."

"Who?" Tali feels a bullet of excitement—the old kind they used to have when sharing secrets.

Zoe gulps. "Blake's sister." She looks like she can't believe she just said it.

There's a pause where Tali's brain has to catch up—she's not sure she heard her correctly. And then, in an instant, it all clicks into place. This is Zoe, moving forward. Getting unstuck. "I don't blame you," she blurts. And she means that, too.

Zoe startles, her face a cross between shocked and amused.

Tali shrugs. "I mean, the girl is smokin'."

Without warning, Zoe flings her arms around Tali, wrapping her in a hug. The relief of Zoe's confession radiates out from her, and Tali squeezes her back, feeling closer to her than she has in a long time. Maybe closer to her than she's *ever* felt. It's clear this wasn't about a single hookup. It was about Zoe, figuring herself out. Maybe Tali wasn't the only blind one.

She wonders if there's a chance they can start over, form a *real* friendship again. Maybe not one involving riding on each other's bicycle handlebars, but something else . . . something new.

Before she can say more, Luce lets out a huge huff, pointing to a long line of people waiting before them at the photo booth.

Tali steps forward. "Excuse me, kiddos, but we're Bunk Blue Heron and it's our last night here so we really need to exercise our line-skipping privileges." When the two eleven-year-old girls in front of her—wearing matching BFF necklaces—look at her funny, Tali rolls her eyes and gives them a nudge, and they begrudgingly shuffle out of the way, letting Tali, Luce, Joy, and Zoe through to the front.

"Nice one," Zoe says, giving Tali an approving smile.

"Thanks," Tali says, smiling back at her, and knowing, without knowing how, that they're going to be okay—that some things are going to be different now, including them.

Once they are inside the photo booth, the thick curtains muffle the sounds of the carnival. The girls are, again, practically piled on top of one another, and there's a mad shuffle to try to get into the exact positions they had in the old photo. Luce is convinced she was sitting on Zoe's left, but Zoe swears Luce was standing, hovering over her from the other side.

"I know I'm right because I had my left arm around Joy," Zoe insists.

"Fine," Luce says breathlessly, once again scooting around to rearrange herself.

"Guys, are we ready? Guys!" Tali says, having to shout just a little for them to pay attention. Sweat lines her palm from gripping Blake's boxers so hard, and in her other hand, she fumbles for the camera remote.

"Hit it," Zoe says.

And so she does. Tali presses the big green button on the remote, and they see the camera light up, then do its 3-2-1 countdown. Then there's a loud snap and a giant, blinding flash.

And then . . .

Nothing. Tali instantly feels for her boobs—the surest sign of what time period they're in—and comes up A-cup only.

Joy grabs at her hair—still long. "It didn't work," she says.

"Hurry up in there, we're waiting!" someone calls from outside, ruffling the curtain.

Zoe lashes out, punching through the curtain. "Back off!" she calls. "We need a minute!"

"Why isn't it working?" Tali asks, her head feeling hot. The photo booth is tiny and smells like her grandmother's attic in the summer.

Luce whines, "We have all the elements together, don't we? What's missing?"

"Just let me think!" Zoe bursts out. "Let's reverse our positioning. Tali, come to the other side. Yeah, exactly. And Luce, you stay there, but Joy, move around her. Good. Okay, let's try again."

No one voices the obvious: that this whole entire plan might have been a dud. It's what they've all been thinking and wondering about, she knows, all week. But somehow, it seems too weighty, too horrifying a concept to fully consider. That the photo booth might not work. That they could be . . . stuck.

Instead, they do as Zoe said. They shuffle back into place in the opposite arrangement and Tali once again clicks the remote.

FLASH.

Pause.

Nothing.

"Oh, come *on*!" Luce cries, clearly on the verge of panic.

"It's okay," Zoe says, her voice wavering. "We'll figure this out." She sounds anything but certain.

Tali's mind is racing. All this time, she's held the fear at bay, the looming, obvious question as to what might happen if this didn't work, if they really stayed stuck in the past. She knows she would still have two more years of high school to relive. She'd have to start all over with Ashlynn and the popular kids—she'd have to decide if that's what she even wants.

She wipes sweat off the back of her neck and tries to stay calm.

"Maybe we need to force the fuse to blow somehow?" Tali suggests.

"I would really rather not get electrocuted if we can avoid it," Luce says.

She looks around at the others. "Any better ideas?"

Joy stands up in front of the camera and pushes Tali into a seated position next to the other girls on the tiny bench. "Okay, everyone sit still for a second," she announces.

Immediately, Tali finds herself focusing on Joy. She notices

306

that the other girls do the same. They sit there, awaiting further instructions.

Joy clears her throat. "Maybe we just haven't given our pasts a proper good-bye. Everyone take a minute to think about what you'll miss."

"But—" Zoe begins.

"Just do it!" Luce says, nudging her.

Zoe grumbles but falls silent, closing her eyes.

At first, Tali feels restless inside the tiny, cramped space, coated in years of graffiti. But then she starts to think about everything that has happened these past few days—the fight and reconciliation with Zoe over Blake. The fight with Luce over Shane. Shane.

What if when they get back to the present, all that has disappeared again? How will she know what sticks and what fades? Will Joy be gone from their lives again? What about Luce and Zoe?

She can't even remember how she managed to get through the last two years without them.

Her eyes fling open in a panic. Maybe this is all a mistake. Maybe they should stay. She's not sure what to do—if she should bring up her doubts—but the other three girls still have their eyes closed, so she begins scanning the graffiti on the walls around them. She feels tears welling up behind her eyes as she reads:

Sammy & Gina, '12.

Dave is da bad ass. Crossed out to say: *Dave is an ass zit.*

Eat me.

Long live the Cruz.

For a good time call Emily Fargo.

Indigo Perez is a ho.

And that's when Tali realizes one piece of graffiti is missing.

"Luce," she says, nudging her shoulder. "Luce! Do you have a pen?"

Luce opens her eyes and searches her bag. *Of course* she has a pen. She doesn't travel without one. She hands it to Tali, and Tali stands up, leaning over Joy's shoulder.

On the wall behind Joy, she scrawls: *Z, J, T & L, friends forever.*

Joy looks at what Tali has written and smiles slowly. "Forever" is all she says.

"Forever," Luce and Zoe echo. Zoe finds Tali's hand and squeezes it, and Tali feels her heart squeeze, too, as though in response.

Joy sits down next to them, takes the remote from Tali's other hand, and hits the green button. At the last second, Tali holds the boxers high in the air, like she's giving a final wave to her past, to her crush on Blake, to her botched romance with Shane, to *all* of it.

Blackness. A soft humming fills her ears, like distant buzzing bees. The whole photo booth is rattling slightly and there's a slim line of smoke snaking up out of the camera. The girls have leaped up with a collective gasp, and now they push through the thick curtains in a jumble. Tali inhales deeply, letting the night air fill her chest.

Her ample, perky, C-cup chest.

She lets out her breath in a huge half laugh, half sigh as she looks around at the faces of her three friends. They are all wearing mixed looks of shock and relief. Gone are Joy's tiara and Luce's badge and Zoe's medal. Their faces each look somehow more sharply chiseled, less blurry and more real than they have since they stepped into the booth in the first place—in the *very* first place. But Joy's most of all—gaunt, almost harshly so, its angles accented by her pixie cut.

"Adorable!" someone booms from behind them. Tali swivels around to see the Cruz holding a strip of four photos that have spit out of the machine. "This will be perfect for the memory wall. Come along to the rec hall so you can sign your names!" She walks off with the pictures, and just like that, the bubble pops and reality sinks in.

It's the present. It's reunion night. Tali's whole purpose in coming here was to get with Blake, but now . . . that seems like a lifetime ago. She snorts and shakes her head just thinking about it.

They follow numbly behind Bernadette Cruz's austere form, and Tali squints as they enter the brightly lit rec hall. She takes in its familiar scent of glue and citronella, watching the Cruz pin up the photo of the girls—the modern photo, not the one from the past. In it, Joy's cropped hair makes her face seem like it's glowing from within. Luce is staring at Joy and not the camera. Zoe is shifting her shirt as though uncomfortable in it, and Tali is checking her iPhone. They look, once again, like four girls long estranged, not close friends. A chill washes over her, and the sounds of other campers and alums talking and laughing and squealing across the room at one another seems muffled and muted. Was any part of the last five days real, or did she just imagine it all?

And what will happen now? They all promised they would stay friends forever. But Tali knows what happens to most promises. And forever is a long time.

Andrew has entered the rec hall and calls Luce over to him. Joy looks a little nauseated, so Zoe walks her over to the corner of the room where there are chairs set up and goes to get her a glass of water. But Tali can't bring herself to move. Staring at the picture on the wall, she feels loneliness and confusion writhing in the pit of her stomach.

She came to reunion night with a simple mission—hook up with Blake. Instead, it's like she tumbled backward down a well, finding herself surrounded by memories: some beautiful, some funny, some painful. She didn't expect to feel this way. She didn't expect to miss her old friends and her old self so powerfully that she was somehow transported back in time. If it even *was* real. And even stranger than all of that is the sense, somewhere in the dark corners of her mind, that she's missing something—that some puzzle piece still hasn't fallen into place.

She turns away from the photo strip at last, looking around the room. She sees alumni and current campers alike traipsing in and out, patting one another's backs, hugging, laughing, catching up. And then, through the throng of people, she sees a familiar baseball cap. He turns so she can see his profile, and she knows instantly that it's Shane.

The heat of mortification creeps up her face. She can't believe she didn't even remember him in the truck earlier—he'd looked familiar, but she'd written it off, when he *obviously* remembered her. She'd been such a dismissive bitch toward him. *Don't I know you?* he'd said. And she'd blown him off. Oblivious.

She isn't about to let that happen again. Steeling herself, she pushes her way through the pack toward him, then takes a breath before tapping him on the shoulder.

He swings around to face her, and he's even more handsome than she remembered. Rugged-looking, with faint stubble lining his jaw, making it look more square. He is strong but lean, like he has grown out of his bulk. He's wearing a faded blue baseball hat, turned backward, accenting his clear green eyes. He has on a grease-stained T-shirt and ratty jeans and smells like car oil. . . .

For a second his eyes light up and she thinks he's about to smile at her, but the smile quickly fades and he takes a step back.

"Wait," she says urgently, touching his arm, even though he's not going anywhere. He looks down at her hand, and she instantly lets go. "Please. Let me say something. . . . Let me apologize."

Shane has a curious look on his face.

"For earlier," she stumbles on. "For not remembering you. I'm an idiot. I don't know how I failed to see it sooner. I don't know how you've *ever* put up with me, Shane, I really don't." She wants to go on, but she doesn't know what she's even saying. She doesn't know what actually *happened*—what's memory, what's dream.

"So you *do* know my name," he says, tilting his head slightly. "You know, from the way you acted earlier, in my truck, I almost thought I had it wrong. You couldn't have been the same girl I recalled from camp two summers ago. But then when you had me drop you off so close to Okahatchee, I figured it had to be you. . . . I just hadn't realized how much you would have changed. I mean"—his face flushes—"not that we really knew each other. I just . . . had a different impression of you from afar is all, but . . . well, never mind."

She fumbles. It's like their new version of the past never happened—at least not for him. He knows who she is, but only as some random camper. "A lot's happened in the last two years . . . ," she starts. "And . . . I really *wasn't* myself earlier tonight." And that's when it occurs to her that she's right: that Tali from earlier *wasn't* her. *This* Tali—the one surrounded by friends, with Shane by her side—this is the real her.

He just doesn't know it yet.

"Well, I'm not gonna lie," Shane says, "I was weirded out by the whole thing. I realize we never really talked that summer— and it was my only summer working there. But I went home and couldn't stop thinking about it, which is why I decided to come to reunion. I had to see for myself. I figured if my hunch was right, I could give this back to you." He digs into his jeans pocket, blushing again. "I've had it for two whole years and I thought you should have it back. It looked valuable. You left it on the dock during swim session that last week of camp. I didn't know how to get in touch with you, otherwise I would have. . . ." He extracts a gold strand—a necklace. As he pulls it out, a pendant swings on the end of it—a tiny Taurus symbol. It's the necklace that Tali always used to wear when she was younger. The one her father bought her, to remind her that she was just like a stubborn bull, and he loved that about her. The one that she lost the night that she and Shane . . .

Wait a second.

"You found it . . . on the dock?" she asks. Tali's face is so hot at this point, she's sure steam must be rising from her skin. *Did any of it happen?* What about the part where she got him fired . . . the part where he hated her and stormed off, never wanting to see her again?

He takes her right hand and positions it palm up, then places the necklace there, folding her fingers around it. "Here," he says, biting his lip slightly.

He starts to back up, but she grabs his arm, forcing him to stay. The feeling she had in her dream, or her past, whatever it was, when she flew off her stolen bike in a neon-green lacy thong and bra, throwing herself into the lake, comes back to her now. Wild. Free. Like nothing anyone else thinks matters—it's just her, and the world lying before her, open to any possibility. Including this one.

"Shane," she says, her words coming out breathy and urgent.

"Yeah?" he says, adjusting his hat with his free hand.

"I have something for you as well."

"Oh, you don't . . . I mean, that's okay, I don't need—"

"Just . . . shut *up* for a second, will you?" She tries to make her eyes look stern.

He puts his hands up in a sign of surrender.

Now another memory comes over her—the sensation of being thrown overboard on Casino Night, crashing backward into the freezing cold waves, thrashing alone out there in the rough, dark water, and then feeling a strong pair of arms wrap around her, pulling her to safety.

She stands on her tiptoes, places her hands on Shane's broad shoulders, and kisses him.

She can tell he's startled at first, but then he wraps his arms around her and kisses her back, his lips warm and urgent and strong, his chin just slightly scratchy against hers.

She pulls away for a breath.

"What was that for?" he asks, searching her eyes. He looks truly startled.

"Saving my life, remember?" she replies, unable to stop the huge dorky grin from forming across her face.

His jaw drops slightly, and he continues to look confused. "I don't remember . . . I don't think . . . Are you sure . . . Wait, when did I save your life?"

For a second, Tali's disappointed. It wasn't real. It *seemed* real, but it couldn't have been—at least, not for him.

But then, she feels relieved. Because this means she can start over, from here, going forward. She can do everything differently from now on. Including this.

She smiles, feeling her face redden. "Just now," she whispers.

He shakes his head. "You might be the most forward girl I've ever met."

She laughs. "Are you okay with that?"

"Okay with it? If I'd known, I would have tried the necklace thing way sooner." His grin takes over his whole face and all she wants to do is ask him about his four older sisters and whether he still listens to the Lost Tigers and whatever happened with his plans to transfer schools . . . but she's got to slow down. He doesn't know her yet.

She needs to earn his trust.

Because—even though she still can't believe it—none of what she just experienced really happened. And yet somehow, anyway, Shane, present-day Shane, is here, in her arms, real and solid. Not the guy she thought she wanted, but so obviously the guy she needed, car-oil stains and all—whether he knows it yet or not.

And she can't wait.

"How did you know?" he asks, looking into her eyes.

"Know . . . what?"

"That I, well, liked you. I thought I kept it pretty subtle that summer. But it was enough of a crush that I couldn't go back the next year. I don't know if I should even admit that. That's why I started up at the tow company instead. It's nowhere near as fun, but I couldn't go back to Okahatchee and risk anyone finding out I'd had a thing for one of the campers."

So he quit. He didn't get fired because of her. He left for his own reasons. He left because of *her*, but the situation was different. And she'd had no idea. Because she'd been blind. Because in the *real* past, she hadn't had a chance to open her eyes.

She's about to tell him more—about how she's changed— when a glass shatters on the other side of the room. A bunch of people quiet down and turn their heads, including Tali and Shane. Her heart thuds in her chest, as though the broken glass has awoken her too suddenly from a dream.

Then someone screams.

It's Luce. "Help!" she's screaming. "My friend is sick!"

Tali's heart stops. Joy has dropped her water glass and collapsed to the ground. Zoe is leaning over her now, shaking her shoulders. "Joy, wake up!" she shouts, as Tali tears across the room toward her friends.

By the time she pushes through the crowd and crouches down beside Joy and Zoe, Luce and Andrew have gathered as well. It's just like finding her in the woods, only worse somehow. She's breathing, faintly, but she's not waking up.

"Come on, Joy," Luce says, urgency in her voice as she clutches Joy's shoulders.

Ryder emerges out of the crowd, kneeling beside them, shouting for someone to call an ambulance. Then the Cruz is there, speaking in staccato into a cell phone. Mr. Wilkinson materializes, too, talking rapidly, urgently, holding on to Bernadette Cruz by the elbow, like she might fall over. It all seems to happen so fast, Tali's not sure if she even remembers to breathe. The wailing siren echoing through the mountains. The red and blue lights flashing through the rec hall window. The crowd parting to let Joy's parents through. Tali hasn't seen Joy's parents in a few years. Joan and Allen Freeman. Joan is crying. She, too, looks thinner and much older than Tali remembers, gray streaking her brown hair. Allen is talking in urgent commands to the EMTs as they lift Joy onto a stretcher. Tali catches only brief capsules of his words—*missed meds, stolen car, unsupervised, nurses were supposed to* . . .

Fear swirls through Tali's chest, spiraling up to her head, making her dizzy. "What are you *talking* about?" she hears herself say, though it sounds like the voice of a little girl. "What's wrong with her? What's wrong with Joy?" Now her voice is getting more high-pitched. Hysterical. "What's happening to her?"

As the words spill out, she feels herself spinning closer and closer to the dark center of the whirlpool, the answer to the mystery she could sense was there all along, staring at her like a black pupil. The secret. The truth.

Joan is squatting down to their level, one hand on Tali's shoulder and one on Luce's. Zoe is curled up with her arms around her knees. "Joy didn't tell you?" Joan asks Luce, then looks to Zoe, then Tali. "Oh, honey . . . girls . . ." Joan shakes her head, tears still trickling down her face. She wipes them with the back of her hand.

"What is it, Mrs. Freeman?" Luce asks, her voice shaking.

And then in a hoarse voice, Zoe says, "You have to let us know. Whatever it is."

Joan just shakes her head again, unable to speak. Allen steps in next to her, helping her to stand. "Joy is very sick," he tells them. His voice, by contrast, is steady and even, filling Tali with sudden rage. "She's been fighting it for the last couple of years, but she's . . . she's no longer winning the fight. She wanted to come so badly tonight. I think she wanted to see you all. She missed you so much."

And then Tali is stumbling through the rec hall doors after them. Mr. Wilkinson is there, holding the girls back, as Joy's parents are getting into their car, slamming the doors with finality, following behind the ambulance as it wails away into the night, and Tali is somehow inside the ambulance and not, standing there on the lawn unable to feel her own hands or her feet, simply watching, helpless, as the ambulance lights flicker behind the trees, before the vehicles turn a bend and are gone.

26

There are certain moments in life that no SAT word can describe. There's no thesaurus in any language that can find the right adjective for how Luce feels as she walks into her house late that night, closely followed by Andrew, her mom, and her twin brothers. Her mom heads inside first, to tuck in the younger kids. Luce sees her father's car in the driveway and, for a second, wishes he was working late tonight, like he does so often. There's a lot she doesn't understand about her parents' marriage, or her perfectly organized and polished family, she realizes.

Then again, there's a lot she didn't know about Joy, either—like the horrible secret she kept from all of them for the past two years. Even as it sickens Luce to think about it, it makes a disturbing kind of sense. The way she vanished so abruptly, refusing to talk or let them visit. The heaviness Luce felt in the air earlier that night, when they first arrived back at camp and saw Joy, so thin and so frail, leaning against the wall, waiting for them. The gravel in her voice when she told them she'd come to say good-bye.

Good-bye to all of it, she'd said.

"Are you okay?" Andrew asks, putting an arm around Luce.

She shakes her head. Of course she isn't okay. Upstairs, her room will be sitting there just like she left it, filled with boxes packed to the brim with stuff she's supposed to bring to Princeton. But this terrifies her. How can she move forward, knowing what she knows now?

"Do you mind if I talk to my mom alone for a minute?" she asks.

"Of course not," he replies, taking a seat at the kitchen island.

"I'll be right back," she says, heading up the stairs to the study, where her mom has plopped down her bag.

Luce enters the room and quietly closes the door behind them. "I need to talk to you," she says.

Her mom looks up, pushing some of her curly dark hair back from her face and retucking it into her bun. She looks tired and overheated, but pretty—her features delicate and refined. "Sweetie, you must be in so much shock," she says, sinking into her leather chair, then bending down to rifle through a drawer.

For a minute, Luce isn't sure whether she's referring to what happened with Joy, or what happened in the past, with Mr. Wilkinson. It occurs to her that while she's been carrying around the burden of this knowledge, her mom probably has no idea that she knows.

It became clear to Luce as soon as they returned to the present that her trip back in time must have been imagined—an extended, if incredibly vivid, hallucination. There was simply no other way to explain it logically, and she knew from the moment she spoke to Andrew that he hadn't experienced it, hadn't remembered anything of their game of Strip Twenty Questions or their rooftop picnic or their attempts to ensnare her mother.

Which made her wonder—did her mom's affair really happen? If it did, was it simply that Luce hadn't noticed the first time around? Did her weird flashback somehow reveal an unconscious suspicion?

She needs answers. That much is clear.

"I am," she says now. "I am in shock. But I need to know something from you. Did you ever—"

Before she can finish her question, she hears a sniffle. It takes her so much by surprise that she can't complete her sentence. Her mother looks up and wipes her eyes.

Her mom.

Bernadette Cruz.

The woman who says crying is a waste of time, who says *achievers don't have regrets*.

Luce is frozen. "Mom?"

Her mother shakes her head. "Can you get your father, please?" Another tear slides down her face.

Luce is so frightened by the sight of it, all she can do is obey, the demands of her planned confrontation instantly forgotten. She hurries to her parents' bedroom, where her father is stepping into his slippers, his straight dark hair matted funnily over his balding head. He's got on his striped pajamas. "Luce?" he says, scratching his head at her sleepily. "How was reunion night?"

She practically chokes. He doesn't know about any of it. But she's in too much shock to say so. She simply shakes her head. "Mom, um, needs you. In the study" is all she can say. Her mind's a blank.

He looks at her like she's grown a third ear but trudges into the hallway and over to the study, Luce following a few feet behind him.

She peers around the bend of the doorway after he enters the room, and she hears him saying, "What is this?" His voice drops an octave to a tone she's rarely heard from him before, except when he's taking care of Amelia. Then her father wraps her mother in his arms. He turns back to face Luce. "Luce, honey. Can you close the door, please?"

And so she does.

She stumbles back down the stairs in a haze.

"Let's get some air," she says to Andrew, who is typing into his phone on the counter in the kitchen. She leads the way through the house to the sliding door facing the backyard. As she slides it open, the automatic porch light illuminates the remains of the picnic Luce set up earlier, rose petals still strewn across the iron garden bench and stone patio floor, wilting slightly. It would be funny if it weren't so awful—her aborted plan to lose her virginity to Andrew seems so stupid now. Just another attempt to control her life, to control the future. On some level, she knows she wanted to sleep with Andrew so he wouldn't break up with her. How pathetic it sounds to her now.

Besides, the problem was never that he might leave her. He loves her. He always has.

They sit down on the bench and he moves to put his arm around her again. After a moment of hesitation, she leans into him, unable to shake the image of her mother leaning into her father. Her mother crying.

"It's going to be okay, whatever happens," he says, sounding, for a brief moment, almost like Joy.

"Will it?" She stares up at him. This boy who is so loyal, so good. The perfect boyfriend. What does Luce do with *perfect* now, though, when everything else around her has fallen apart?

"What can I do?" he asks her. "What do you need?"

She shakes her head, trying to find the right vocabulary. "I just need . . ." She thinks of Tali's strength, of Zoe's independence, of Joy's quiet depth. How when she's with her friends, she feels somehow bigger than when she's alone, more powerful.

She looks out at the dark yard beyond their pool of light, the trees thick and looming, and beyond them, a seemingly endless smattering of stars blinking down on half the world at once. "Space," she says now, realizing it. "I need space." The confession burns her throat like a vodka shot. "Maybe forever. I'm not sure." She's never had to say anything this hard before. She feels destructive. Out of control. Like she is sinking in quicksand and she wants to grab on to him, but would only bring him down with her.

Andrew puts his arm down and looks at her, stricken for a second. His face twitches, and she prays that he won't cry. She's seen him cry only twice: once when his grandfather died last

November, and once when he broke his leg skiing and had to miss out on varsity soccer. It kills her to be the one hurting him now.

"I'm sorry," she whispers. She wants to take it back, but she can't.

He clears his throat. "No, I . . . I get it," he says finally.

Now it's her turn to stare. "You do?"

"We're both going to different colleges. We have our whole lives ahead of us. And . . . it's like Mr. Wilkinson said. You can't plan for everything."

"You remember that?" she asks, stunned, like she has just stumbled upon a trick question on a pop quiz, and the more she studies it, the further she drifts from the right answer, deeper into confusion.

"Yeah, he used to say that all the time. Like when the sailing team lost because of some sort of westerly wind." Andrew gives her a small, sad smile. "You know I remember it all, babe," he replies.

The familiar saying hovers in the air between them—ironically confirming both that the past never changed, and that Andrew hasn't either. It's just a statement, a final admission of how much he loves her, how much *real* history they've shared. And the words cut some invisible tether inside her, loosen the rope holding her above the quicksand. Gravity pulls her under. The emotion rattles her small frame, a tide coming through, a wave she has been holding back for so long she forgot it was even there. Now it rises to submerge her, sobs choking through her.

She doesn't know the last time she cried. Luciana Cruz isn't a crier; she's a fixer. She holds it together for everyone. But here she is, crying for the first time since she was a little kid, since before she was the one who had to make sure her siblings did their homework after school. Since before she had to make sure that at least 76 percent of her Brewster classmates passed the SATs with Ivy-level scores, before being captain, or leader, or valedictorian kept her up and sleepless, before she was the one who had to make sure that Amelia took the right pills each morning, that the driveway lights were on for Dad at night, and her mom's Tupperware-sealed meals were each properly labeled in the fridge for tomorrow.

She cries for her parents, who never had the perfect happy marriage she believed they did, and more, she cries for the whole idea of perfection, which feels like a giant red balloon that has finally popped, or slipped from her grasp and fled into the sky. She cries for Andrew, who is sitting beside her so stoic and solid and, she knows, so totally heartbroken. Curling into her body, she cries for herself, and how much she'll miss him.

She even cries for her *former* self, the girl who struggled so hard to fit into a mold, that she became just that: a mold, like the kind they once used to make clay sculptures at camp. Just the shape of a girl. An idea of a girl. A shell.

But most of all, she knows, she is crying for Joy.

27

Zoe's blond head hovers like an alien sun just to the side of Joy's bunk bed. *I can't sleep,* she's whispering. And then she climbs up the ladder and they're lying side by side, giggling in the darkness.

Dimly, Joy hears the sound of machines beeping. She turns her head slightly, trying to breathe in the smell of the night. Outside, the cool, clear lake goes on forever, deep and glacial. Giddy laughter echoes off the trees.

She sucks in oxygen, its tubes leaving a familiar plastic, sticky feeling on her face. The sound of it is like the *shush* of the lake itself, lapping at the rocks. And now Joy is standing in the shallow water near the footbridge, the moon casting violet ripples on the surface. Ryder is facing her, looking into her eyes, touching her, kissing her and kissing her. Love wasn't so hard to find after all, once she stopped running from it.

And now she's holding Tali and Luce's hands, leaping past the tire swing, over the cliffs, as though flying.

She *is* flying.

Joy wakes up and must immediately close her eyes again against the bright florescent hospital lights above her. She opens them once more and blinks. She feels dizzy and nauseated. Until she remembers: The water. The laughter. Her friends. Her past.

When she snuck out the other night, yanking the oxygen cords from her face and stripping out of her hospital gown, changing shakily into her jeans and boots, then slipping the car keys from her mom's purse while she went to get dinner (her parents had been taking turns staying the night), Joy had expected one evening of escape, a chance to bury all the memories and say good-bye.

She had gotten so much more than that.

"Oh good. You're awake," says a voice.

It takes effort for Joy to turn her head—she's *so* tired—but she does, and sees George Townsend, her nurse, taking her vitals. "Boy George," she says. "How long have I been out?" Her lungs hurt when she breathes, but she tries to ignore it.

He smiles at her. "It's good to have you back. You shouldn't have run off like that. You know you need your beauty sleep."

He leans over and sticks a needle into her arm. She hopes it'll make the breathing easier.

"What time is it?" she asks. Through the window, the sun appears to be setting.

"About seven. Your dad's napping and your mom is on the phone. Visiting hours are over, but we've made an exception. You've got friends here who have been asking to see you," he says, removing a tray from below her bed. "Oh, and you got a phone call from someone."

"A call?"

"Kid named Doug," he says, shrugging. "Dialed the main line. Said he got the number on a cruise or something."

"From the Cruz," she fills in.

"You know him? Let me find the message," says George, rummaging through a pile of notes in one of his long scrubs pockets. "There he is. Doug Ryder. Gina wrote down his number, just in case." He puts the note down next to her bed. "Should I tell your friends they can come in now?"

"Actually," Joy says, her breath coming short. "Could I . . . could I have a phone? I want to make this call first."

"Ooo-ooh," George says in a singsong voice. "I get it. No problem, sweetie. I'm on it."

Joy smiles, plastic tubes crinkling against her cheeks. "Don't be a dork, George," she says.

Moments later, he appears with a phone, saying, "I'll tell them to come in a few, okay?"

She nods. It's a little easier than speaking. "Thanks, BG," she says to his back as he leaves the room.

It seems like the phone rings forever—a concept Joy now believes is fully possible. If she thought hell were a real thing, she'd be sure it was an unanswered call. But in this moment that seems to stretch infinitely in two directions, she has all the time in the world to wait for his voice, which comes, at last, like a wave breaking. "Hello?"

"Hey, Ryder."

There's a pause. "Is this Joy? From camp?"

She smiles. "The very same."

He takes in a breath. There's another pause—a long one. Finally he says, "How? How did you find it?"

"You taught it to me," she answers.

"No, I didn't," he protests. "I would remember. I've never shown anyone those lyrics before."

"I memorized them," she says simply.

Another pause. "I don't understand it. I don't understand it at all, but . . . Joy?"

"Yeah?"

"I don't even know how you got ahold of it and I know we never got to know each other that well at camp, and I'm sorry about that. But . . . I just can't believe it."

"Can't believe . . . what?" she asks, her words flowing out of her with only the slightest effort.

"How good my song sounded in your voice," he says. "It's incredible. I had no idea this song was any good until I played your recording. It popped up in my email this morning kind of like a miracle. I'd forgotten I even wrote it."

She finds her hand is clutching the phone hard, her breathing is more painful. She wants him to *remember*. She wants it to have been real. She thinks of his lyrics:

> *Now I climb another wall,*
> *Look out from another height,*
> *Trying to remember it all*
> *Scared that I just might.*

But it's clear, oh so clear
You'll never be here
Because every day, a little more
You disappear, you disappear, you disappear.

"Joy? Are you still there?" he asks quietly.

"Still here."

"I thought you'd disappeared," he says, practically a whisper. "Are you okay? I saw you fall at the reunion. The ambulance came . . . I know you're still in the hospital, but they wouldn't tell me anything."

There's too much to say, and every word hurts. So she settles on the most important thing. "I *will* be okay, Ryder."

He lets out a breath. "Maybe we could . . . maybe when you're feeling better, we could, I don't know, hang out. Get to know each other. Maybe play some music together. If you want, that is."

Something between laughter and tears is happening inside her right now, but she's not sure she has the strength to get it out. She nods, though he can't see her. She manages: "That would be really nice."

"Okay, then," he says. "It's settled." Just like he said when they were rock climbing. In the past. In the dream. In the memory. In the future. In the summer days that existed completely outside of time, where Joy found herself again. Where they found each other.

"Good-bye, Doug," she says.

"Good-bye, Joy," he says.

* * *

It would be so easy to close her eyes again. So easy to go back to the dreams, or the memories—not that it matters which. She tries to convince herself that she doesn't hate this place. Here at MCCP, just ten minutes south of Portland, everything is black and white. Everything is long Latinate words that should belong on one of Luce's SAT study spreadsheets, not in her medical files. *Peripheral primitive neuroectodermal tumors.* Such ugly words, for such ugly things. Unbelievable how our own bones, our own cells, can betray us. Inexplicable. Unfair. And in her case, unavoidable, no matter how hard she has tried to run from it for two whole years.

But her friends are here—gathered together like the four elements, to see her. While she waits for them, Joy tries to decide who would be which element. Luce, the swimmer and always the organized, reliable one would likely be water. Zo would be earth—steady, loyal, grounded . . . and often covered in *actual* mud. Then there's Tali—impatient, hot-tempered, constantly blowing things out of proportion. Also, she's a runner and can travel faster than any of the rest of them, even if, sometimes, she carelessly destroys things in her path. Yup, *definitely* fire.

So that leaves wind for Joy. Which kind of works: sometimes gentle, sometimes fierce. *Check.* Usually a little bit invisible, except in the way that she affects others, bringing them together and then letting them scatter again. *Check.* Sometimes, when the music's right, causing them to dance, like leaves. At least, that's how it used to be.

Wind.

Touching everything.

Just passing through.

They come through the doorway in a noisy jumble, their voices dissolving the silence. In that moment, Joy can breathe again. The ache in her bones, in her whole body, seems distant, easy to tune out—just faint white noise, fading into the background.

"So serious," Joy says with a smile, because if she doesn't make a joke, she might cry. Tali has her arms folded across her chest and is picking at the elbow of her purposefully shredded off-the-shoulder sweater. Luce looks pale and shocked, dark bags beneath her eyes. Zoe looks as though she was just yanked from bed only moments ago.

This is why she didn't want them to know for so long. This is why she never told them.

"Come on," she says, trying to make her voice louder, firmer. "Get it together, people. Who's here to cheer up who?"

"Whom," Luce corrects automatically. And then she's smiling, too.

Relief washes through Joy's chest. "I'm so happy you guys came," she says. "I had . . . the most bizarre dream. We all went back in time—back to our last summer at Camp OK. It was . . . it was so real."

Zoe shakes her head. "I had that dream, too," she says.

Tali and Luce look at each other, and then back at Joy. "I think we *all* did," Tali says carefully.

"Whatever happened to us," Luce says, "we all felt it. It was *real*."

Joy blinks. Somehow she already knew that this was true—that the four of them must have been given a miracle: a second chance, one golden bubble of opportunity to go back and try again. And maybe one version of the past wasn't better than the other—maybe that isn't the point.

After all, she's still dying.

Maybe the only thing that really stuck from their trip back in time is inside them now, just a spark, evidence that there's more to this world than everyone else thinks. Maybe that's what forever really means.

"Just promise me you guys will . . . hold up your end of the bargain, then," Joy says, each word coming out slow and labored now. But it's too important not to say.

"Our end of the bargain?" Zoe repeats.

Joy nods. "What we wrote . . . on the photo-booth wall."

Tali takes a deep breath. "That we would all be friends forever?"

Joy lets out a breath and smiles. "Promise."

She sees a tear streaking down Tali's cheek, bringing with it a dark trail of mascara, but Joy no longer has it in her to tell her to stop, to tell her it will all be okay. Even better than okay—fantastic. It's what she always used to say.

Zoe leans down and hugs her gently. "Of course we promise," she whispers.

Luce leans in, too, taking Joy's hand. "You can fight this, Joy," Luce says, serious, like she's coaching her on a difficult SAT question. "I know you can do this. It's going to be all right."

Zoe is crying now, too. Joy wants to hug her, to make her feel better, to fold her into her side on the narrow hospital bed. But she is so tired. Movement is too hard. So she lets the girls cry, lets them hug her, lets them try to dry their own eyes on the backs of their sleeves. Inexplicably—despite everything—Joy feels oddly, wildly happy.

This was all she wanted. To feel whole again.

And then, the weirdest thing happens. As her friends pull away to give her some space, she sees the *sun*.

They're standing on the Okahatchee soccer field, breaking from a huddle. *I'll sneak off after the second relay,* Zoe is saying. *I'll take the path through the woods,* Tali responds. *And I'll stay on lookout, then meet you at the Stevens,* Luce says with an official nod.

Behind their heads, the trees are swaying, sunlight breaking through the leaves at the edge of the field where the woods begin, making white spots in Joy's vision. Shadows and light, dancing across her skin. She can feel the warmth of the sun and closes her eyes, watching the shapes behind her eyelids grow brighter and brighter into just white.

This is forever, the light says. She smiles, realizing there was never any proof of it, just this feeling, just this truth.

EPILOGUE

ONE WEEK LATER

Zoe hunches forward and switches off the car radio. At the funeral, there was a lot of music—Doug Ryder played his guitar, and several girls from Joy's old choir sang a hymn. Right now, she just wants silence.

She keeps picturing the ashes, Joan and Allen standing at the end of the pier and sprinkling them out over the lake. It's only the first day of September, but a light breeze already stirs in the mountains, and at that moment, it seemed to pick up, causing the ashes to lift on a gust and separate, blending with water and sky, becoming nothing.

As her car rises up over the hill on Ossipee Trail, Zoe passes the ENTERING LIBERTY, NEW HAMPSHIRE sign and shakes her head. She and Cal have always joked that they should print the sign on both sides—because it's even truer when you're leaving town.

And she *will* be leaving, for college, in precisely seventeen hours. She can't quite believe it, but all her bags are packed and her mom even requested tomorrow morning's shift off to take her to breakfast before the drive.

She catches a glimpse of her face in the rearview mirror—she looks like she hasn't slept all week, which is basically true. There's smudged mascara under her eyes, which are tinged red at the edges. She has gone through so many emotions in just a few days—sorrow, anger, confusion, guilt—that she feels exhausted somehow, like a wrung-out towel.

Zoe fumbles with her cell phone, taking a breath before dialing. As she looks through her windshield at the town she has known all her life—the spire of a church poking up over the next hill; ski shops directed at the tourists who head through here to North Conway, currently closed for the season; Mr. Jenklow returning his lawnmower to the shed at the side of School Road—a sense of calm settles in. She knows, without knowing how she knows, that wherever Joy is, wherever her soul has gone, she's going to be okay now. Even better than okay.

Calvin answers on the third ring. "Zobo." His voice is restrained, like he's not sure what tone to take. What tone *do* you take with the girl you were friends with all through high school and then who you dated, briefly, and who broke up with you out of nowhere, and then whose best friend died less than a week later?

"Hey, Cal."

"My mom wants to know if you're still coming over for lasagna tonight. She's planning a big good-bye feast for both of us, so you won't want to disappoint her." But she knows what he really means—that even though they broke up, they'll always be friends. That *he'd* be disappointed if they didn't get one last chance to say good-bye before leaving town.

Zoe smiles. "Yeah, of course I'm coming."

There's a pause. "I would ask you how your day was," Cal starts, "but that just seems sort of . . . wrong."

Zoe sighs. "Sometime I will tell you all about it. After I even figure out how I feel."

"Any time, Zo. So, I'll see you in, like, an hour?" he says.

"Actually, I was calling because there's . . . something I wanted to say . . . to tell you . . . before I come over tonight."

"Okay, shoot," Cal says, and she can hear him bracing himself, though what could be worse than telling him she didn't feel the way he did?

And so she tells him: about *her*, about the secret she has been pressing down inside for so long she *almost* didn't know it was there. She tells him that she likes girls. How Ellis—maddening, elusive Ellis—made her see it finally, though it felt like she was the last person to know. She wasn't being used, or messed with. Or maybe she was. It doesn't matter. *She* was the one who couldn't admit that she actually wanted it, actually *liked* it. More than liked it. It had been a taste of freedom.

Hopefully only her first.

She hasn't really had any practice saying the words, so they come out jumbled and awkward, and during the brief silence that follows, she's sure she has somehow said it wrong, that she failed to explain what she really means, that she has made things even more confusing between them.

Finally, she hears Cal let out a breath. "All right," he says slowly. "So . . . that's it?"

"Wait, you have no reaction? You aren't, like, shocked or mad or something?"

"Why would I be mad? Look, Zo, you've been one of my closest friends for the last few years. This doesn't change that. It's not like you're telling me there is no spoon," he says with a small laugh.

"Oh, the Matrix is very real, Cal," Zoe replies, feeling a nervous smile creep onto her face. "Spoons are just an illusion."

"Then what have I been eating my soup with?"

She laughs, surprised by how good it feels. "Your brain?"

Now it's Cal's turn to laugh. "That's disgusting." He sighs. "But . . . thank you."

"For what?" Zoe says, with a new sense of relief. Over the hills, the sun is still shining high, turning a faint peachy orange as evening eases in.

"For telling me." He pauses. "At least I know you didn't dump me because you secretly hate my taste in music or think my feet are gross."

"Your feet *are* gross."

"I'll ignore that. And now that all that's out of the way, we can move on to discussing the mix I'm making for your drive tomorrow. I thought I would start off with something more indie and then move toward pop hits to represent your journey into the—"

"Cal!" Zoe says, shaking her head.

"What?"

"We can talk about that later."

He sighs. "Fine. So Zoe, just tell me one more thing and then I'll hang up."

"Sure, what is it?" she asks, tapping her steering wheel as she makes her way onto her street, the one she has lived on for her entire life. She can see her house down at the end of the block.

"I just want to make sure"—his voice gets quiet—"that you'll, you know, be okay."

Zoe squints into the distance and takes a moment before answering. She thinks again of the funeral—how she held Luce and Tali's hands through the whole service, feeling like if they unlinked, even for a second, she might not be able to stand anymore. How, afterward, they promised to get together over Thanksgiving break, and how relieved Zoe felt, knowing they would still be there—somewhere—caring about her, inextricably linked to her. And not through the shared experience of losing Joy . . . but of finding her again, of rediscovering the invisible thread that had always tied them together before and lifted them up, made life better.

They've been given something that most people never get: a second chance.

Of course, she can't help hearing Joy's voice in her head, too, always insisting that life improves with time, that someday when camp was long over, they wouldn't have to settle for just okay.

She feels herself choking up all over again. "You know what, Cal?" she says. "I'm going to be better than okay. I'm going to be fantastic."

ACKNOWLEDGMENTS

Thank you first to Lauren Oliver, a dear friend and phenomenal writer, whose courage, brilliance, and hard work inspire me daily, and without whose support I may never have written this book. Thanks also to my remarkably relentless, genius, kick-ass agent and invaluable conspirator Stephen Barbara; and to the most nurturing and insightful editor in the world, Rosemary Brosnan, who has helped turn my first baby manuscript into a full-grown book with a wild mind and heart of its own.

I'm indebted to Susan Katz, Kate Jackson, Jessica MacLeish, and the rest of the very vibrant HarperTeen group, including Erin Fitzsimmons, whose brilliant design made the book beautiful on the outside. To Rhoda Belleza, Angela Velez, Kamilla Benko, Tara Sonin, and Alexa Wejko, the sharp-minded and fashionable editors at Paper Lantern Lit (you all wear my clothes so well!); to Jessica Regel and the rest of the formidably awesome Foundry team; and of course, to my writing retreat rivals in Type A-ness: Jess Rothenberg, Rebecca Serle, Leila Sales, Courtney Sheinmel, and Emily Heddleson . . . not to mention puppy mascot, Rufus, and honorary writing partner, "Bebe" (Theo) Barbara.

Thank you to EVERYONE in my big, loud, boisterous family for forcing me to have a voice, believing in it always, and even, occasionally, listening to it. Thank you to Laura Schechter, my "first marriage," who has encouraged me to let go, to leap toward that which scares me most, and to fly.

And of course, thank you to my husband, Charlie, who has offered patience when there could have been none left, who has fed me in many ways but especially the literal way, and most of all, who has shown me the tenderness of great love.